The Homecoming War

THE
Homecoming
WAR

ADDIE WOOLRIDGE

Underlined

Text copyright © 2023 by Alexandra Massengale
Cover art copyright © 2023 by Ana Latese
Confetti art by Ifti Digital/stock.adobe.com
Sunglasses art by th3fisa/stock.adobe.com

All rights reserved. Published in the United States by Underlined, an imprint of Random House Children's Books, a division of Penguin Random House LLC, New York.

Underlined is a registered trademark and the colophon is a trademark of Penguin Random House LLC.

GetUnderlined.com

Educators and librarians, for a variety of teaching tools, visit us at RHTeachersLibrarians.com

Library of Congress Cataloging-in-Publication Data is available upon request.
ISBN 978-0-593-56866-8 (trade pbk.) — ISBN 978-0-593-56867-5 (ebook)

The text of this book is set in 11.3-point Warnock Pro Light.
Interior design by Cathy Bobak

Printed in the United States of America
1st Printing
First Edition

For Great-Aunt Patty: thanks for sharing
your love and books with me.

Chapter One

"I CAN'T BELIEVE THEY'RE FORCING THIS ON US. THIS WAS not the plan."

"Definitely not the plan. Definitely hate it."

Nadiya and I stood still and squinted up at the freshly christened Huntersville High building. The nervous pit that had been growing in my stomach since the announcement last week that Hirono High was being combined with our rival, Davies High, was expanding by the second. The district had been too cheap to spring for new signage before the school year started and instead opted to hang a vinyl banner in front of what used to be Davies to welcome everyone. Guess the school board wasn't joking when it said it was strapped for cash.

"We're going to get so many complaints." Nadiya stamped her foot, and I would've laughed, but this was serious. I'd already heard from no less than half of Hirono's junior class about how much it sucked to have to change schools. If given the choice, some of my classmates would probably rather have gone to class with the toxic mold at Hirono than show up here.

Worse, I kind of agreed with them. But I was junior class president, the bridge between the administration and the student body, so it wasn't like I could put *Yeah, it blows* in an email and send it off.

Instead, I had to be diplomatic, and so far, it wasn't going great.

"This was supposed to be our year," said Nadiya, Hirono's junior class vice president, then started listing off all the supposed-to-happens on her fingers, her electric-blue manicure flashing in the sunlight: "Planning homecoming, student-store policy revisions, updating the dress code . . ." Nadiya's general energy was always around a sass level seven, but when she was mad, it could crank up to ten. If someone didn't calm her down soon, she'd be in the school board president's office threatening to tie herself to the old building until they revised their verdict. "We were going to make all the important decisions that we'd write about on our college applications. Instead, we'll be dealing with this."

"I'm sure we can still do some of that." I tried to sound enthusiastic as the buzz in the parking lot picked up around us. Nadiya and I had arrived early to greet our classmates and try to win over a few of the Davies students to our voting bloc just in case new elections were held for our combined school.

Instead, we wound up with a front row seat to everyone pointing out that the former Davies Kraken was still proudly outside of the school while the Hirono Mustang was in a junk heap next to our now sealed off old building.

"Hi, Meg," a fellow junior on the debate team called to me from the back of the parking lot.

"Happy first day!" I waved back, mentally cataloging that she and her boyfriend hadn't arrived together, which may mean that the rumors of their breakup were true. I'd avoid mentioning him to her until I was sure. Wouldn't want to alienate anyone on the first day.

"Satan's favorite Barbie at three o'clock," Nadiya mumbled out of the side of her mouth.

I turned to see Freya Allanson walking directly toward us and tried to stop my lip from curling. As usual, she was perfectly put together, with her slick blond ponytail and her long features just a little too pinched to be pretty. "Of course she's here early. Probably with a list of grievances, too."

"Where do we think she got that sunburn she's calling a tan?"

"Likely in hell, but she'll probably say Barbados."

I smiled, waved, and put my sunglasses on so she couldn't see me looking for a place to hide. I didn't feel like dealing with Freya's backhanded compliments or outright jabs about how I won class president only because I was "lucky" or because "diversity is in now."

The idea that I won because people like me and I'm good at this job never crossed Freya's mind. Harder still was knowing that she'd managed to pull about 25 percent of the votes, which meant that a good chunk of Hirono's junior class agreed with her.

I was just about to dig deep and accept the fact that I didn't know Davies's layout well enough to hide when someone pounced on my shoulders, sending my pulse racing as my knees locked to keep me from collapsing.

"Holy—"

"Got you!" Riley Fischer, our class secretary, shouted, and they bounced around to face me and smiled like they'd won a prize.

"Riley. Are you trying to kill me?"

"Sorry, Meg. Didn't you hear me calling for you? I've been yelling from the front door for, like, five minutes." Riley's face faltered slightly as they looked at the two of us.

"Obviously not," Nadiya said, clutching her chest, then immediately pulling her hand away so she didn't wrinkle her crisp white tuxedo shirt.

"Don't worry about it," I said, smiling, and elbowed Nadiya. Riley had been a trickster since we were in the second grade, but they had a heart of gold. Nadiya was really only mad that they scared her and probably forced her to forget whatever she was planning to say to scare Freya off. "How was your summer?"

"Fairly excellent. Spent most of it working at Mayfield. Like my suntan?"

"Mayfield? What tan?" Nadiya asked, looking for even a hint of sun on Riley. "You are still exceedingly pale."

"Jewish summer camp four hours from here." Riley shook their dark shaggy hair out of their eyes and smirked like they couldn't wait for the punch line any longer. "The tan I got from working in the kitchen for three meals and two snacks a day, far, far away from the pool, horseback riding, or anything even remotely fun."

"So, basically, you wish you'd stayed home and been bored with us?" I asked as the three of us watched the parking lot fill up.

"Pretty much. Nadiya, how was your summer?"

"Let's see. I spent it being bossed around at my mom's office and watching Bengali soap operas with my grandma while helping my little cousins with their math workbook. So, pretty exciting."

"What about—" Riley stopped as Nadiya looked around them toward the parking lot. In fact, it felt like the entire class stopped to watch a red vintage Mercedes convertible pull into the lot, its speakers blaring some old-school music. The wind whipped the driver's hair around in the impossibly cool way that people's hair moved in car commercials and not the way it actually got destroyed in convertibles. As the car crept toward the front of the lot, a guy, standing next to the open door of his big truck, shut it, obviously freeing up a spot so the convertible driver could park.

"Clever," Nadiya mumbled as all three of us realized what had happened. The driver had managed to reserve a good parking space up front without having to show up early or actually do anything to get it.

"Who is that?" Riley asked as the driver shut off his engine and got out to do some kind of complex handshake-hug with the guy who'd saved his space.

"Is that—" Nadiya started, and then stopped as the driver turned to face us.

The first bell rang, and my stomach dropped three inches as students began to file inside. I'd underestimated the Davies junior class president. My social media research had turned up that he was a baseball player who had an awesome sweet sixteen party for his entire class this summer that people were

5

still talking about. (What? Don't judge me. It's not my fault some of his friends have open profiles with too much personal info on them.) But I didn't know about the classic car, which made my vintage-sunglasses collection look mundane. That entrance put me and Nadiya's smile-and-wave plan to shame.

"That's him." I sucked in my breath and tried not to panic. Even with big black Wayfarer sunglasses on and from twenty-five yards away, he was unmistakable. "Let's go inside."

"Good thinking. Establish dominance. Make him come to us." Nadiya tugged Riley's arm toward the door as if ignoring him had been my plan all along.

"Okay," Riley said, then grinned. "But then will you tell me who convertible hottie is?"

"Sure, but you aren't gonna like it," I said, refusing to glance back at the parking lot. I knew who was there, and the internet hadn't lied. Chris Chavez was undeniably cooler than us.

And he had excellent taste in sunglasses.

"Oh, come on." I had wandered down the wrong crimson-and-gold-striped hallway. Again. Sure, I could admit that Davies was bigger, newer, and shinier and had better air-conditioning, but I missed the old, dented hallways of Hirono. Here everything was so sterile that it was impossible to remember which of the five hallways in this wing would take me to the atrium.

Any minute now, the bell was going to ring, and I would

be late for Life Skills, just like I was late for Precalculus and American History—another shining first impression for me, courtesy of a school district too cheap to have an orientation for upperclassmen. At least half of Hirono High would be late right along with me.

I turned in a circle, trying to pick which of the hallways I should attempt next, when I spotted Riley, huddled with someone in a corner.

"Hey, do you know where room fourteen-B is?" I asked.

Riley jolted upright. I realized they were talking to Spencer Lam and tried not to wrinkle my nose. Spencer was walking trouble. He thought it was hilarious to torment me in the third grade. The pranks only stopped after I took matters into my own hands: I'm not proud of it, but I snapped and filled his entire desk cubby with wood chips. Then, to be sure he got in trouble, I typed a note to our teacher saying that Spencer had put the chips there so he could throw them at her later. It was diabolical. I never told him what I'd done, but I'm pretty sure he figured it out, because after that, Spencer treated me with a healthy dose of respect bordering on fear.

"Hey, Meg," Riley said, trying to look less guilty. They had zero poker face. The two of them were up to something.

A crooked grin plastered to his face, Spencer said, "Hey, Prez. How do you like our new school?"

"I'd like it better if I wasn't lost all the time." I shrugged, trying to figure out what angle he was working. "And I love that the Davies Promise is plastered everywhere."

"'Pride. Character. Excellence.' The Davies Promise," Riley

said in their best stern-announcer voice. "It's like Hirono doesn't exist."

"My favorite," Spencer piped in, "is the giant banner in the parking lot that says DAVIES, WHERE ATTENDANCE MATTERS." He laughed and nudged Riley. "Not that those signs will be up there for long."

Something in the way he said it gave me pause. Why wouldn't the signs be up? "I don't get it. Why—?"

"You kids need help?" A teacher I didn't recognize rounded the corner, and all three of us stood a little straighter.

"No. Just helping Meg look for room fourteen-B," Riley called, their tone all innocence.

"It's down the B Wing." The teacher raised his eyebrows, sending wrinkles halfway up his bald head, as if the location of the room should have been obvious to all of us. "You better get going. The bell's gonna ring any second."

Spencer opened his mouth to say something, but I cut him off, hoping to keep all three of us out of trouble. "Thank you."

Giving Spencer a wave, I tugged on Riley's arm so that they could fill me in. "Where are you supposed to be?"

"There was a mix-up and the computer put me in gym class twice. I'm supposed to report to the counselor's office for a corrected schedule. And I will, eventually."

Riley winked, and I knew there was no way I was talking them into going to the counselor's office anytime soon. I looped my arm through theirs. "Walk with me, then?"

"Why not?" Riley shrugged. "I can always say I got lost."

"What did Spencer mean about the signs not being around?"

Riley froze for a moment, torn between whatever promise they made to Spencer and our friendship. Finally, they sighed. "It might be better if you don't know."

"Now you *have* to tell me."

"Yes, but, Meg . . ." Riley trailed off, their eyes wide as if the look alone would convey something to me. It didn't.

"What?"

"It's just, you're such a rule follower."

"Am not."

"When was the last time you cut class or were even intentionally late?" Riley looked down at me as we sauntered through the hallway, and I frowned. "It's probably killing you that I'm walking this slow and might make you late."

They were right: I did wish they'd hurry up. Not that I would admit it now. "Okay, so I'm not a truant, but I can keep a secret." Riley quirked an eyebrow at me. I grinned and batted my eyelashes. "Please."

"Fine. But you can't tell anyone."

"Except for Nadiya," I added, just to be safe—she was the one person I didn't keep secrets from.

"Obviously." Riley nodded. "Anyway, me, Spencer, and a couple of the guys from the swim team are going to 'fix' the signs." They put air quotes around the word *fix* with their free hand just in case the meaning wasn't clear.

"Oh." My heart skipped a beat. Riley always had a prank ready, and knowing they were going to occasionally TP a house or whatever was just part of our friendship. But this seemed like the kind of thing that could go sideways. "How bad?"

"Not super bad." Riley frowned, then quickly added, "I don't think. We're just gonna make sure that Hirono is also represented here. You have to admit, the crimson and gold everywhere is a lot."

"It's not great. But I'm sure the school is going to fix it. The plan was always to close Hirono after the tungsten mine finally shut down. They just didn't plan to do it until after we graduated. The school board is trying to save money and avoid hefty maintenance costs, so . . ." I let that sentence trail off as Riley leveled a don't-make-excuses look at me. Clearing my throat, I adjusted the strap on my backpack, which was heavy thanks to my two new textbooks and the fact that I couldn't find my locker. "Just don't get caught, okay? I can't afford to have someone from Hirono student council suspended."

"Wouldn't dream of getting caught." Riley grinned. "Does this mean you won't tell?"

"May as well let the administration know who's really running this place." I smiled up at Riley as we reached room 14B. "See you at lunch."

"Assuming I have a lunch," they snorted, unlacing their arm from mine.

With that, Riley wandered back down the hallway at the same slow pace. At that rate, they'd get to the counselor's office halfway through third period. Taking a deep breath, I pushed my curls over my shoulder and opened the door to Life Skills right as the bell rang.

I was overwhelmed as I looked around and tried to figure out where to sit. The Life Skills class was almost double the size of the other classrooms and packed with stuff. In one corner sat two rows of sewing machines, with a series of tiny cubicles staged to look like kitchens on the opposite side. Another corner held several older desktop computers and a copy machine, and the last held a half dozen massive metal filing cabinets that likely held tools for the shop unit. In the middle, the teacher, a balding man with dark skin and big glasses, had jammed all the desks together.

The issue that had me bothered was that the only available desk was next to Freya and her pack of Hungry Girls. We didn't call them that because they all looked hungry, although that was true, too. It was more that they seemed to want to consume everyone's soul. They would destroy your pride if you had so much as a stain on your shirt; if you wore the wrong designer or got dumped, they would be the first to laugh at you from behind their manicures.

Not that I cared what they and their circle of pseudo-friends thought of my breakup. I was done with dating in this too-small town of Huntersville anyway. I couldn't have any distractions if I was going to get into a good college and get out of here.

"Welcome to Life Skills. Take a seat," the teacher said, pulling me out of my thoughts.

Sighing, I dropped into the open chair between Freya and Christine, aka the Brunette Hungry Girl, praying that the teacher, who'd just written MR. AGGARWAL on the whiteboard, wouldn't do that thing where you're forced to sit all term in the same seat you first sat in. Four desks over, Nadiya mouthed *Sorry*, not looking the least bit sorry as she rested comfortably next to some girl I'd never seen before. If I had to guess,

I'd been abandoned for one of Nadiya's infamous love-at-first-sight crushes that would fade in a week. I wrinkled my nose at her, then widened my eyes so she knew exactly what kind of grilling she was in for at lunch.

"Since some of you are new to Dav—Huntersville this year, I'll just go over what Life Skills is, and then we'll jump into our sewing unit." Mr. Aggarwal cleared his throat as if he hadn't just forgotten about the merger, then started speaking again, interrupting my nonconversation with Nadiya.

I put on my best I-am-engaged smile and let my mind wander as Mr. Aggarwal went over the old Davies High commitment to "producing whole adults," an ethos that had miraculously survived the school merger. He sure seemed excited as he talked about learning how to budget, change our cars' oil, put together a résumé, cook, and about fifteen other skills I was almost positive none of the adults in my life had and I, therefore, would never need. Not that I wouldn't learn them: if I had to get an A in fixing drywall or frosting a tiered cake to get into college, then I would.

"I'm sure we have a whole host of sewing skill levels here today," he said. "Can any of you use a sewing machine?"

The closest I'd ever come to sewing was watching my dad stitch up Bell Pepper, my ratty old teddy bear. It's one of the few clear memories I have of him from before he passed. My dad, I mean. Bell Pepper still lives on my dresser.

Out of the corner of my eye, I saw Freya's hand shoot up, along with those of a few other students. At the same time, Christine stage-whispered, "Ew."

It felt like everyone in the room turned to watch the two of them, trying to figure out which of the Hungry Girls would back down. After a moment, Freya shrugged, put on a bored expression, and said, "What? My grandma sent me to a fashion camp a few summers ago."

"Right," Christine said, her forehead still creased, as if Freya's diplomatic solution to a Hungry Girl battle didn't really change her opinion of sewing.

"It was in the Berkshires," Freya volunteered, then crossed her legs the other way, as if trying to brush off the conversation and everyone's gaze at the same time.

"Well"—Mr. Aggarwal jumped in to defuse the tension between Freya and Christine—"no matter where you all learned, I'd like to see what you can do so that I know where to start our lessons. In the cupboard, there are some fabric scraps and basic patterns for those of you who have some experience. The rest of you can grab a scrap and show me your best stitches, whether that's fixing a hem, or poking holes and talking with friends. I'll be walking around to answer questions. You've got twenty minutes."

The class broke into a low hum of chairs scraping across the linoleum and students chatting as we all made our way to the scrap cupboard. I reached for a large square of dark blue fabric with tiny stars sprinkled across it just as another hand darted out and snapped it up. I looked up at the owner of the hand and winced. For a moment, Freya blinked at me, then both of us pasted on our best disinterested smiles.

"Hi, Freya. Have a good summer?"

"Amazing. I summered in Mexico with my grandmother. Lots of time by the pool. I'm sure you saw the pictures." I was just about to lie and say I hadn't seen endless pool selfies when I remembered that it was in my best interests to stay quiet. Freya managed to sound bored as she continued to pick through scraps on the table. Selecting a soft white fabric, she held it next to the blue swatch she'd just stolen from me and said, "You should know: people are talking about you."

"Oh? Who?" As soon as it came out of my mouth, I hated that I'd asked the question. My whole goal was to avoid interactions with Freya, and here I was, falling for her gossip garbage again.

"I mean, just a couple people in first period, like Jamie and her group." Freya picked up another piece of fabric, rubbed it between her fingers, then dropped it casually like she hadn't just mentioned our star soccer forward. "And Trevor in second."

I felt my stomach contract as if Freya had punched me in the gut. My ex was talking about me. To Freya and apparently everyone in their English class. "What were they saying?"

"Just that it seems like no one here is sticking up for Hirono. Which I'm sure isn't true." Freya sounded like she thought it was 100 percent true. "It's just that you're such a goody-goody, I think people are worried you won't have the spine to do what it takes to make sure Hirono is still here."

"Right." I nodded. I wasn't sure what else to do. I would've brushed it off if I hadn't just heard Riley and Spencer talking about the same thing. Albeit without me in the center . . . that I knew of.

"Anyway. Just trying to help." Freya eyed me, then the Hungry Girls huddling over by a group of sewing machines, a chair for her conspicuously absent. Flipping her long blond ponytail over her shoulder, she angled toward the group and raised her voice slightly: "Like I said, it's just Trevor and a couple other people. I'm sure not everyone thinks like that. See you at council tomorrow."

"Bye." I turned my back almost as fast as she did, determined not to let her see so much as a muscle flinch. I didn't care what Freya thought. And I was working very hard not to care what Trevor thought. In fact, over the summer, I'd made great strides toward not caring at all. It was just a little harder to not care now that I knew he was somewhere at school . . . talking about me.

Chapter Two

IN HINDSIGHT, I SHOULD'VE JUST ARRANGED TO MEET Nadiya at the car. It wasn't like I'd had a lot of luck *not* being lost on our first day, so thinking I could find her French class was a vast overestimation of my ability to navigate.

Sighing, I took my phone out of its pocket in my backpack and leaned against a locker to text her about meeting by the car. My plan was simple: wait until the hallways cleared and then try to find my way out, avoiding anyone from Hirono who might grumble at me about how much they hated Davies.

Eyeing the corridor for any teachers who seemed eager to hustle students out of the building, I popped my earbuds into my ears. I loved a lot of things about my big, curly hair, but right now my favorite was my ability to hide my earbuds behind it when I needed to drown out the world.

Finding one of my older sister Mac's lo-fi playlists, I let the mellow tempo wash over me and tried not to think about my day. In Life Skills, Nadiya almost persuaded me to ignore Freya's jab, but at lunch, no fewer than three people approached me with their complaints, including a member of the old Hirono bowling team, which admittedly, I only kinda knew existed. By the time Brianna Kempner, one of the tumblers from Hirono's cheer team, slid into the free seat at the end of our lunch table, just to, "y'know, check-in," I might have actually thrown my lunch across the room if Riley hadn't been so busy eating it.

I got their concerns. Brianna had been working on tumbling passes all summer, but it wasn't like our cheer team had money for expensive lessons. While our squad was out washing cars to afford a day at a gym, the Davies squad was practicing in the air-conditioning with Chavez Flowers money. No one from Hirono was rolling in that kind of dough. Not that it was Chris's fault that his family ran one of the trendiest ethically grown flower businesses on the West Coast, or that every time I opened anything on the internet, I got an ad for a Chavez business venture of some kind, but it sure didn't help me like him.

"Holy—" I clutched my phone to my chest as rich brown eyes met mine. His lips were moving for a second before I realized that my earbuds were still in. Reaching under my hair, I yanked one out and swallowed hard. "What?"

"Sorry. I didn't realize you were wearing earphones." Chris Chavez took a half step back, pushing a wave of dark hair out of his face. Up close, he looked different than in his photos, less angular and brooding. Like someone had softened his cheekbones, then dusted his brown skin with a sun-kissed glow that was typically reserved for people standing outside.

Wearing a look that was just a little too practiced to be

real guilt, he adjusted the strap on his backpack. "You're Meg, right?"

So he knew my name, too. Had he been checking *me* out on social media for the last week? My socials were closed, and while I was well-liked at Hirono, I was not a town golden child. He would have had to look a lot harder. . . .

Not that I was flattered. I was supposed to make him come to me, and come to me he did. Now I just had to take Nadiya's advice and establish dominance. Clearing my throat, I tried to look unhurried as I took my other earbud out.

"That's me. And you are?"

"Chris. I'm the Davies junior class president." He gestured to the center of his chest without a hint of irritation that I had no idea who he was. So much for establishing dominance.

"Nice to meet you."

"Are you walking to the parking lot?" He gestured down one of the halls. A small part of me was grateful he'd pointed me in the right direction. Nadiya still hadn't texted back. If I didn't find her soon, she might forget she was my ride and leave.

"Uh, yeah."

Eloquent, Meg. Real eloquent. I started walking, hoping that Chris would develop amnesia and forget this whole interaction.

"So I heard you're into collecting vintage stuff?" Chris said, following my lead and walking down the hall.

"Mostly vintage sunglasses. The clothes are just a byproduct of being in thrift stores."

"That's cool. Do you want to be a stylist or something?"

"No, not really. It's just a hobby." I shrugged. The question took me by surprise. It was one thing to have researched me. It was another to actually commit the details to memory and ask questions. That was something you did for friends, enemies, and employers. Chris and I weren't friends, no matter how friendly he sounded, and my mom didn't work for Chavez Flowers, so that just left . . .

"How'd you get into that?" Chris asked, smiling over at me as we ambled along like he had all the time in the world to have this conversation. Something about his being so friendly while doing opposition research started to irk me. Sure, I needed him to find the parking lot, but I was not about to tell him my life story and my five-year plan just because he was maybe a little better-looking than I'd anticipated. For all I knew, this whole thing was a charade to distract me so he could take over the presidency without my suspecting a thing. That would fit with the whole enemy-recon thing he seemed to have done.

"How'd you find out that I like vintage?" I asked, trying not to sound suspicious as I sidestepped his question.

"The internet. Hirono's old school newspapers, mostly. But also, my mom serves on the local business bureau with the woman who owns that thrift shop, I think it's called Beth's Place, and she mentioned you. So I put two and two together."

"That's funny, I didn't look you up," I said, trying to regain my footing and the upper hand in a conversation that was now officially the opposite of whatever establishing dominance was. Nadiya would be ashamed if she could see me.

"Of course you didn't." Chris shrugged like this made sense, but he sounded like he believed me about as much as he believed in the tooth fairy. Shaking his head, he watched me for a second as if sizing me up. Finally, he said, "So, what do you want to do about class president? I mean, we already had elections, so I don't know that it makes sense to do them again, but—"

"Are you suggesting that, because Davies already had an election, you are the new junior class president?" The implication that I might not be president snapped my brain back into focus. I narrowed my eyes at him and ignored the aw-shucks expression he wore.

"I mean, not like that. But I'm the Davies president. And this is Davies High School."

"Technically, it is Huntersville High School, which also now includes Hirono High School, of which *I* am the junior class president."

"It says *Davies* on almost everything."

"Not for long," I mumbled.

"What?"

"Nothing."

"It didn't sound like nothing."

"Just like it didn't sound like you were trying to unceremoniously strip me of my elected office."

"*Unceremoniously.* Nice word." He dodged the issue. I rolled my eyes and kept walking toward what I hoped was an exit to the parking lot.

"I'm sure you're not suggesting that I simply surrender my

school's representation over to you," I continued. "A core tenet of the American system of government is no taxation without representation, and you are not Hirono's representative."

"Unless you're in Washington, DC." Chris grinned.

"What?"

"Washington, DC. It's not a state, so the people there don't have representation. Same for a number of territories, like Puerto Rico and—"

"I know that," I said, spying the trees in the atrium at the end of the hallway.

"Just checking." Chris shrugged, as if this entire discussion was amusing. Maybe for him it was. I, on the other hand, was exasperated.

"And *I'm* checking to see if you are willfully missing the point."

"Not at all. We will apparently stay in some sort of weird deadlock until the school is forced to call an out-of-cycle election." He looked down at me, a hint of the joke still playing at the corners of his mouth. The tension between us stretched as we stared at each other, waiting for one of us to back down. He had impossibly brown eyes. They might even have been nice to look at if I weren't irritated. Which I was. Very irritated.

I needed to focus. I really did not want to notice the color of his eyes right now. Trying hard to mimic his level of casual charm, I shrugged. "I didn't really think of it as a weird deadlock, but yes, I guess you're right."

As he arched one eyebrow at me, the right side of his mouth quirked up and caused a faint dimple to appear in his cheek.

"Then we understand each other. I'm guessing you know how to find the parking lot from here." Chris half smiled down at me as he called my bluff. Walking backward away from the front door, he said, "See you tomorrow in Leadership."

"Looking forward to it," I called, trying to sound light and not like I wanted the last word.

"Is that our president?" Grandmama called the second I closed the front door.

"Yes." I dropped my backpack on the floor and nudged it against the wall, then took my shoes off. It wouldn't matter if I was being chased by an ax murderer: if I brought shoe dirt into Grandmama's house, she would throttle me.

"You want a snack, baby?" she called.

Right as Mom yelled, "Come in here. I want to hear about your day."

"Okay. Let me wash my hands."

I darted into the bathroom and tried not to think too hard about my day. On the ride home, Nadiya had filled me in on what she'd heard about the merger from Hirono students, in between random updates on everyone's summers and almost running a stop sign. She hadn't heard anything great either, but Riley's prank would help calm people down and send the administration a message that Hirono wasn't here to be forgotten. Hopefully.

Then there was Chris. Something about him had rattled

me more than I wanted to admit. Before school started, I wrote him off as special enough for Huntersville but nothing for me to adjust my plan for this school year over. Now ignoring him didn't seem like it was going to work. Worse, his smirk when he called my bluff was stuck in my head.

I pressed the damp towel to my face. There was no hope of hiding my flush from Mom or Grandmama. No amount of melanin was going to save me, and being half white didn't help. It was either cool myself down or pretend I had sprinted really hard from the bathroom to the living room. Not a likely story.

I exhaled slowly and walked out of the bathroom. A small part of me wanted to just stay in the hallway and decompress, but that wasn't an option. Mom and Grandmama always made it a point to be home on the first day of school. And, in the tradition of Black grandmas everywhere, she'd probably fixed my snack an hour ago while Mom watched for me from the window.

Sure enough, Grandmama, Mom, and Mac were all sitting in the living room grinning at me from around a plate of snickerdoodles. As soon as she saw me, Mom grinned and said, "Okay, spill. What was the new school like? Classes? New teachers? Any cute boys?"

"Mom, let her breathe," Mac said. She picked up a cookie, then smiled at me playfully. "But once you do, could you please answer her questions? I gotta get on the road soon, and I would like answers."

"You're not staying for dinner?" Mom's tone was light,

but a little bit of the sparkle in her eyes dimmed. This happened every time Mackenzie left. I bit the inside of my cheek. Mac was only an hour and a half away. What would Mom do when I went even farther and couldn't come home to do laundry?

"I want to try to beat traffic," Mac said, flipping her long braid over her shoulder. "I was just waiting because I wanted to hear about Meg's first day at Davies."

"Not Davies. Huntersville," I chided. If even my own family was calling it Davies, I was doomed.

"Right," Mac said, nodding. She bit into her cookie.

"You know that San Jose traffic is bad, so you could stay and—"

"What I want to know is, how are the academics at that place?" Grandmama cut in, giving Mom a pointed look that said *Ditch the guilt trip* and bringing the conversation back to me. "And how are your friends? Anyone do anything cool over the summer?"

"It was fine." I took a bite of cookie and leaned back against the couch, starting to feel sleepy. "The school is huge. I spent all day being lost. My classes seem fine. I have Life Skills with Freya."

"Ugh." Mom looked how I felt. "Guess she still hasn't moved to Bel-Air, then."

"The one person who seems like she should have left town by now, and yet she never does." Mac wrinkled her nose. "It's like you're cursed."

"Leave that girl alone," Grandmama shushed Mom and

Mac, then looked back at me. "What other classes are you taking?"

"Precalculus, French III, American History, PE, and Leadership, but that is only on Tuesdays and Thursdays after school."

"Sounds like a decent schedule. Is Mrs. Cabrini still there?" Mac asked.

"Still there. Still hates teaching math." I giggled, and Mom sighed next to me, likely because she was already mentally preparing for a teacher's conference.

"When will she retire?" Mac asked. "How did she survive the merger when Principal Rodgers left? He was, like, the nicest man." She rolled her eyes.

"And I hate to repeat myself," Mom said, bouncing back from Grandmama's chiding as if she hadn't been an inch away from feeling sad, "but any cute boys? Did you meet your future husband?"

"Who is she marrying in Huntersville?" Mac asked, more offended than anything. "Have you seen these boys?"

Grandmama giggled. "Your mother met your father when she was Meg's age."

"Yeah, but he was probably way better than what we've got, right?" Mac asked. I held my breath, hoping Mom would say more. I tried not to look at the picture of my parents on their wedding day tucked away in a corner of the living room with all the other photos he was in. They were glowing, Mom's white dress highlighting her figure, Dad clean-cut in his Marine Corps dress blues. Mom almost never talked about Dad directly anymore.

"He was a work in progress," Mom said, shaking her head, then laughed. "Maybe if we got your yearbook, we could spot one you missed?"

Deflected again. I knew better than to ask for details about Dad, but that didn't stop me from getting my hopes up.

"Dad was a fluke, trust us," Mac said, reaching for another cookie.

"After the whole Trevor breaking up with me for being 'no fun' and 'too ambitious' thing," I said, "I think it's better if I commit to school and avoid these wastes drenched in body spray."

"That's right, baby, you focus on your grades." Grandmama cackled, then shook her phone at Mac as if to emphasize that she could use technology. "Although your mama and I looked up that little Davies junior class president, and you know, he ain't half bad-looking. And his granddaddy sponsors the senior center flu shot drive every year."

"Name three things in this town the Chavez family and their 'ethically sourced flower' empire don't fund," I replied, citing their marketing copy just to add sarcasm.

"Someone's cranky." Mom's eyebrows shot up, and she placed a hand on her chest as she looked from me to Grandmama to Mac and back at me. "Did you meet him?"

"I did, and I think it's safe to say he is *not* my future husband." I focused on eating a second cookie and not on the way my stomach had flipped when Grandmama mentioned him. That response was based on loathing with a side of nice eyes, which I was a big enough person to admit to myself that he had—but absolutely not a big enough person to admit to my mother or literally any other living soul in Huntersville. Except for maybe Riley's cat, Süleyman—she was pretty chill.

"And why not?" my mom asked, pulling me out of my thoughts.

"Besides his trying to convince me to give up being class president?"

Mom's face fell and Grandmama said, "Ohh."

"We know Meg is not about to date anyone who tries to derail her ambition," Mac said, "and we know that no one around here is as ambitious as she is, so she didn't meet her future husband. Quelle surprise." She threw her hands up, saving me from the giant Trevor-shaped elephant in the room. Standing up, she said, "All right, it's time for me to get packed up and head out."

"I'll help you," I said and jumped up, grateful for a way to avoid my mom asking next if I'd seen Trevor.

Mac looked at me like I'd lost my mind. She had all of a duffel left in her room, and both of us knew it. I flicked my eyes between Mom and Grandmama, then back at Mac in the silent *Sister, help me* gaze, and she nodded. Pasting on a big smile, she said, "Thanks, Meggie Bear. I'd love help."

"So soon." Mom's face fell.

"Kendra, she is two hours away, not in Siberia." Grandmama waved her hand in front of her face as if she could brush Mom off. "Meg, after dinner, do you want to come over to church with me? We could use a little help getting the thrift closet organized."

"Oh." I paused as if giving church real consideration. She knew this was for show. "Sorry, Grandmama, I just really want to buckle down and get a head start on some of my homework. Junior year is already killing me."

To be fair to Grandmama, she wasn't asking because she was convinced I'd become a devout practitioner. Rather, she legitimately wanted me to organize, hand out, or do some heavy lifting while she and her other retired friends gossiped.

"All right, baby. There's always next week." Grandmama grinned and reached for a cookie, clearly in no rush to get anywhere.

I turned and dashed down the hall to catch up with Mac. "So, I know you're gonna go through my clothes while I'm gone," she said without so much as looking up. "I just ask that you wash them and put them back like you found them so we can both keep up this charade of pretending you didn't. Got it?"

"I can do that." I laughed as a little piece of my heart cracked. I didn't want my sister to leave me here with nothing but Dad's ghost and the grieving that Mom refused to do. After Mac left last year, I felt like loneliness would swallow me whole. If it hadn't been for Hirono student council activities, it might have.

For a moment, both of us were silent as Mac folded, then refolded, a T-shirt. Finally, she said, "His anniversary is on a Wednesday this year. I can't come home."

"It's okay." I swallowed the lump in my throat.

"I don't think you mean it's okay." Mac stopped folding

and looked at me, her honey-brown eyes drilling into mine. "I think you mean you'll make it through."

For a moment, I considered telling her the truth. Last year, I threw myself into school. If Mom wouldn't let a negative emotion into our house, I could take my frustration out on the homecoming parade float. A failed candy-gram sale was a good chance to cry. I could get angry over changes to the dress code or feel downright awful about the swim team losing the district meet, just as they did every year. Hirono gave me a place to feel sad when I needed it. But now, with everything at school in tangles, I wasn't sure that I could be alone with that sadness again.

Shaking my head, I said, "Sometimes making it through is all you get."

Mac smirked, but it wasn't funny, and both of us knew it. Taking a deep breath, she picked up her massive makeup case. "Just wait. You are gonna love college," she told me, an intensity to her voice. "It will make the sad stuff less sad and put the hard stuff in perspective."

"That's what I'm counting on." I reached over and tugged on either side of her duffel as she tried to simultaneously cram the makeup in and zip the bag. "I've been counting on it for years."

After a moment of yanking and pulling, Mac let out a laugh before walking around to give me a hug. Wrapping me in a tight squeeze, she said into my hair, "I know. But have some fun, too. Don't tie yourself up in knots about the future. Try to enjoy yourself, okay?"

"I have fun." I let her go to arm's length just so I could make a funny face at her.

"I mean real fun. Do-something-you'd-never-do kind of fun. You never know, there could be some cool people from Davies. I know you want to get out of here, but you don't have to run out the door. Your exit will come soon enough." Mac wrinkled her nose at me before letting my arms go. Snatching up her duffel, she shrugged. "Maybe you won't marry someone from school, but you may as well practice making out with some people."

"You need to go to school now." I rolled my eyes and followed her into the hallway. "Bye, Mac."

"Whatever. I know you'll miss me. Love you, Meg."

"I love you, too." I said it like I was over her, but both of us knew there was no way I could say those words and make them untrue.

Chapter Three

"OH MY—"

"What?" I stopped trying to put on my makeup as Nadiya's herky-jerky driving slowed to a crawl outside the parking lot.

"You don't see that?" She pointed to a sign hanging on the chain-link fence that separated the school grounds from the sidewalk.

Part of me wanted to tell her to keep her eyes on the road. "It's just their motto."

"No. Read it." The traffic in front of us had fully moved on, but Nadiya waited for me to get a good look.

"Oh wow."

I wasn't sure what else to say. Whoever had changed the sign had worked extremely hard to find a font that matched the old one, so unless you were looking closely, you might miss the change. What used to read DAVIES, WHERE ATTENDANCE MATTERS now read DAVIES, WHERE ASSHOLES GATHER.

"It's not as bad as it could be." I shrugged, doing my best to swallow a twinge of guilt. Riley was right: I *was* a rule follower, and I totally did feel bad about the vandalism, even though Davies got what was coming to it.

"Really, Spencer has done much worse," Nadiya said, sounding about as guilty as I felt. A horn behind us honked, and she turned around to give the driver a nasty look—as if she hadn't been in the wrong—before pulling forward.

"If the administration didn't want this problem," I said, "they should have made rebranding a top priority." I bent down to pop my mascara back into my bag.

"Exactly! And it isn't even that bad. The tape probably peels off and— Oh, that's actually bad."

"What?" I looked around the parking lot. Someone had taken the time to paint over the streetlight pillars with Hirono's forest green and white colors. By itself, that wasn't so bad. . . . It was the posters stuck to the fresh paint, the politest of which read DAVIES SUCKS.

Around the parking lot, students pointed at posters. Tabitha and Ashley from the Hirono softball team were laughing, while a guy big enough to be a professional linebacker stood there in his letterman jacket, shaking his head and furiously scraping at a bit of paper that was still stuck to the pole where he had ripped the sign down.

"I'm sure Davies has a power washer," said Nadiya.

"Yeah." I put on my sunglasses so no one could tell I knew something. I wasn't the best liar, but it wasn't like all the teachers here knew me. "They have to. Remember when our Class of 2017 bought all that cow crap and put up that blowup animal pen in front of Davies for the homecoming prank?"

"That was, like, a zillion years ago." Nadiya parked the car and looked at me like I was nuts. "No one is hanging on to a pressure washer for ages just in case Hirono repeats a prank for the first time in sixty years."

"I mean, it used to just be one prank per school each homecoming, so there's a first time for everything." I got out of the car and walked around to meet Nadiya.

"Wait." She stopped short, her eyes wide. "Do you think they'll retaliate?"

Crimson-and-gold nightmares swam before my eyes. Every year, the Hirono student council was forced to be part of the Davies-prank cleanup crew. *If they glue birdseed to the principal's car again . . .*

"But where would they play a prank this year? It's not like they're gonna fill their own fountain with dish soap and food coloring."

Nadiya sighed in relief, putting a dramatic hand over her heart and her other arm through mine. "You're right. Davies can't retaliate, and now Hirono has put everyone on notice, so—"

"Hey, Williams."

How had his voice already worked its way into my memory? A small piece of me hoped I was wrong. I didn't want to recognize Chris's voice. Yet here he was, using my last name in front of other people, like a pet name for a relationship we weren't in.

Where had he come from? His car wasn't in the parking lot. I'd checked for it just in case I needed to avoid this exact scenario. Maybe if I just didn't stop . . . I looked over at Nadiya right as she looked over her shoulder to see who was calling me, then her head whipped back around and her eyebrows shot up. *Don't leave me,* I mouthed.

Nadiya grimaced. "That's all you. I want zero of that problem." Angling her face slightly over her shoulder, she called, "Oh look, it's Tabitha. I'm going to say hi."

"Traitor," I whispered as she let go of my arm and made a beeline across the parking lot, leaving me to scramble for a hiding place or someone else to talk to. I was desperate enough—maybe I'd talk to a teacher . . .

"Hey." Chris pulled even with me. The way the light hit his hair exposed glints of reddish-brown highlights.

"What's up?" I forced myself to focus on getting into the building. The last thing I needed was to notice his hair right now.

"Do you know who did this?"

"Nope." I reminded myself that this answer wasn't a total lie. Technically, I didn't know exactly who did what. I just had a strong hunch about who might have been around for it, which is not what he asked.

"Huh." Chris bit down on his lower lip and raised a skeptical eyebrow. "Why don't I believe you?"

I snorted, which is very possibly the least attractive sound on the planet. But, in my defense, it was the best I could do to cover up nervous laughter. "Because you are a naturally suspicious person?"

"Not at all. True story, I fully accepted candy from someone in a van as a kid."

"You're lying. No one is that stupid."

"It *is* true. You can ask my friend Russ; he was there. It was one of those energy drink promo vans with DJs and big splashy stickers. But still, what kind of kid goes up to one of those to take candy? My mom lost it, drove down to the park and yelled at them."

"That is bad." This time I laughed before I could catch myself.

"So you really don't know who's behind this?" I could feel him watching me as he reached for the handle of the school doors. I was about to deny it again, when I saw the atrium. For a moment, both of us stood still, just taking in the Hirono handiwork. Someone had wrapped Hirono's forest green- and white-colored streamers around every single tree in the center of the room. They'd even managed to get the sad little shrubs that seemed to especially hate living under the skylight. How had Riley gotten back into school? It took them a year to figure out how to sneak into Hirono after hours, but somehow they'd managed it in a day at Davies. They really were a mischievous mastermind.

"If you do know, it's better if you just say." Chris turned to face me. Narrowing his eyes, he gestured to the streamers. "This kind of thing can get out of hand."

That caught my attention. "It's already your school. Why would this get out of hand? You'd be playing pranks on yourself."

Something hovering between panic and guilt flashed across his face and left as quickly as it had come. "This kind of stuff always does."

"What do you know?"

"As much as you know."

How did he manage to turn the tables on me? At least I had a reason for lying: Hirono was the aggrieved party, not Davies. And certainly not Chris. Not that it mattered. Reason alone said any retaliatory prank couldn't be as bad as this without their damaging Davies. I shrugged. "Then I guess you don't know anything."

"Guess not." He didn't break eye contact, those brown eyes searching for something.

I didn't know what he was looking for, but I was also certain I didn't want him to see it. "Well, since we both don't know anything . . ."

"If that's the story you're sticking to. Just do me a favor, okay?"

"Not a story." The look Chris leveled at me was withering, and I backed off. "What's the favor?"

Walking backward toward the A Wing, he said, "Try to keep your school in line."

I crossed my arms and squinted at his stupid smirking face. Who walked backward with confidence? Someone who was used to getting his way. But not this time. "That'll be easy . . . once I'm the only president."

Chris shook his head like he was listening to a nonsense story from a kid. "Way to dream big. See you in sixth period, Co-President."

"How did we change schools and Warm Fuzzy is still here?" Nadiya asked, tilting her drink toward the door to the Leadership room, above which Mr. Bednarik, our advisor, had hung a sign that said YOU ARE YOUR BEST YOU! in a wine-mom font.

"At least he's consistent," Riley said between slurps. Huntersville was supposed to be a closed campus, but Riley had somehow managed to get out and buy all of us blended coffees from Debbie's so we didn't have to go into our extra period undercaffeinated.

"Come on," I said. "I want to get seats together before the Hungry Girls get here."

I pulled on the heavy door handle and felt like I had been transported back to Hirono as several posters with cats and encouraging slogans greeted us. In the corner stood Mr. B's tiny shrine of plants, each of which had a glass bulb stuck in it to measure water or something. And of course, there was Warm Fuzzy himself, earnestly talking to the massive person in the letterman jacket I'd spotted trying to clean up the Hirono sign earlier in the parking lot.

"Well, hello. Welcome, welcome," Mr. Bednarik said. He was wearing a mint-green shirt and a bright pink tie with his favorite pair of red toe running shoes, all of which made his pale skin look even paler. "Take a seat." He pointed to a row of desks placed in a horseshoe shape. "I just want to give everyone a few more moments before we get started. This school is just so big. . . ."

Sliding into a seat, I looked around the room, trying to get a sense of which students I would be working with. Most of the Davies students sat on the opposite side of the horseshoe from us, including the girl Nadiya had made friends with in Life Skills, talking to someone in a Davies marching band

T-shirt with bleached-blond hair, the ends dyed bright green. All in all, I counted fifteen of them. Then the door opened and Chris strolled in, holding a guitar case.

"Hi, Mr. Bednarik." To the rest of the room, it probably felt like Chris was smiling at Warm Fuzzy in all his good-natured-and-perfect-orthodontiaed glory. But that smile sent chills down my spine like a wolf was grinning at me. For all I knew, his warning this morning wasn't about retaliation at all. Maybe it was about who would be our new class president.

"Hello, Chris, we were just waiting on you," Warm Fuzzy replied, then gestured around the room. "Take a seat and we'll get started."

There were exactly two empty chairs. One was next to Freya, who was twisting the end of her ponytail between her fingers and smiling in a way that made me want to gag. My stomach squeezed as, instead, Chris dropped into the other open chair, next to Nadiya's new friend, and set his guitar case down carefully. It put him directly across from me, but at least he wasn't sitting next to Freya. If I was going to lose my title as president today, at least she didn't get to have what she wanted in the process.

"Welcome to Leadership! There are so many places you could be after school, and I'm honored that you all opted to add a sixth period to your schedule. It is my pleasure to be your student government advisor this year."

Mr. Bednarik paused to look several of us in the eye, doing his best to communicate his absolute sincerity, then started again. "Now, I know there's a lot of hurt in the building, and

I truly believe that this group can heal our school's divide. So for the next hour, I encourage you all to set aside the labels of Davies or Hirono and just be humans with each other."

The green-haired person on the Davies side laughed and immediately tried to turn it into a cough when the large person in the letterman jacket glared at her.

Unfazed, Warm Fuzzy continued: "To that end, I want to open this year with a healing compliment circle. Let's get to know each other through the best of ourselves. We'll alternate sides of the horseshoe and work our way to the middle. When it's your turn, please share your name, pronouns, and one compliment about someone or something from the other school."

A volley of murmurs and snickers went around the room, and I braced myself. For those of us from Hirono, this was pretty far out, even for Warm Fuzzy. Typically, he just asked us to share a color that described our mood that day or something. Demanding compliments was new.

Ignoring the groans, he said, "I'll go first. I'm Mr. Bednarik, or Mr. B for short. I use he/him pronouns, and I love that the teachers at this school are thoughtful about the smells of the foods they put in the teachers' lounge fridge."

He turned to look at the green-haired person, who was laugh-coughing again, inclined his head, and said, "When you're ready."

Blinking like someone had turned a spotlight on her, Green Hair said, "Hi, I'm Amber Marsh, she/her, aaaaand . . ." Amber dragged out the word as she thought. Finally, she said, "I think it's really cute that all the Hirono kids get lost because our school is so much bigger and nicer than theirs."

"Cool," Nadiya said under her breath as she narrowed her eyes at Amber. Next to her, Riley pursed their lips to one side as if Amber were something growing mold in their kitchen.

"Thank you for that creative compliment, Amber," Mr. Bednarik said, frowning slightly over the sounds of Hirono students shifting in their chairs. Turning to the end of our side of the U, Warm Fuzzy gestured to Trevor, and my heart sank. With everything going on, I had almost forgotten that he would be here. In fact, I had so much else on my mind that I hadn't even noticed him when I walked in the room. I'd been trying to forget about Trevor all summer. Of course, now that I finally managed to go a day without thinking about him, here he was, reminding me all over again that I'd been dumped.

"Hello, I'm Trevor Nelson, he/him." His tenor voice rolled around the room and seeped into my bones. Unfortunately, summer had been good to him. Looking down the U toward me, he smiled briefly, then said, "I think it's great that the Davies football team are so proud of themselves even after getting stomped in last year's playoffs."

"Hey," Letterman Jacket said, looking genuinely affronted.

"It's good to have confidence," Warm Fuzzy said, nodding and looking uneasy as the Davies side continued to grumble. "Who's next? And, reminder, let's reach into the kindest version of ourselves today."

"Hello. America Martinez, she/they. And I think it's great that Hirono has so many people who really don't care how they look."

"Well, I think it's cute how everyone at Davies dresses like they're dumpster-diving," Freya shot out, glaring at America. "Oh, Freya Allanson, she/her."

"Freya, thank you for your enthusiasm, but we are going in an order—"

Riley leaned around Nadiya to make wide eyes at me—the universal sign for *This is going off the rails*—when someone cut Warm Fuzzy off.

"Hi, Tori Smith, she/her, and I don't have anything nice to say about the person who defaced our attendance sign. Talk about a bunch of sore—"

"Yeah, hi. Still Freya, and I'd rather be a sore loser than—"

Warm Fuzzy quickly cut in, bouncing off the desk he'd been leaning on: "I just realized that we'll run out of time if everyone goes today, so we'll pick back up with introductions on Thursday." The tension in the room stretched as each of us looked around, trying to get a feel for whether we were headed for an all-out brawl or people would calm down.

Inadvertently, I looked straight ahead and felt my breathing hitch as Chris looked back at me and then away just as fast. Forcing air back into my lungs, I glanced over to see if either Riley or Nadiya had noticed anything but found them engaged in a stare-down with America and Tori.

"Let's move on to something I think you all are really going to like," Mr. Bednarik said, thawing some of the cold that had settled around the room. "While we may have started out as different schools, we are now one, which means you fantastic people will get to establish new traditions and make important decisions about the future."

"Are they fantastic, though?" Nadiya mumbled around her straw, forcing Riley and me to try to stifle giggles.

"This administration is dedicated to unity through joint decision-making and letting you all shape the future of Huntersville." Warm Fuzzy intertwined his fingers like a basket and held them up for us, as if the gesture would convey the gravity and dignity of a task that was basically left to us because the administration didn't have time to hold public discussions. Picking up a marker, Mr. Bednarik turned to the whiteboard and said, "In that spirit, today, I'd like for us to envision new—"

"Excuse me, Mr. Bednarik." Chris's formal I'm-talking-to-a-person-with-authority voice pulled the attention of the room to him.

"Yes, Christopher?"

"I think some clarification about the structure of our government would be helpful."

"Structure as in?"

"Right now, we have doubles of everything. Two secretaries, treasurers, presidents . . ." He let his voice trail off, and he looked over at me. It took everything I had not to give him a very unpresidential middle finger. Instead, I forced myself into a neutral smile, folding my hands together on the desk as I watched Mr. Bednarik's face shift from stumped to surprised.

"Ah. Well, that's easy. Since we are one school, we'll just share. You are all now co-senators, treasurers, et cetera." Warm Fuzzy waved the pen around as if sharing were the most obvious solution and not something that would send shots of panic down my spine.

How were any of us going to survive this for a year? In hindsight, I should have anticipated that a man with a poster of a kitten standing on a golden retriever that said TEAMWORK! would have come up with this solution. He probably loved participation trophies, too. Never mind that his everyone-wins mentality would destroy my résumé and college applications, not to mention my peace of mind for the rest of the year.

Across from me, Chris's face went pale. The corner of my brain that wasn't busy spiraling about my future was just a little bit delighted to see him caught off guard. Clearly, he thought posing that question was going to work out differently for him. Now we were formally stuck together.

"Anyway, as I was saying," Mr. Bednarik continued, "we've got a fun year ahead of us. We need to select a new set of colors for the school, and that's what I want us to focus the remainder of our time on." He beamed, writing the words NEW COLORS on the board. Turning back to face us, he said, "So let's brainstorm. Then we'll narrow it down to our top five and let the student body vote. Who's got suggestions?"

"Why not crimson and gold?" Tori said, looking as if her suggestion of just using Davies's colors was no big thing. Catching a look from Letterman Jacket, she added, "What? It would save the district money. Isn't that why we're here?"

"Or, why not forest green and white?" Trevor said. "I mean, if we are looking to save money, buying new jerseys and sporting equipment would be more expensive than new paint."

I tilted my head and tried not to make a face. Trevor was my ex, but his argument didn't make sense. After all, Davies also had sports equipment. Across from me, Chris quirked an eyebrow as if the same thought had occurred to him. I forced myself to look over at Nadiya. I did not want Chris to know we agreed on anything. Even the fact that Trevor might be a little stupid.

"People. We are looking for our humanity here. Compromise, work together. We want unity colors." Mr. Bednarik sounded like he was starting to believe this might not be fun.

"Oh. What about forest and crimson?" Freya said, letting go of the end of her ponytail and bouncing in her chair.

"Is our mascot Santa Claus?" Chris slumped over, sounding incredulous.

Right as I said, "We cannot be a Christmas tree."

A smile spread across my face, and Chris sat up and grinned. For a second, the two of us just looked at each other, trying not to laugh at being in sync.

The room erupted into giggles, and I caught myself. We did not need to think the same way. My job was to represent Hirono and get myself to a top-tier college. I didn't want to be understood by Chris Chavez. We were not friends, and we did not need to agree. Not even on the basic principle of Freya being as useful as a box of weasels.

"Well, gold and white is tacky," Freya huffed.

"Again, everything in the school is already crimson and gold," Tori said as the laughter died down.

"Again—"

"You know, I actually think we should let the seniors select the unity colors," Warm Fuzzy jumped in. "This group can work on something else." His eyes went to the clock. "This is a really great start. We'll pick it up again on Thursday. Good work, all. I'm proud of you."

Another volley of giggles went around the room, mostly from the Davies students, who weren't used to Warm Fuzzy's class dismissals. Technically, we still had twelve minutes left, but we seemed to have exhausted all his creative problem-solving for today. So much for a good bonding experience. I looked over at Riley, who shrugged. Nadiya grabbed her bag and said, "I'm gonna say hi to someone real quick. Then we'll leave. Cool?"

"Sure." I nodded, not that I had another option, since Riley rode their bike to school. It was either waiting for Nadiya to talk herself into a stupor or walking, and I had on new yellow shoes that matched my vintage culottes.

"See you tomorrow." Riley waved and scooped up their backpack simultaneously.

"See you."

I grabbed my bag off the floor and set it on the desk, determined to rearrange my textbooks so that one of the edges would stop poking my back. I was in the middle of giving my bag a solid shake when a deep rumble of a voice interrupted me.

"Hello. I'm Russ Dentler. He/him pronouns. I like that Hirono students care about being present and respected."

I blinked up at the fluorescent lighting, trying to get the giant in the letterman jacket in focus. For a second, I thought he was joking. After all, Warm Fuzzy was not forcing us to introduce ourselves anymore. But as I squinted up at his friendly, copper-tone face, it didn't look like he was laughing at me. In fact, he was holding out a massive hand, patiently waiting.

"Hi, Russ. Meg Williams. She/her. Nice to meet you." I felt his giant hand wrap around mine and waited for it to be crushed.

Instead, Russ gently shook it, then grinned at me as if this were a momentous occasion. "Pleased to meet you. I'm the Davies vice president. Chris and I have been friends since the seventh grade, when my mom and I moved here. He's a good dude."

"Oh. Well, Nadiya Huq is the Hirono vice president," I said, feeling oddly more cheerful in his presence. Nothing about Russ felt like a trick. At least, not as far as I could tell. "We've been friends since the second grade, when she moved here."

"See! I told Chris you two were old friends, too. I can tell. I just know these things." Russ lit up. "I think this is gonna be okay. Once I get the posters all cleaned up, Tori will be less upset. And you gotta ignore America—they sometimes come off as mean, but—"

"Ready to go," Nadiya said, leaning around Russ and pointedly eyeing the corner of the room where Trevor and Jasmine, another student council member and leader of Hirono's mock trial, stood close-talking. I had to admit, she wasn't half bad-looking, with her curls pulled back into a tight bun and her preppy but decent sense of style. The little bit of cheer Russ had given me deflated, and I tried not to keep looking.

"Sure. Nadiya, this is Russ, Davies vice president."

"Nice to meet you," she said, nodding at Russ as if it were anything other than nice. Stepping into my line of sight, she linked her arm through mine and said, "Sorry we can't stay. We gotta talk about her birthday."

"Is it your birthday?" Russ asked, not sounding the least bit distressed by Nadiya's brush-off.

"Not yet. A couple more weeks," I said, reaching for my bag as Nadiya began to tug. Whatever was going on with Trevor, she clearly didn't want me to hang around and see it.

"I love birthdays," Russ said. "Let me know if you want a song or anything. Chris is very good at the guitar, and I'm good at piggyback rides."

"Okay, well, she'll think about that. Bye, Russ." Nadiya tugged hard and wheeled me out of there.

"Thanks for the offer. Nice to meet you," I called to Russ, and when I looked back over my shoulder at him, I knew exactly what Nadiya had been trying to keep me from seeing: Trevor and Jasmine fully goodbye-making-out as if their lives depended on it. Ouch.

My heart sank as heat burned in my cheeks. It was one thing to know you'd been broken up with and another thing entirely to see it on full display. Intellectually, I accepted the breakup. I just wished my heart felt the same way.

"You okay?" Nadiya asked as soon as we were in the hallway.

"I mean, Jasmine seems a weird choice for someone who doesn't want to date an intense girl. She's on mock trial." I scowled, looking over my shoulder to make sure they hadn't followed us into the hallway, then remembered that I'd been claiming to be over Trevor for weeks. Pulling my shoulders back, I added, "I'm fine. Totally over him."

"That PDA screamed 'Claiming my turf.' I give them two weeks. Three tops." Nadiya squeezed my arm and tried to get a good look at my face.

"It's okay. We're broken up." Really what I meant was that it *would be* okay, which seemed to be a theme for me lately.

"All right, then, we don't have to talk about it." She watched me for a moment, her eyes scanning my face for any sign that I might crack and burst into messy tears—a thing I hadn't done since June, when he broke up with me. When nothing happened, she shrugged. "What we do have to talk about is your birthday. The baby of the class is finally turning sixteen, and we have to do something better than get you a piggyback ride from Russ."

We both laughed. I had almost completely forgotten about that bizarre offer to have me serenaded during a piggyback ride—a thing I was almost certain Chris would be opposed to, even if his best friend since the seventh grade suggested it.

Nadiya pushed on the door to the parking lot. "The weirdest part was that he was serious."

"I know." I shook my head and laughed. "Maybe I'll take him up on it, but I'm also sure we can do something better."

Nadiya giggled. "That's the spirit. Why choose when you can have both?"

Chapter Four

I CLOSED THE BLANK DOCUMENT THAT WAS SUPPOSED TO be my French essay and rubbed my eyes. My brain was tired of trying to focus over the sound of Mom's music blaring in the kitchen. Any other time of year, it was fine. Mom was loud. She liked to dance. But this close to the anniversary of Dad's death, the music was more like a shield, the thud of a bass chasing away her sad thoughts.

Sometimes I wondered what would happen if I talked to Mom about it. Would she turn off the music or make one of her jokes? She might be angry. After all, what kind of daughter wishes someone could just admit they were sad? And really, how do you talk to someone about a broken heart they won't feel?

The opening bars of a Mariah Carey song floated around my room, and I stretched up. If I wasn't going to work on my French, I may as well use the time wisely. And by that, I meant use the time to fall down the rabbit hole of vintage sunglasses. There were people who were willing to pay astronomical amounts for certain glasses. And then there were people like me . . . i.e., people who were working with babysitting money and had time to look for a deal.

I'd been looking for a pair of 2008 navy-blue octagonal Tabby Brichmans. Like the ones that were my dad's favorite, a splurge he got after getting a promotion. There's even a picture of him and me when I was about four and I'm wearing them upside down while he smiles at me. He loved the right pair of sunglasses for an outfit. After he died, I started collecting them. Not the cheap ones, like he often wore, but the good ones when I could find a deal. By now, I had about a dozen pairs of designer glasses, but no Tabbys.

Since my breakup and the announcement of Hirono closing and the schools merging, I'd wanted a pair badly. Everything just felt messy, and I figured I was due for a cosmic win. Some people didn't change their socks when they wanted luck. I wore my sunglasses. The problem was that Tabbys were like the de la Renta dress of sunglasses. Their resale value was ridiculously high, and most people who bought new ones knew what they were buying, so the used market was slim.

I started with my usual spots. First Goodwill's website, which was probably being stalked by eleven other collectors right now. Then the social media accounts of some of the thrift shops closer to Santa Barbara—the local ones knew me. I'd even convinced a few of the sellers to email me pictures if any navy sunglasses came in.

I was just about to give up when I remembered the Monterey Flea Market message board. Nothing obvious was going on, but I saw my friend Sharon's post about coming back to the Monterey market. She had to be close to Grandmama's age, but she was cool as hell. An old hippie with snow-white hair and an impressive collection of muumuus, she always kept an eye out for a good deal for me.

Typically, you don't want a seller to know they have something of value, or the price shoots up, but Sharon had tipped me off about a seriously underpriced pair of Oliver Goldsmith Audreys at another stall once. I snagged them for thirty-five bucks, thanks to her.

Hunting around the market's dated website, I found the Email Seller button.

> Hi, Sharon, it's Meg, the collector you helped find the Audreys last June. I'm in the market for a pair of navy-blue octagonal Tabbys circa 2008. If you happen to find them, I'd love a heads-up. My number is below, so you can text me. In case it's helpful, here's me wearing my dad's pair when I was little. No worries if you don't run across any. Thanks!

I attached the photo of me and Dad and sent the message, then closed the browser immediately. Mentioning my dad felt scary, and I wasn't sure why.

Over by my bed, my phone dinged, and I jumped up to see who'd texted me, grateful to get away from my computer. Riley's name scrolled across the screen, and I unlocked the phone to see what they said.

So is it too soon to say the prank worked?

I mean, Warm Fuzzy is out here having students pick new colors. And Nadiya's little cousin said the freshmen are in charge of a new fight song, so . . . I think it's fair to say you saved Hirono.

I grinned as I hit Send. It had been so hard not to talk about what Riley had pulled off while we were at school.

It's kind of a shame. I had so many great pranks planned.

Part of me laughed. They had literally been plotting Davies pranks since the first day of freshman year. Before the mold fast-tracked Hirono's closure, they'd even gone so far as to call a preliminary meeting of the pranksters to talk about our senior class joke. Of course Riley was sad. Some of their pranks were truly legendary.

Guess we'll have to find a new rival.

As long as my skills can be put to good use. Now we just gotta manage these Davies clowns in government.

I have a plan for that! We'll just make sharing so painful they quit. You only need one or two and the floodgates crack.

On the ride home from school, Nadiya and I had moped about it. Then I got home and ate about six cookies—What? Grandmama and Mom weren't here, and I was too hungry to make a real snack—and it hit me. Just because Chris and I started out as co-presidents didn't mean we had to stay that way. If he quit halfway through the year, class president still went on my résumé next year. Riley's response buzzed in my hand.

I like how you think, Williams.

Right back at you, Fischer.

Tossing the phone back onto my nightstand, I sighed. Tomorrow was going to be the start of a fantastic new Huntersville High era, I could just feel it.

"What I don't get is why I even need to learn to sew," Nadiya said. "Life Skills is such a weird class." She flipped on her blinker and, at the same time, swerved onto the road that led to the parking lot, effectively defeating the purpose of a blinker.

"I can see where being able to fix a hole in something without asking Grandmama might be good."

"Yes, but how is making pajama bottoms gonna— Oh shit." Nadiya slammed on her brakes as she came to a line of cars at a standstill. "What is going on?"

"Maybe it's an accident?"

"It's probably Tori. She drives that massive truck like it's a tiny two-seater," Nadiya growled, and I had to wonder how she had already figured out which car was Tori's in the exactly one week that we'd been in school.

Reaching for my buzzing phone, I said, "I hope they move soon, or we'll be late."

"Tori's too dense for that."

Riley's name scrolled across my screen, and I opened my phone to see a video call of the Huntersville High parking lot.

"You will not believe this," said Riley. They started to walk toward what should have been the available parking spaces. Except someone had set up inside the lot a makeshift soccer field, its boundaries defined by the trees that had previously been in pots at the front of the school, construction barriers, and what proved, once Riley zoomed in, to be massive bags of mulch and random construction debris.

"What's happening?" Nadiya asked, putting the car in park and leaning over to look at my phone.

Riley's voice came through the video again as the picture changed to a bunch of students running around, calling for the ball and laughing while just about everyone else from Davies watched. "They are literally holding a soccer match in the middle of the parking lot."

"But we need to park," Nadiya shrieked at the phone, as if the Davies students could actually hear her. "We are going to be late."

"I think that's the point." I squinted at the students in the video, trying to figure out if I could identify any of them. I didn't see Chris's car in its usual parking spot close to the front of the school, but Riley was too far away from the crowd for me to be able to tell who was playing.

"Yeah," said Riley. "I think they coordinated this so that Davies students got here early to set up and no one from Hirono would be able to park. It's actually kind of genius . . ."

"No, Riley. Forced truancy is not genius," Nadiya grumbled. "It's just evil."

"Sorry," Riley said, flipping the video around so we could see their face right as the warning bell started to ring. "I'm gonna go to class, but text me when you park. I want to know how long this takes."

"Bye." I hung up, trying to keep the irritation from my tone. Of course Riley would find this funny. They rode their bike to school every day.

"What are we gonna do?" Nadiya asked, starting to panic. Unlike my mom, her parents were a lot less forgiving if they got a tardy notice from school.

"Right now? Nothing. But this won't go unanswered." I sighed, looking out the window at the other parked cars. "So much for Hirono getting respect."

By the time Principal Domit waved Nadiya into the parking lot, we were already twenty minutes late to class. On the upside, half of the Davies football team was also in the parking lot, hefting goalposts and barriers out of the way, so at least it wasn't only Hirono students who were late. We got out of the car just in time to catch Russ heaving a massive potted tree back into place by himself.

Releasing the plant with a shout like an Olympic power-lifter's, he stopped to flex at absolutely no one before spotting Nadiya and me. Waving, he shouted, "Hey, Prez, I cleared you a parking spot."

"Thanks, Russ." I grinned and started to wave back. Nadiya grabbed my arm.

"What are you doing?" she hissed.

"Waving at Russ."

"Stop. People are pissed." Nadiya nodded in the direction of other Hirono students.

"But Russ is nice to literally everyone. I don't think he did this just to clean it up." It was the best I could come up with as Trevor narrowed his eyes at me like I was the one who put sandbags in the parking lot. I shrugged.

"I don't think that argument is gonna make it better," Nadiya said, dragging me through the front door. "Maybe we give it a couple days before we put our new friends on display. Otherwise, everyone is going to hate us, whether or not you are co-president. Okay?"

"Fine." I sighed. Chris may have been right: this whole rivalry might be getting out of hand.

"So, Meg, what are you gonna do for your birthday?" Nadiya asked, focusing too intently on her sandwich. Since this morning, Hirono students had been on edge. A few were happy that some teacher or other was cool about attendance. Others had stopped us in the hall to talk about retaliation, or how messed up it was that Davies made us all late. And then there were a surprising number who avoided me, ignored me, or gave me a weird look, like I had something to do with the prank. Or should have known about it, at the very least.

"I haven't talked to my mom yet. Maybe just something chill, like the movies." I poked at the sad grocery store salad my mom had stuck in a Tupperware for me. Whenever Mom decided the family needed to eat more vegetables, Grandmama suddenly got the urge to be in charge of making lunches for a while. Clearly, she didn't check my lunch bag this morning. Mom was getting sneakier—

"Earth to Meg." Riley waved their fork in front of me. "Are you listening? This is serious."

"Yes. Totally listening." I pushed my salad aside to give Riley and Nadiya my full attention.

"Then what are you gonna do?" Riley asked, humor hiding just under their scowl as they exchanged glances with Nadiya. Neither of them was in the mood to give me a break or a hint, apparently.

"Okay, I'm sorry I wasn't paying attention. What were you saying?"

"My god, girl. Help us help you." Nadiya gestured around the table with her sandwich. "We were saying that you gotta do something big with this party. Invite everyone from Hirono. Use it to bolster your credibility, like Chris did. Because

I don't know if you noticed, but people aren't exactly on our team right now."

"I don't think it's that—" I was going to say *bad* when I caught Freya laughing two tables over. She was talking to Jasmine, then both of them looked directly at Riley, Nadiya, and me. Shaking my head, I turned back to my friends and tried to push Freya out of my mind. "Okay. I hear what you're saying, and I'll talk to my mom tonight."

"You said that last week," Riley pointed out, right as the warning bell went off.

"I know, but this time I really will." I wrinkled my nose at them and stood up to walk my salad to the compost.

"You better." Nadiya scowled at me, then relaxed. "Don't forget, I'm helping out at my mom's office after school, so if you two plan anything, text me. Okay?"

"You got it," I said, hoping Grandmama would give me a ride without trying to make me walk halfway home so she didn't have to sit in the pick-up traffic with all the freshman parents and school buses.

I stood looking at the parking lot, wondering where Nadiya's car had gone, then remembered she wasn't around. I had every intention of texting Grandmama before fourth period started, but then I remembered the state of my Life Skills homework and then I stopped to talk to Brianna about her cheer tryout and *BAM*, the day was over, and I didn't have a ride yet.

Stepping away from the front door and the flow of traffic, I tucked myself away under an overhang. On the upside, by the time Grandmama got here, she wouldn't have to sit in the pick-up line, so at least there was—

"Hey, Meg, you got a second?"

My heart started pounding before I even looked up, and I hated it. Exhaling sharply, I put on my best casual smile for my ex.

"Hey, Trevor, what's up?"

He stopped an extra foot away from me, and I was painfully aware that he was keeping his distance. Nothing said *This is my ex-girlfriend* like all that space between us. Pulling on the straps of his backpack, he looked down uncomfortably and said, "It's about Hirono."

"Uh-huh." Inside I felt like screaming, but I'd rather be caught naked in the middle of the grocery store than let him see me rattled. "What about it?"

"Look, I know you're trying to adjust like the rest of us, but you gotta do something to get Davies in line. These people are not our friends."

"Who said they were?" I pocketed my phone and gave him my full attention. A thing he claimed he never got from me.

"Jasmine saw you talking to Russ, and—"

"So you think that because I said hello to a Davies student, I don't care about Hirono. Is that right?"

"I'm just saying, you used to be really intense about Hirono, and it seems like you don't care as much as you did when we were together."

"First, that is not true. I waved at one person, and I think that if you spoke to Russ, you'd probably wave at him, too. Second, you broke up with me *because* I was too intense."

"But that's exactly what I mean. You were like a bulldozer, and now you barely make a sound."

"Did it ever occur to you that I am trying to resist this in a different way? Maybe with a tad more subtlety than your profoundly stupid football insults."

For the space of three heartbeats, Trevor just blinked at me, his cheeks getting redder. I narrowed my eyes and tried not to feel guilt creep into my conscience. It was a low blow, but then again, so was making out with your new girlfriend in front of me and then taking her word over mine, despite the fact that we'd been together most of sophomore year.

Exhaling, Trevor took a half step toward me, his voice raised slightly: "Well, at least I said something. You're so desperate to get out of here that you probably would have—"

"Hey, Williams, can I talk to you for a minute." Chris's voice—the tone making his words sound more like a request than a question—cut Trevor off and made both of us jump before turning to look at him. His baseball cap shaded his eyes, so I couldn't be sure if he was upset, but his full lips were pulled into a frown. Seemed like I was due for a fight with everyone today. Goody.

Admittedly, having Chris ask for my time in the middle of this exact fight might not have been ideal, but I would literally have paid money for anyone to interrupt whatever it was that Trevor thought he needed to say right now.

"Sure." I shoved past Trevor.

Chris squinted at Trevor and tilted his chin at him in an acknowledgment that wasn't entirely friendly. "What's up."

Again, not really a question. For a second, Trevor looked like he might argue. Instead, he just gave Chris a nod that implied they were the opposite of friends. "'Sup."

Chris turned to me. "Let's go."

We ambled in the general direction of the parking lot, although I couldn't see where his car was parked. Maybe in the reserve lot? For a moment, Chris said nothing, which left me with the sound of my heart thudding from the fight with Trevor and my mind racing to figure out what Chris could possibly want from me.

We were about halfway to the lot when Chris looked over his shoulder at me, a gentle smile working its way across his face. "You cool?"

"What?"

"That guy. He was yelling at you. It seemed weird." Chris turned to face me and pushed up the bill of his hat so I could see his eyes. In this light, they were almost amber.

"Oh." I didn't mean to sound surprised. It just hadn't occurred to me that Chris might check on me. A half dozen people must have walked past Trevor and me without blinking. They probably weren't even listening. I could feel Chris watching me, and I took a deep breath, pulling my thoughts together before speaking. "That was just Trevor. I think being my ex made him pushier than he would have been. I get under his skin sometimes."

"You dated that guy?" Chris sounded incredulous, like he

couldn't see Trevor's face, which frankly explained a lot of how our relationship happened as far as I was concerned.

"Don't hold past me against present me."

"I'll try not to if you agree to do the same. Stick around long enough and I'm sure you'll find things I'm not proud of."

"I'll keep that in mind if I ever need blackmail."

Chris laughed, then grew serious again. "You want a ride home or something?"

"Don't you have practice?" I pointed at his baseball bag. "You're, like, big into baseball, aren't you?"

"How do you know?" Chris quirked one eyebrow.

I opened my mouth, then closed it when I realized the answer would have been "social media sleuthing." A slow smile spread across one-half of his face as he put the pieces together without me.

"Probably just a guess," he said, "since I know you haven't tried to look me up." He shook his head, still with that ironic smile. I imagined that if he didn't have the hat on, his hair would have fallen into his eyes. "My parents are into baseball. I can miss the first few minutes of practice. It's fall ball, which is basically not baseball at all."

"Trevor isn't about to harm me. Don't worry."

"You can still get a ride, even if you aren't in mortal danger." Chris grinned, and I felt myself laughing in spite of the fact that I should be grilling him about today's prank. The problem was, he was a little bit funny. "We're co-presidents and, really, I don't mind."

"Thanks, but I'm okay." I forced myself to swallow the rest

of my laughter as I leaned forward. It was actually a really thoughtful thing for him to offer. Without thinking, I reached out my hand, then stopped. What was I planning to do? Hug him? Pat his arm? Flag down a cab to take me away from myself? Chris looked at my hand awkwardly hovering between the two of us. I folded my arms quickly. "I have a ride. In fact, my grandma is probably sitting up the hill waiting for me so she can avoid after-school traffic."

"Yeah, I think she missed the traffic jam." Chris snorted a laugh, pointedly ignoring whatever weirdness my body was doing without my knowledge or approval.

Looking up the road where Grandmama was likely parked by now, I turned back to Chris, who was watching me, a hint of disappointment around his eyes. That was unexpected . . . unless maybe he was avoiding line drills at practice?

Whatever the reason was, it was 100 percent none of my business. I shouldn't have even asked about baseball in the first place. Not-friends don't ask questions, and they don't take rides from rivals. Refocusing, I pushed my sunglasses down over my eyes. "Florence Bausley doesn't do waiting around. See you tomorrow?"

"If you say so. Bye, Williams."

"Bye, Chavez." I waved, then started walking up the hill. I had just pulled out my phone to check for a text from Grandmama when I realized that I never even asked Chris about his involvement in this morning's prank.

Whatever. He was sweet to me, so he could have an afternoon's reprieve. Tomorrow, we'd be rivals again.

Chapter Five

I HAD JUST ENOUGH TIME TO WONDER WHY SOMEONE IN my family put a bag of marshmallows in the fridge when my phone buzzed. Snagging a cheese stick, I sat down and watched Riley's name scroll across my screen.

> So I have a plan to deal with today

> Which is?

What had gotten into me? Last year, I wouldn't have asked questions; I would've just told Riley, *Don't do it.* I wasn't usually someone who encouraged the homecoming pranks when we were at Hirono. But this year felt different. I'd tried to do everything that had worked for me in the past—talk to teachers about concerns, listen to peer complaints, smooth over bumps with cookies, and remember birthdays—and all it had gotten me was a bunch of dirty looks at lunch. Strange as it felt to be encouraging bad behavior, if I wanted to have class president instead of "shared presidential responsibilities" on my résumé when I applied to college next year, I might have to deviate from the plan. At least for a little while, until I could get everyone and everything back under control. My phone buzzed again as Riley texted back:

I don't think youre gonna like it.

Will I like the outcome?

I bit down on my lip and waited for the blinking dots to disappear with Riley's answer. A smidge of guilt scratched at the back of my brain, and I tried to shove it aside. It wasn't that I felt bad about the prank, exactly. More that I felt conflicted. Davies deserved a prank, but I wasn't so sure that Chris did.

I know how you feel about animals

Riley, no live animals. I am NOT cleaning up after that again

My shoulders relaxed. This was an easy one to put a stop to. The time Riley had put a goat in Principal Rodgers's office had been an unmitigated disaster. If I hadn't already been uninterested in 4-H, shoveling crap and bits of chewed-up paper would have done it for me.

But what if they weren't . . . living?

"What?" I shrieked, practically choking on my cheese stick. Coughing, I typed back:

> Is this The Godfather? No. No dead animals, no severed heads

> I'm not a monster!

> I meant like plastic or something

"Oh." I looked around the kitchen trying to figure out what to do next. If no one from Hirono was putting an actual goat anywhere on school property, how bad could it be? And yes, Chris had been nice to me today, but that didn't mean that I was about to pledge allegiance to all of Davies High. Chris was a big boy. He'd be fine. Taking a deep breath, I typed back:

> Well, as long as there is no blood, guts, or dead things, I'm fine with it

> They made me miss part of precalc. Retaliation is only fair

> Exactly. This one is gonna take more people and time than the last one. People will love it

I could practically see Riley grinning at the screen as they typed this, their diabolical mind spinning into overdrive.

> Just don't tell me exactly what or who, and I'll have plausible deniability

Sooner or later, I'm gonna get you to help me plan one of these. They are fun

Keep dreaming, friend

I tried hard not to grin as I set the phone down. Someday, if Riley wasn't careful, they'd get caught and expelled. Instead, they were out here plotting revenge and still giving me credit by pretending I sanctioned the prank. The truth was, Trevor was kind of right about me not standing up for Hirono like the school expected a president to. Someone else was doing my work as class president. Riley.

The little voice in the back of my head said that I shouldn't be encouraging them. Was it really fair that they were doing all of my dirty work while I was getting all the glory? Was I the one in the group project not pulling my weight? Drafting off of everyone else's good grades?

I hate that person.

My phone buzzed again, and I looked down, expecting to see Riley, but catching Nadiya's name instead.

Riley text you yet?

Just did. If you know something don't tell me. We gotta keep plausible deniability.

Okay, but...

I could almost feel Nadiya's eyes rolling as I waited for whatever followed the *but* in that sentence. There came a point in every prank where Riley would enlist Nadiya's help to try to convince me to do something they deemed fun. Apparently, today was the day.

> I'm starting to feel like we should be doing more. Freya and like 12 other people cornered me about Davies's stupid prank today.

> They didn't threaten you, did they?

I frowned down at the phone and tried to steady my breathing. Nadiya didn't get bullied much anymore, but it was still a soft spot for both of us. Our friendship was the bond of two lonely playground kids—Nadiya for having an accent and a mom who wore hijab, me for being young and scrawny for my grade and looking a mess in mismatched outfits. We met right after Dad passed but before we moved in with Grandma so she could help. Mom hadn't finished social-work school yet, and between the grief and the sleep deprivation that came with working and trying to get her degree at the same time, dressing two little girls wasn't always at the top of her list. It was a hard year for both of us.

> Nothing like that. More like menacing "maybe we should force a recall"

I exhaled as I read. Nadiya hadn't been threatened so much as our plan had been. When Riley moved to town, the three of us formed a quirky trifecta. We weren't cool, but we managed to carve out a niche for ourselves that would help us survive Huntersville and get out of town. Our being class officers wasn't an accident; it was the result of years of thoughtful planning, strategic friend-making among our classmates, careful fashion choices, and the sort of friendship between the three of us that didn't need words to know we were on the same page.

> I get it. But I feel like we should at least give diplomacy one more try

> If thats what you want to do, fine

> BUT we need to make your birthday Hirono exclusive. And its gotta be better than what Chris did

> You talk to your mom about it yet? What did she say?

I stopped to stare at the message. I hadn't talked to Mom yet. I'd been avoiding it, but I couldn't wait much longer or I'd be sixteen without anyone knowing it.

> I haven't asked her yet. I'm gonna do it tonight

> You better! If you don't, I will

> Only YOU can save Hirono High

I snorted as a picture of Smokey the Bear appeared on my screen.

> Got it. I'll let you know what she says. Hirono party, here we come

I set the phone down on the counter and took a deep breath, holding it for a second to process today. Everything felt off, like wearing a flip-flop on the wrong foot. Typically, I would have blamed the unease on the whole being-forced-to-be-late thing. But it wasn't just that. Everything just seemed so messy, like I was standing in the middle of a snow globe. I'd finished sophomore year right on track, going full steam ahead with my plan. Now I was trying desperately to find a fixed point in order to stay upright in the storm. With every flick of an imaginary wrist, the world around me became more turbulent.

The room rotated again, and I took another deep breath. Snow globes eventually settled. And when all the glitter has fallen, the little world remains fixed to the bottom of the dome, still firmly upright without so much as a stray sparkle to betray its previous turmoil.

All I needed to do was stay standing until the world around me stopped swirling. And I could do that. I'd waited out much worse than this.

I got up and then stuck my head into the hallway before I could lose my nerve: "Mom."

"In here." Mom didn't shut the music off so much as turn it down a sliver and then shout over it. When I poked my head around the door, I could see paperwork laid out all over her desk and about fifty tabs open on her laptop. "What's up?"

"Nadiya asked me what I want to do for my birthday. I know we don't usually do big things because of Dad . . ."

Mom placed a hand on her forehead as if she had completely lost track of the date. Given that I could see one of Dad's old shirts tucked into a corner of the bed, the gesture wasn't exactly believable, but I left it alone. "Baby, you are turning sixteen. I actually meant to ask you about it the other day. What do you want to do? Dinner? Movies?"

"I was thinking I might throw a party." I glanced at the floor, and I wasn't sure why. I knew what the carpet looked like.

"Oh." Mom sounded surprised, and I glanced up just in time to see her eyebrows hit her hairline. "Like, a house party? Because I trust you, but that's how your father and I ended up—"

"Ack! Not like a house party." I cut my mom off before I got any more unwanted details.

"I figured." Mom grinned as if grossing me out had been the goal. "Rule number one of a house party is *Don't tell your parents*. And you are such a good kid that I would be big surprised if you missed curfew, let alone threw a rager."

"Thanks?" I wasn't sure that was the compliment she seemed to imply that it was. Did everyone think I was a staunch rule follower? When Riley said it, I brushed it off. Of course, I wasn't gonna TP Principal Domit's house, but even my own mother thought I was incapable of breaking a rule. That was just insulting.

Mom's computer dinged as a message came in, and her

eyes flitted to the screen before coming back to me. "So what did you have in mind?"

"I'm not sure yet. But it's gotta be better than Chris's pool party."

"Chris as in the other president?" Mom tried to ask this like she hadn't googled him at least twice, driven by his parents' business, and asked six coworkers about the family. She was so not sneaky I almost laughed.

"Yes. Davies keeps one-upping us, and he threw a massive pool party for his birthday, so I have to come up with something better or risk being the 'boring president.'" I put *boring president* in air quotes.

"I get it." Mom nodded and sucked on her bottom lip as she thought. No one loved a theme more than my mom. She even decorated for Groundhog Day when we were little. "What about a theme party? You could do something like disco—"

"No disco. I mean, Grandmama can come, but I really don't need people seeing her dance."

My mom grinned. Let's just say that being on the club scene ran in the family. According to Grandmama, she even danced in drag onstage with Sylvester. Grandmama's seventies disco dancer put Mom's nineties club girl to shame. Although, come to think of it . . .

"What did parties look like in the nineties?"

"We can't rent a warehouse, so . . . Oh! I got it." Mom jumped up, all excited, and ran over to her packed closet, still talking. "We gotta rent out the roller rink. Get a DJ. My closet has a plaid and a crop top with your name on it. I still got my hoops . . ."

As my mom mumbled about slap bracelets, which sounded painful, and Fun Dips, which sounded gross, I tried to take stock of what was happening. I wasn't exactly a great skater, but Mom was so excited that maybe it didn't matter. If it meant we weren't going to spend my birthday dreading the forty-eight hours before and after it, then maybe it was worth it.

I hadn't really had more than a friend or two over to celebrate my birthday since Dad died. Last year, I stayed over at Riley's house just to avoid celebrating with Dad's ghost. When I thought about it that way, I was overdue for a big party.

"Come try this on. I think I might still have dark purple lip liner . . ." Mom interrupted my thoughts as she dug through her closet with one hand while holding up a bright yellow tube top and overalls in the other.

I grimaced. With my luck, she'd have my hair bone-straight and in pigtails with butterfly clips. Then again, I'd said I wanted over-the-top, and whatever Mom was planning sounded like people wouldn't forget it.

"You're shorter than me, so we'll see how this goes." Mom stopped digging in her closet and looked at me. She was genuinely happy, not the pretend happy we usually were this time of year. I could live with a yellow tube top in exchange for that. "Come on, girl, we gotta get an outfit together. And I got an idea for invitations . . ." She went back to furiously pawing through her closet, then stopped suddenly. Turning to look at me, she seemed to finally remember that I hadn't actually agreed to anything. Her voice faltered a little as she started to speak. "Unless you don't want a nineties party. Because we don't—"

"No, no. This is perfect." My voice was a little louder than I meant it to be as I ran over to the closet, as if the volume of my voice alone could both reassure her and ward off whatever sadness was waiting to pounce if I said no. "I was just trying to figure out if I want my hair like yours or Auntie Kim's from that picture at the Jodeci concert."

She and Auntie Kim went to that concert dressed like they were going to marry two of the singers.

"Joke if you want, but we were real cute, and you're about to be, too. You'll see." Mom nudged me with her hip as I teased her. She handed me the first outfit she wanted me to try on. "Now, where is that blue plaid?"

Chapter Six

"SO FAR, NO GOATS." NADIYA SOUNDED AS RELIEVED AS I felt as she turned into the parking lot.

"Let's just hope they keep it that way."

I grabbed my overstuffed backpack and scanned the lot for Chris's car. I didn't see it, and I couldn't decide if I was relieved or nervous. On the one hand, without him here, I could figure out the prank first. On the other, it was easier to feel settled when I knew exactly where my brown-eyed sorta-kinda-maybe-or-maybe-not enemy was. Not that the eyes part was necessary in this equation. It was more a complicating variable that I had to set aside.

"What's everyone doing?" Nadiya's voice pulled me out of my personal math problem and redirected my attention to the stream of people poking their heads in the front door, then walking down the sidewalk toward the gym entrance.

"Please, God, don't let there be roosters in there," I mumbled as we got closer to the front door. Standing on my toes, I peered around a couple of freshmen and saw what the holdup was. "Wow."

"How did they even do that?" Nadiya's jaw was practically resting on her collarbone.

"They must have had a bunch of ladders."

Both of us shuffled forward to get a better look as a few more students backed away from the door. Making our way to it, I could see the full scope of just what Riley and a team of people had done. Cups of water packed the atrium from wall to wall spelling out HIRONO. Some of the cups were green, others white. In the center of the atrium, where the planter filled with trees was, someone had taken the time to blow up dozens of balloons to create a giant column that spelled out DAVIES SUCKS.

"It's really not that bad." I nudged Nadiya away from the door so other students could gawk. Looking over my shoulder to make sure none of the Davies students scattered around were listening, I added, "Riley made it sound like they were going to build a barn in there."

"True." Nadiya shrugged as we walked through the gym entrance.

"Maybe they won't even bother to retaliate."

Nadiya looked at me as if I were denser than a swimming pool full of Jell-O. "Seems unlikely, but I love your optimism. Just promise me that if they do try something else, that you and I can be done with diplomacy. No more sitting on the sidelines and getting snide comments from Freya or whatever."

"Sure." I shrugged. Realistically, they would probably do something. But if the water and cup situation was as bad as it got, I could deal with being party to a little payback.

Only the water cups weren't as bad as it got. By lunch, I learned that the full extent of Riley's work included sliming Vaseline all over Davies students' lockers. Labeling all the outside lunch tables where the Davies students sat with various rude signs that added up to TABLES FOR LOSERS. And the coup de grâce: creating a circular sticker for every member of the Davies junior class with their yearbook photos and the words AIM HERE, then conveniently placing them in every toilet, urinal, sink, and chair on campus. Oh, and adding rubber chickens to the Davies trophy case.

I tried to keep a straight face as I put my precalc textbook back in my locker. America was trying to open their locker with a tissue to avoid the Vaseline, her face contorting with disgust as the tissue stuck to the lock. I grinned and looked down at my backpack like maybe there was something funny in there. Then looked up to find Chris standing next to my locker, a guitar strapped to his back. He started to lean toward the lockers, then straightened at the last moment, likely remembering they were covered in goo.

"Smooth," I deadpanned, refusing to let him think I hadn't seen that.

Chris shook his head. "In my defense, it would have been smooth if someone from Hirono hadn't covered every locker in diaper rash gel. Happen to know who did it?"

"I'm sure I don't know what you're talking about." I pulled my French book from my locker and shut the door, giving the lock a spin for good measure. The last thing I needed was for Chris to figure out my combination and fill my locker with crickets or something.

"Of course you don't. And I'm sure you didn't know that a pack of freshmen are currently trying to pee on my face in the B Wing bathroom."

Chris's tone was flat, but he couldn't quite get a handle on the smirk playing around the corners of his mouth.

My laugh echoed off the walls before I could catch myself. Over Chris's shoulder, I could see Freya, wearing a bright pink blazer, and a few of the Hungry Girls at the end of the hallway glaring at me. Refocusing, I flattened my facial expression. "Did you go looking for yourself, or did someone find you?"

"Russ found me, but swears he aimed elsewhere."

"What a gentleman."

Chris laughed gently, then looked over his shoulder, where America stood frowning at us, as conscious as I was of our growing audience. "I know you aren't going to tell me anything. So just scowl and say something so it looks like I tried."

"Fine." I crossed my arms and tried to look angry, then dropped my voice. "What's the name of your band?"

"What?" Chris asked, his eyebrows shooting up.

"May I remind you that this was your idea? It doesn't work if you don't play along." I kept my arms crossed and narrowed my eyes at him as Freya walked by.

"I just didn't expect that question." Chris lowered his voice and scowled. Unfortunately, he was worse at keeping a smile off his face. "What makes you think I'm in a band? You didn't find someone to share my socials with you?"

The warning bell dinged, and I turned to walk to my next class. "Don't flatter yourself. I'm still not checking for you. You're wearing a guitar; it's a natural question."

"I guess I'm used to people knowing." Chris smirked, then shrugged, but didn't say more. This irritated me. I had done enough googling that I should know the name of his band. It wasn't like we were mutuals or anything, but it's not like the guy's life had a ton of mystery. Half the town was employed by some kind of Chavez enterprise. This seemed to be the one thing he kept to himself.

This time I scowled at him for real as we reached my French class door. "Are you seriously not going to tell me the name of your band?"

Chris looked down at me, tilting his head to one side and biting his bottom lip as if debating something. The second bell went off, making the two of us officially late, although with the disruption this morning, it seemed unlikely that a teacher would care. The sound seemed to make up his mind. Grabbing onto the straps of his case, he moved closer to me.

My heart started beating so hard I felt like everyone in the hallway could hear it pounding. He was close enough that I could smell him: clean and spicy. It made me want to grab onto him and bury my head in his chest just to wrap myself in his scent. He watched me, his gaze scanning my face as I looked up at him, trying not to let him see that I was even the tiniest bit distracted by his smell. Finally, he half smiled and whispered, "I'm seriously not going to tell you."

With that, he straightened, his lopsided smile spreading into a full grin as he took in my face. Belatedly, I realized that my mouth was hanging open. How could he just not tell me after all that buildup? Not three seconds ago, I had been ready to wrap my arms around him or try to steal his shirt or something just to get closer to the smell of him. There are only two reasons to be that close to someone: either you share a secret or you kiss them.

Not that I thought he was going to kiss me. My face flushed with the thought. He grinned as if reading my mind, then turned to go to class, sauntering as if he'd won a prize. Why wouldn't a sinkhole open in Davies's stupid new linoleum floors to swallow me whole?

Chris waved but didn't turn around and singsonged, "Bye, Williams."

"I'm gonna find out, Chavez." I was sure Mme. Chaminade could hear me, but I didn't care. Chris had gotten under my skin.

I could almost hear the smile on his face as he called back, "I'm counting on it."

I knew something was off as soon as I opened the door to Mr. Bednarik's class. First, because he didn't greet me. In fact, the entire room was dead silent, making everyone uneasy. Second, because he had arranged the room in our usual horseshoe but had positioned himself squarely in the center in a regular chair, as opposed to his usual jaunty perch on top of his desk.

Nadiya and I eyed each other as we settled into our seats next to Riley, who was studying their hands as if their life depended on it. For all I knew, it might. I'd never seen Warm Fuzzy this distraught. Maybe he could cause people to spontaneously combust.

We continued to sit in silence until Amber and Russ walked in, the goofy grin sliding right off Russ's face as he tried to wedge himself into his tiny chair.

Sighing heavily, Mr. Bednarik said, "I'm really at a loss here, people. I know we're supposed to start thinking about ways to bring the school together, but it feels like every morning I walk in here and something else has happened to pull us apart. Today's prank was just too far. Now, I don't know who is behind this, and I don't want to know . . ."

Mr. Bednarik paused for dramatic effect and proceeded to try to make eye contact with just about everyone in the room, which forced everyone to look anywhere but at him. Finally giving up on eye contact, he continued: "Do you know that the maintenance staff is still trying to clean up after this? Do any of you have any idea how long it takes to scrape stickers off of lunch tables and urinals? Or to empty hundreds of cups of water? Not to mention the waste!"

His hand dropped to his thigh with a thud, causing half the room to jump. Next to me, Riley squirmed like they might actually melt to the floor and re-form as a puddle of goo if that were possible on a molecular level. Standing up, Warm Fuzzy began to pace. "You know what? Today, we aren't gonna work on government. Take out some paper and a pen. We are going to hand-write messages of support to the maintenance staff. And that's better than all of you deserve. If something this bad happens again, I have half a mind to give everyone detention. I'm disappointed in each of you."

"Why us? We didn't create the stickers." Everyone in the room turned to face Amber, who looked incensed at being asked to write a letter. A few other Davies students nodded and murmured their agreement. In his corner, Chris frowned slightly, then lowered his gaze and started fussing with the zipper on his backpack in an exaggerated manner, as if it gave him an excuse not to engage with the rest of the Davies student council's complaints.

Mr. Bednarik opened and closed his mouth a few times, his face getting redder with each passing second. Finally, he said, "Davies students may not have made the stickers, but did you do anything—and I mean *anything at all*—to make the Hirono students feel welcome?"

Amber's eyebrows scrunched together as if she hadn't expected Warm Fuzzy to offer a counterargument, let alone a forceful one. Mr. Bednarik looked around the room, daring some other student to respond, and when none did, he continued: "That's what I thought. Now, I'm putting a half hour on the timer. You all start writing, and it better be legible."

With that, he pulled his phone out of his pocket, tapped the screen a few times, then glared at us.

Every time I looked up, it felt like Mr. Bednarik was piling on another layer of guilt. The man was slumped over in his chair, wallowing in the deep sense of failure and remorse that only someone utterly committed to being a student advisor who brings people together can feel. At one point, I actually saw him sniff and rub his eyes like tears were a very real possibility, which I was not emotionally prepared to handle. The sight was truly horrific.

By the time his phone alarm chimed, my hand was so cramped that I thought I could be stuck holding a mechanical pencil for the rest of my life.

"All right. That's class. If you will please drop your letters on my desk, I'll make sure Mr. M and the rest of the maintenance team receive them."

On my right, Riley squirmed in their chair for the zillionth time, then neatly folded two pages of perfect handwriting before springing up and dropping their letter into the box on Mr. Bednarik's desk. Nadiya sighed heavily, looking at her pages of loops and swirls before adding a little heart above the *i* in her name. Across from me, Russ's tongue was partially sticking out of his mouth as he continued to concentrate on writing what appeared to be the fourth page of a densely packed letter, while Chris stood next to him waiting with his letter in one hand and the guitar hanging off one shoulder. I still didn't know what his band's name was—

Nadiya raised an eyebrow at me to hurry up, and I shoved the thought aside. Dropping my letter in the box, I grabbed my bag and started walking toward Nadiya and Riley, who was waiting with one hand on the door, practically vibrating with the need to get out of the room.

"Meg, if I could have a word with you and Chris, please."

My stomach sank as I turned around to see Mr. Bednarik looking at me with the same level of disappointment and an added layer of not-a-question-so-don't-try-to-get-out-of-this. "Umm. Sure."

"See you in the parking lot," Nadiya whispered, then shoved Riley through the door, a stream of awkward, silent class officers following them out.

"All right, you two." Mr. Bednarik dragged two chairs from the U-shape into the center of the room in order to form a tiny circle with his own chair. Chris looked at me, then dropped into the chair closest to the door. Great. Now I'd have to run past him to get to the exit if things took a turn and Mr. Bednarik started crying uncontrollably.

Swallowing a sigh, I dropped into the other chair and put on my best I-didn't-do-it expression. Judging by Chris's puppy-dog eyes, he must have had the same thought.

Not that it did us much good. Mr. Bednarik looked from one of us to the other and said, "Look. I'm sure neither of you was involved with this—"

"Not at all," Chris said.

At the same time, I said, "I don't know anything."

Mr. Bednarik put a hand up to silence us, his mouth drawing into a thin line. Exhaling loudly through his nose, he continued: "But you are both leaders. Students look up to you. They will follow your example. I need you two to work together and put an end to this homecoming war. The staff needs this. The community needs this . . ."

The community needed us to save a botched high school merger? That seemed like a stretch. Out of the corner of my eye, I caught Chris trying to press a smile into a scowl that didn't quite work. At least I wasn't alone in thinking Mr. Bednarik was exaggerating.

"Even your own classmates need this. They just don't know it yet. This school and its students need to heal, and that kind of cohesion is something no teacher or administrator can give. This kind of fusion can happen only from within." Warm Fuzzy continued with his impassioned speech, oblivious to the looks Chris and I were exchanging. "I've told Principal Domit that we are finally on a path to true unity, that this was the worst of it, and that an intervention isn't required. Can I count on you two to work together to heal the division in this school?"

"Uh. Sure." Chris fidgeted with the handle of his guitar case, then nodded at me.

"Of course."

Mr. Bednarik smiled, and his shoulders relaxed for the first time all class. "Good. You two come up with a plan for how to work together. You don't have to use me as a resource, but I'm happy to work with you if you'd like. I have some great trust-building exercises that—"

"I think we can figure it out, Mr. B," Chris said, jumping up and grabbing his guitar.

I jumped up, too. I wasn't missing my chance to get out of there. Otherwise, I might have to experience another forty-five minutes of guilt with a side of trust falls. "If we need help, we'll let you know."

"Meg, do you have time to talk about it right now?" Chris asked, pointing toward the door, mischief barely masked on his face.

"Yes. Yes, I do. See you later, Mr. Bednarik."

"All right, but I am trusting you two—"

"Talk to you soon." Chris waved over his shoulder as he yanked the door open and held it for me.

We didn't look at one another until we heard the classroom door click and walked around the corner into the hallway.

"Wow, that guy is dramatic." Chris looked at me. "Was he like that at Hirono, too?"

"Same general energy, but less guilt and more . . . feelings." I wiggled my fingers in the air to better convey the extent of Mr. Bednarik's woo-woo.

"It makes me miss the days when Coach was in charge of student council," Chris said with a laugh. "Although it's nice not to have to talk about baseball season six months before it actually starts."

"You say that, but wait until Mr. B busts out his hard-truths baton and we are all forced to say something true and scary for an hour."

"He did not do that to you all?"

"I'm unwilling to relive it," I joked. "Suffice it to say that at least three people cried."

"Were you one of them?"

"Not that time."

Chris's laugh filled the hallway. It had a musical quality— a sweet sound that felt whole and gentle. I let silence fall between us as the remnants of it rolled around in my mind, trying to make itself stick to my memory without my permission.

"So what are we going to do about—" I waved my hands

around in front of me as if to grab a word that was just out of my reach.

"About . . ." Chris mimicked my gesture, and I wanted to shove him, although that wouldn't really help the great Hirono-Davies divide.

"You know what I mean."

"The never-ending homecoming prank war? Which, if we don't get this under control soon, will likely result in someone burning the building down." Chris offered this in a cheerful tone, as if mentioning arson would be helpful.

"I hope it won't come to that." I deliberately did not make eye contact with him. I would not give him the satisfaction of laughing at that joke, even if it was a little funny.

"Is now the time to mention that I said this would happen?"

"Definitely not." I squinted up at Chris, just in time to catch him looking particularly smug.

"Then I won't mention it." Chris grinned, the slight dimple on his cheek reappearing. "Maybe we start by giving each other a heads-up when we know something is going down. That way we have time to pull our respective classes together to try to discourage them from doing anything rash in retaliation. We don't even have to tell anyone we knew about the pranks before they happened."

"I can live with that." We reached the door to the parking lot, and I waited for him to hold it open for me.

"Okay, then. See you tomorrow?" Chris smiled down at me, looking a little confused. I looked over at the door, then back up at him. His brow furrowed, and then he put two and two together. "Oh! Sorry. I didn't realize that the Hirono junior class president doesn't open her own doors."

"Not when there is a Davies junior class president to open it and get all those door germs for me." I pulled my round, double-bridge sunglasses out of my bag, then turned to face him and grinned. He may have gotten to say I told you so, but I wasn't the one leaning on a germ-covered handle. "Are you not going home?"

"Not yet." Chris patted the strap on his guitar case.

"Then thanks for walking me to the door and opening it." I laughed. I assumed he was going to the band practice rooms, which meant he was officially on the opposite side of the school for no other reason than to talk to me.

"Anytime."

The weird part was that he sounded like he meant it. It felt like he'd offered me something, but I didn't know what and I wasn't sure I understood the terms. I couldn't just let him walk away with an unspoken promise hanging in the air.

"Hey, Chavez."

"Huh?" Chris reached back and stopped the door from closing to look at me, the sunlight highlighting the angles of his face.

"I'm going to learn the name of your band sooner or later."

For a moment, he looked surprised, then a slow smile crept across his face. "Like I said, I'm counting on it."

Chapter Seven

"WHAT ABOUT THIS?" NADIYA ASKED, HOLDING UP A PATCH-work denim overcoat. It was early on a Saturday and we were basically the only people poking around Beth's Place, one of the slightly more upscale thrift shops Huntersville had to offer. We didn't have a large tourist industry here, but sometimes deal hunters or antiques collectors came through on their way to Monterey, and this was one of their primary stops. Mostly because nothing in the store was taxidermy, it didn't smell like shoes, and it avoided the dreaded overstuffed-room-of-doom layout so people could actually find things in there.

"I'm pretty sure that's seventies, not nineties."

"You're right." She sniffed, then eyed the rack of eccentric clothes she had pulled it from. "Bethany better hurry up. We gotta leave soon, or I'll be late for work."

"She'll show." I laughed. Work for Nadiya meant watching the phones when her mom opened up her dental practice one Saturday a month to squeeze in patients who didn't have dental insurance or couldn't get sick leave to come in during the week.

I'd dragged Nadiya here on the false pretense that we were party shopping. Mostly, I was looking for the Tabbys, but that didn't stop me from browsing some of Bethany's new additions while we waited. I'd just spotted a pair of pink high-heeled boots on a display shelf that I absolutely didn't have space in my closet for when Nadiya waved a pair of embroidered jeans in my face. I wrinkled my nose and shook my head. Nadiya sighed and put them back.

"It's funny, I thought they'd have more sparkly jeans like your mom had in that picture from the Blackstreet concert."

"Still has them, and she'd be delighted to dress you, too." I held up a tie-dyed crop top for Nadiya's inspection. She shook her head, and I put it back.

"Dude! Doesn't this look like that outfit Freya wore last year to the academic awards?"

I looked up from my browsing to find Nadiya clutching a mod-cut paisley dress. I remembered it because, loath as I was to admit it, the dress was really cute, and if we hadn't gone to the same school, I would have tried to buy it for myself. The little tag on the inside read DRESS WAREHOUSE. The pattern was so distinctive that if I hadn't known Freya was a label snob, I would have sworn it was the same exact dress. But Dress Warehouse was about six levels below her self-proclaimed minimum budget.

"Freya would never wear Dress Warehouse. We should take a picture and tell her that she ought to demand her money back from whatever designer store ripped her off."

Nadiya laughed. "Remember when she told us she wasn't taking driver's ed because she planned to have a driver once she graduated and moved to New York?"

"That was so weird. The two aren't mutually exclusive." I picked up a furry vest and immediately hung it back on the rack. "And even if they were, I want to get out of town, too, but not so I can have a driver."

"Is Huntersville really that bad, though?"

I stopped flipping through graphic T-shirts to throw Nadiya an *are you serious?* look.

"What? I mean, I know you don't plan to stick around, but it's not like it's that town in Florida where that man keeps trying to domesticate wild animals or anything."

"Okay, but that's not much of a bar, is it?"

"True." Nadiya rolled her eyes, then went back to browsing. "I always wondered why Freya didn't go to Davies anyway. I feel like her family lives on that side of town."

"Who knows? Maybe her parents wanted her to know how the half without swimming pools lives?"

"I was just thinking about it because, for someone with so much in common with Davies, she sure seems to hate all of them—okay, except maybe Chris. For someone who thinks everyone from Davies is beneath her, she sure was flirting hella hard with him in Bio."

A flicker of something close to irritation snuck through my brain. I was probably just irritated that Freya would hold me to a different standard than the one she held herself to. Not that it mattered. I'd given up dating. And even if I hadn't, Chris was absolutely not mine. I didn't care who he talked to, or why he talked to them.

I cut the thought off before it showed up on my face for Nadiya to read. "Maybe they deserve each other."

"That's funny. It seemed like you two were getting along well." Nadiya stopped shuffling hangers around. I could feel her eyes on me, and I did my best to keep breathing normally, even as the back of my neck began to heat up. "You'd tell me if there was something going on, right?"

"You serious?" I asked, even though all traces of any joke had left her face. She arched an eyebrow at me, and I exhaled, slouching to get my point across. "There is nothing going on."

Nadiya eyed me for a moment, then grinned. "Okay, but I'd just like to say that while I'm not overly here for the boys, I can acknowledge that he is cute. And you know you can trust me."

A little voice said that maybe I didn't need to keep Nadiya in the dark about the deal I'd made to share info on pranks with Chris. Then again, that really wasn't what she was talking about. And if I told her about the deal, she'd have all kinds of questions about me and Chris, and there really wasn't much to say. I didn't like Chris, and he didn't like me. No, it was better to just keep this plan to myself. Realistically, once the home-coming war ended, everything would just go back to normal, including me and our plans to get out of town. Nadiya would never need to know.

"There is nothing, and I mean nothing, going on. If there were, you'd be the first person I'd tell. I told you when I had a crush on Trevor, didn't I?"

Nadiya blinked at me, as if debating whether to accept my past behavior as proof. She must have decided I was being honest, because her face broke into a wide grin. "Good. 'Cause you know that a crush on him would be bad for you? Socially, at least. And I would stand by you, but there are plenty of boys left to date from Hirono— Don't make that face."

"If you were here for the boys, would you date any of them?"

"God, no. I'd start collecting cat figurines and hope those would ward off Hirono boys for the rest of my natural life."

I snorted. "Nadiya, you don't even like cats."

"Well, I'd learn to if the boys in this town were my only option."

She kept a straight face for exactly three seconds before both of us burst into giggles, Nadiya leaning against the rack of skirts and me doubling over at the thought of her surrounded by a million creepy little glass cats.

Eventually, we both straightened, and she looked at me seriously again. "All I'm saying is that you don't have to hide stuff from me."

"I know." And I did know it. Even if I wasn't ready to tell her about the deal I'd made with Chris just yet.

"Good." She nodded as if she were listening to a solemn vow, then held up a hot-pink puffy vest and said, "In that case, when are you sending out these invites? Because I am wearing this to the party for sure."

"Oh. There's a pair of high-heeled boots over there that matches." I nodded toward the shelf.

"You know I wear heels exactly twice a year." Nadiya laughed. "You just want me to get them so you can borrow them."

"Guilty." I held up my hands in an exaggerated wince. "But is that such a bad thing?"

"Not when the boots are cute." Nadiya giggled.

Mom's sweater nearly thwacked me in the face as I walked in the front door. She had the stereo up and was ostensibly vacuuming, although, given the number of layers she was shedding, it seemed like there was more dancing than cleaning going on. She was listening to extremely hokey-sounding country music—the kind my very white dad was raised on. When he was alive, none of us could stand to listen to it, but now that he was gone, it was a silly reminder of him.

"Sorry, baby! You have fun?" Mom hollered over the music and the vacuum.

I nodded, then laughed as Mom hopped from one foot to the next, shaking her backside and the cord to the vacuum in time while making a silly face.

"You want to join me?" She added a weird arm motion to the dance as if pulling me in would make joining her more enticing.

"I'm good. Gotta get my party invites out." I shook my head as I yelled, just in case she couldn't hear me.

"Suit yourself." Mom gave me the *you're no fun* eye roll, then went back to shaking it with renewed enthusiasm.

I walked down the hall to my room and closed the door, which did little to dampen the sound but at least gave me the illusion of privacy. I hadn't expected Bethany to have the Tabbys, but it hadn't entirely stopped me from getting my hopes up. Now that I'd come home without them, I wasn't in the mood to dance-grieve for Dad. Not that Mom would ever admit that that was what she was doing. . . .

Instead, I took out my laptop and looked to see if Sharon had gotten back to me about the sunglasses. I pulled up the message board website, and my heart skipped a beat when the little letter icon popped up next to my name. Holding my breath, I opened the message.

> Meg, sweetie, of course I remember you! I've been out here rambling around the California coast in this van, and I haven't seen anything like the Tabbys you described. But if I do, I'll make sure you're the first to know. Hope to see you in Monterey!

"Bummer." I typed back a quick note thanking Sharon, then clicked on the invitation Mac designed for my party. A picture of me as a little kid wearing pink roller skates popped up just as Grandmama cracked my door open.

"Just checking in on you. See if you were busy tonight."

"What's going on?"

"Well, the church volunteer corps needs help moving some boxes of donated clothes for the community closet, and Wilma Crowder tried to say that her grandson would do it, but I don't like him—"

"You mean you don't like Wilma and you don't want her to

get credit for something?" I raised an eyebrow at Grandmama. When I was twelve, that excuse about Wilma's grandson might have worked, but by now I'd been suckered into helping out enough times to know who all Grandmama's church rivals were.

Grandmama shook her head at me as if she was considering telling me off for sassing her but laughed it off instead. "Fine. I don't like Wilma. She's always falling all over Pastor Berryman to get credit like doing good work is solely for recognition."

I giggled and Grandmama's smile spread. "Thanks," I said, "but Mac helped me with an invite for my party and I want to get it sent out tonight."

I flipped my computer around so Grandmama could see the invitation on my screen, then watched as a slow, sentimental smile crossed her face.

"All right, baby. I just don't want you to feel like you have to be alone in the house right now." She said the words *right now* slowly as if they were standing in for some other words she couldn't say. Big, scary words about my dad and grief we couldn't feel. My grandmother feared almost nothing. If she couldn't say the words, what hope was there that anyone else would ever say them? As long as I was in this house, I'd probably choke on them before they ever left my mouth.

This was why I had to get out of town. Someday, I could talk about my dad. But not while I was here. Not in this breakable place.

I took a deep breath and exhaled, hoping it conveyed some

universal sign of understanding. "I'm okay. Thanks for checking, Grandmama."

"Anytime. Love you, baby."

"Love you, too."

Grandmama closed the door, walling me off from the full force of the stereo again. The air in my room felt thick, and I had a weird urge to open the window even though it was solidly 92 degrees outside. Forcing a few breaths into my lungs, I calmed down. I would get out of this house eventually. I wouldn't be stuck with his ghost forever. Hell, when I became a lawyer, maybe I'd even fly Mom and Grandmama to me for special occasions. Christmas in Hawaii. Easter in New Orleans. New Year's in Paris.

The idea of Mom and Grandmama in berets and striped shirts, sipping wine under the Eiffel Tower, made me smile. Less than two years to go and I'd be on my way to taking us there. First, I just needed to throw a killer party and make sure Hirono High stayed on my side. And complete my precalc homework before that class swallowed me whole.

Chapter Eight

"WHAT KIND OF JERK DEFACES A CHAMPIONSHIP BANNER from 1986?"

"I know. And the poor sophomore class worked so hard to get those brought over and hung up in the gym."

I tried to drown out the sound of Freya and Christine discussing the latest Davies prank by focusing on the extremely wonky-looking pair of pajama shorts I was sewing. Luckily, I was bad at sewing, so I really did have to pay attention. Otherwise, my facial expressions might have given away the fact that Chris had given me a heads-up about the prank yesterday.

Unfortunately, Freya was very much not bad at sewing. This meant that she finished her project on the second day of our sewing unit and was officially assigned by Mr. Aggarwal to be a "helper," which she took to mean that her duty was to socialize, with a side of bothering me.

"The worst part is, no one is even going to do anything about it. The administration is just out here pretending that we're all getting along, and no one is brave enough to stand up to them."

I gritted my teeth and continued to pretend I couldn't hear Freya's insult. A tiny, petty part of me was enjoying the fact that while I couldn't call her out to her face without risking getting in trouble, the more I ignored her, the more peeved it made her.

Next to me, Nadiya picked up a seam ripper and began pulling apart some tragic-looking stitches with enough force to rip out half the sleeve she was trying to fix. "I wish she'd shut up."

"Meh." I shrugged, careful not to let the gesture reach my hands and mess up my shorts. "Who cares? It's not like she's clever enough for anyone to listen to."

"I mean, Christine is listening."

"Well, it's not like Christine is a Mensa candidate."

"What is Mensa?"

"A special society for geniuses. Or just people who test well. Standardized tests are garbage." I looked over at Nadiya, who was watching me like maybe I wasn't that clever either. "You know what. Never mind. The joke doesn't work if I have to explain it."

"You spend time in weird places on the internet," Nadiya grumbled. "I wouldn't care if it was just Christine, but she was also talking to Spencer during passing period."

"Don't worry. I got a plan."

"To do what? Say you found out Freya shops at the Dress Warehouse?" Nadiya cackled.

I started to say "Retaliate" when I heard Freya's droning falter. Was she listening to us? I looked over at her just in time to catch her looking at me, her eyes narrowed and her cheeks pink.

Definitely listening. I couldn't tell if she was angry or upset or what. For a heartbeat, I almost felt bad. Then I remembered that she'd spent all class talking trash at me, and I no longer cared. The only person who would feel bad about someone thinking she shopped at Dress Warehouse was Freya. And only Freya would think that I'd bother spreading rumors about her. She didn't need my help for that to happen. The other Hungry Girls did enough of that without me.

I turned my attention back to the sewing machine, a cue for Nadiya to do the same. Waiting to make sure my sewing machine was whirring at full tilt, I whispered, "Can't talk about it here. Just know that Spencer will be in on it and the Hungry Girls are most definitely not."

"I can't believe you came up with this." Spencer was practically shouting at me, despite the fact that I had specifically asked him and Riley to keep it down before I told them my plan.

Next to me, Riley waved their hand in a shushing motion. "Okay, but how do we get everything to the pool?"

"I haven't worked that out yet. We may need an ATV or something. . . ." I leaned farther into the group, hoping the motion toward secrecy would get Spencer to calm down. It did not.

"I just really can't get past this. You are, like, such a Goody Two-shoes." Spencer nodded at me, his eyes wide.

"Am not." I wrinkled my nose. "And who says 'Goody Two-shoes'?"

"Your favorite expression is 'I don't want details.'" Spencer grinned.

"That's not—"

"He has a point." Riley shrugged at me.

"Okay, well, this is different—"

"Hey, team!"

We jumped apart as Russ waved at us from down the hall. To be fair, half the hall jumped out of Russ's way even when he wasn't shouting. The guy was just big.

"We'll finish this later. I'll text you. Keep this quiet, though." I looked from Riley to Spencer as they nodded in confirmation and straightened.

Riley cupped their hands around their mouth and yelled, "Hi, Russ."

"Since when are you and Russ friends?" I asked.

"Who isn't friends with Russ?" said Spencer. "He's like the world's nicest linebacker. It's like if a teddy bear smashed into people and gave great hugs." He looked at me like I was totally out of touch, then waved at Russ, who dodged around a confused-looking freshman to stop in front of the Leadership classroom.

"Hey, buddy!" Riley proceeded to engage in a complex

handshake with Russ that ended in the aforementioned fantastic hug.

"Sorry about your championship flags," Russ said. "I'm gonna see if Mr. Aggarwal can help fix the originals so the dates of all your losses aren't there anymore."

"Thanks, man." Spencer nodded at Russ with reverence as if we hadn't just been plotting revenge, then, pointing at me and Riley, he said, "I'll see y'all later."

"I hear Prez doesn't open her own doors." Russ reached for the door handle and looked down at me with a mischievous grin that was whatever the opposite of menacing was.

"I do not. Thank you for your service," I joked and let Riley walk through first. I was halfway through when I remembered my promise to Chris and stopped—"Oof."

"Sorry." Russ walked into me, and I stumbled forward. He reached out to keep me from falling over. "I didn't expect you to stop walking."

"It's my fault." I took a step forward and adjusted the collar of my shirt, which had gotten snagged on my backpack in the collision. I looked to make sure Chris wasn't in class yet, then turned to Russ. "I was gonna ask, do you know the name of Chris's band?"

"You mean the Wicked?" Russ looked surprised.

"Yes! I just wondered if . . . if they'd always been the Wicked," I fibbed. The last thing I wanted was Chris getting tipped off about my reconnaissance.

"I get that." Russ nodded. "It's a stupid name, but they don't want to change it with everything that's going on."

"Going on?"

"You know, with the producer, the EP, and his family and all that." Russ circled his hand in a follow-along gesture.

"Right." I nodded. There was no way for me to follow along with the information I had. Apparently, social media sleuthing through third parties left a lot of information out, and Chris wasn't volunteering any more.

"I just hope it all works out, you know?" Russ continued, complete sincerity in his expression. "He's such a good guy, and he really wants to do this on his own."

"Totally. Do you—"

"Hey, Meg. Got a minute?"

I knew it was Trevor who'd interrupted me, and it didn't help with my level of annoyance with him. We hadn't really talked since the parking-lot thing.

"What's up?" I crossed my arms and stepped to the side of Russ a little—still close enough, though, that there was a buffer in case Trevor was upset about the banners and wanted to yell at me again.

"Are we cool? I know I lost my temper at you the other day. But then Tabitha and Brianna were talking about your party, so I just wanted to make sure it was cool if me and Jasmine show up . . ."

Trevor trailed off, looking at the floor, then back at me. For a moment, I considered telling him the truth—that I would rather eat glass than have him and his new girlfriend show up at my party. But that would defeat the purpose of inviting all of Hirono.

"Everyone in the class is invited. So, yeah. You and Jasmine can come if you want."

"You're having a party? When? Where at?" Russ grinned at me, and my mouth fell open. Trevor's eyebrows shot up like it hadn't even occurred to him that someone from Davies wouldn't figure out the deal. And of course it was Russ. The whole school's beloved teddy bear.

"Um. Yeah. This Saturday at the Skate Deck."

"I love skating."

Russ bounced on his toes, and I didn't have the heart to uninvite him. Maybe I'd just try to dissuade him.

"It's nineties-themed. You probably don't want to—"

"I love the nineties. Like, Backstreet Boys and stuff? My mom listens to them."

"Uh-huh." I nodded and tried to keep the horror off my face. Surely, he'd talk to other Davies people and figure it out.

"All right, can everybody grab their seats?" Mr. Bednarik called over the din of chatter.

"Eh, see you two on Saturday." Russ grinned and then reached out with what I'm sure he thought was a pat but felt more like a slap on me and Trevor's arms.

"See you." I winced, rubbing my bicep.

Trevor arched an eyebrow at me like I had lost my mind.

"What?" I shrugged.

"Nothing. See you Saturday." Trevor gave me one last look, then walked back to his seat.

I considered calling after him to explain myself. Then I remembered that it was my party. Honestly, if it wasn't for the whole rivalry thing, I'd rather have Russ there than Trevor. If Trevor really didn't like it, then maybe he wouldn't show up and I wouldn't have to watch my ex skate around with someone who was supposed to be less ambitious than me.

I dropped into my chair right as Chris slid through the door, dressed in baseball gear complete with the socks worn with sliding sandals. "Sorry, Mr. B. I have fall practice right after this."

"No worries. I'm happy to have any of you in my class at any time." Warm Fuzzy delivered this speech with a heavy undertone of *You are safe here*, then bowed slightly at Chris to drive the point home.

Chris slipped into his chair next to Russ, set his bag down, and looked up at me. He was doing that half smile thing again, like the two of us were in on a joke. I started to smile back, then froze. Why did he have to smile like that? It was easy to forget we were rivals when that smile was aimed at me.

"First," said Mr. Bednarik, "I want to thank you all for your thoughtful letters to Mr. M and the maintenance team. They were all very touched by the gesture."

"I bet they'd be more touched if we stopped playing pranks," Riley whispered, and I smiled. What I had in mind wouldn't require the maintenance team to fix. The swim team, on the other hand . . .

"So today, I want us to focus on the future again! The junior class is always responsible for planning the homecoming dance, so we have some themes to work on and—drum roll, please . . ." Warm Fuzzy held out his hands as if he were an emcee winding up an excitable crowd. Russ began pounding on his desk, oblivious to the fact that he was the only one. When no one else joined in, Mr. Bednarik simply shrugged and shouted, "A mascot to choose!"

Most of the class looked somewhere between stunned and horrified. Warm Fuzzy must have picked up on it, because he rushed to add context. "As you've likely heard, our senior class has decided to make our upcoming football game a grand unveiling. We'll be unveiling the colors the seniors worked on, the fight song the freshmen are developing, and the mascot you all choose. Isn't teamwork amazing!"

"That's one word for it."

Nadiya snickered at my joke, and Mr. Bednarik stopped to look over at us. I folded my hands together and tried to smile like I wasn't the source of the disruption.

"To kick things off"—he paused, then giggled. "See what I did there? A football pun." He laughed again, then turned to the board to write, first saying, "A few ground rules."

1. NO PUTTING DOWN OTHER PEOPLE'S IDEAS.
2. NO ANIMAL IS OFF-LIMITS.
3. TOP FIVE VOTE-GETTERS GO FOR A SCHOOLWIDE VOTE.
4. REMEMBER: WE'RE 1 SCHOOL WITH 1 GOAL: UNITY!

Mr. Bednarik tapped each rule as he read it off. Letting his hand fall to his side, inadvertently getting whiteboard marker on his pants, he said, "Any questions?"

Tori's hand shot in the air.

"Yes, Tori."

"Can we keep our current mascot?"

"If it is nominated and gets enough votes."

"Then I nominate the kraken." Tori smirked.

"Is the kraken even an animal? I thought it had to be an animal," Trevor asked.

"We'll make room for mythical creatures," Mr. Bednarik said without a hint of irony as he turned to face the board and wrote KRAKEN.

"I nominate a unicorn, then," Nadiya said.

"All right."

Mr. Bednarik had barely written UNI when Riley said, "Obviously, the mustang has to be there."

"Is this going to work if we all just stick to our original mascots?" asked Chris. "Maybe we pick something new." All eyes turned to him, and the room grew quiet with an uncomfortable tension.

"What?" Amber said, her jaw dropping. Tori's lip began to curl like she'd just stepped in something gross.

"New animals are welcome," Warm Fuzzy said, nodding, which did not help Chris's case at all.

"Not when you already have a mascot." Amber narrowed her eyes and stared at Chris as if his life depended on his next words.

Pushing his hair off his forehead, he shifted in his chair, then said, "I'm just saying this feels like a place where we could try something new."

My insides squirmed with secondary humiliation. This

was clearly not the crowd for that suggestion, but he tried anyway. Was he intentionally aiming to ruin his social life? Chris looked unfazed by the awkward silence setting in around the room.

"Or maybe we combine them," Russ said, nodding like someone's dad trying to force everyone to get along. "A krakenstang."

"That is the most profoundly stupid thing I've ever heard," Jasmine said. She was squeezing Trevor's hand, and he nodded along in support.

"No put-downs," Warm Fuzzy chided as he tried to figure out how to spell *krakenstang*.

"What about a mustanken?" Nadiya snickered. "Why should their name go first?"

"All these suggestions are ridiculous. How about otters?" Freya said, looking over at Chris.

"No one is afraid of an otter," Christine said, the bony features of her narrow face pulled tight as she flipped her long brown ponytail over her shoulder, looking at Freya as if she had never seen her friend before.

"Maybe we don't need to be scary. We could be the Pufferfish." Trevor snickered, but Mr. Bednarik wrote it down anyway.

"I really think a krakenstang could be great." Russ nodded his head and looked around the room as if people were going to agree this time.

"Nope. But we could be the Dragons," a blond person with a poorly executed undercut said from the back of the room. I was pretty sure their name was Dax and they were part of Davies's anime club.

"Is Jackson's mascot the knight?" Amber asked. "I don't want ours to be too close to our new rival's."

"Who said Jackson is our new rival?" Nadiya asked. "If we have a rival, it should at least be a school that has won a division championship in something other than bowling." She slumped to the side like being forced to argue with Amber was a big lift.

"Hey!" Kyong objected from the back of the class, causing everyone to jump. She was on Hirono's bowling team and even wore her letterman jacket with the bowling patch to advertise it.

"No offense," Nadiya mumbled, which didn't seem to do much to lower Kyong's offended level.

"I'm pretty sure Jackson is who we're playing for the homecoming game, which makes them our rival," Amber said, sounding like a Valley girl stating the obvious.

"Playing them at homecoming this year doesn't mean they should be our rival for all years," Nadiya said, mocking Amber's tone.

"All right, let's stay on track," said Mr. Bednarik, raising his voice and clapping his hands. His face said that he was dead serious about keeping us on the rails this time around. "We have about seven more minutes. Last call for mascots."

"What about a stallion," Nadiya said.

Which prompted Riley to add, "Or just a horse."

"Mr. B," Tori piped up, then pointed in our direction, "they are clearly trying to pack the ballot full of things that look like mustangs."

"All animals are welcome."

"I'd like to add pony, then." Chris grinned and I glared at him. What happened to Mr. Compromise?

"Any last—"

"How about a squid," I said, crossing my arms and leaning back in my chair. If Chris wasn't playing nice anymore, then neither would I.

"All right, then—"

"Miniature horse." Chris looked directly at me, almost laughing as he spoke.

"How is that different—"

"Octopus," I interrupted Tori, raising my eyebrow at the challenge.

Chris's entire face lit up with laughter as the room watched the two of us. Taking a deep breath, he started again: "Shetland—"

"Oh, look at that, time is up," Mr. Bednarik said, causing half the room to jump as he slammed down the marker to get our attention. "Everyone take out a piece of notebook paper and write down your favorite. I'll collect them at the door as we leave."

"Everyone vote for krakenstang, okay." Russ looked around the room and smirked as he began to write.

I looked over at Chris, half of me wondering what he would vote for, when he looked up and caught my eye. It should have been a playful, fleeting look, but something changed. The smile on his face shifted, the playfulness in his gaze replaced with something more dangerous. Hotter even. I held my breath, my heart slamming around in my chest as the electricity stretched and crackled between us.

Then he winked at me, like a full, mischievous wink,

and that broke the spell and whatever was between us. Heat flooded my cheeks, and I went back to focusing on my paper, trying to regain my composure. I wasn't sure what that look was all about or what game Chris was playing, but whatever it was, I was going to win.

I wrote down *octopus*.

Chapter Nine

IN HINDSIGHT, I SHOULD'VE PRACTICED SKATING BEFORE the party. But Mom assured me that it was just like riding a bike. The thing was, I wasn't that great at riding a bike either, so that really should have been a sign.

"Cute outfit!" Brianna called as she zipped by with a few of the Hirono cheer team members.

"Thank you!" I hollered, then looked down to make sure everything was still in its place. In the end, my go-to nineties consultant, my mom, had been extremely persuasive in convincing me that grunge-prep was the look I should be wearing, especially since her baggy jeans were too long on me. So here I was in a gray miniskirt that no nun would ever let a girl wear to school, a white collared crop top, fishnets, and knee socks, all of this covered by one of my dad's old plaid shirts with the sleeves rolled up so I could still use my hands to crash into the carpeted walls.

"Hey, birthday girl." I managed to turn around just in time to see Nadiya rolling right at me, her arms flailing as the plaid shirt she had wrapped around her overalls flapped in the wind.

I shot to the side of the wall so she could run into my former spot.

"You're getting better at this," I teased as she tried to straighten up.

"Whatever. We can't all be Spencer." Nadiya rolled her eyes, and the two of us looked over to where he was doing an unexpectedly dainty one-legged spin. Apparently, his parents had put him in ice hockey when they lived in Connecticut, and he had been biding his time since moving here to show everyone what he could do.

"Let's get a slushy before we break something." I grabbed Nadiya's arm. It seemed like a friendly gesture, but if anyone was looking closely, they'd see us clutching each other like a life raft to keep from falling.

We stutter-stepped over to the table that my mom and Auntie Kim had smothered in balloons and streamers, and gracelessly climbed up to sit on the back of the bench so that we could see the entire skating rink. Riley waved at us from over by the pinball machine and started to skate over right as my mom appeared with cups of mini slushies.

"Hey," Riley shouted. They managed to stop just before hitting the table and then smiled at my mom. "Hi, Ms. Williams. Grandma Florence said she wants you to take a picture of the three of us. Then she wants pictures of her and Meg."

We all looked over to where my grandmother was standing by the pinball machine with some of her church friends. Grandmama waved to let us know that she meant business about the picture.

Mom shook her head, then gestured for Riley to climb up

on the back of the bench with us. "Three, two, one: Say 'Birthday girl!'"

Mom took the picture as Auntie Kim tried to pry some sugar away from my ten-year-old twin cousins. It wasn't going to work. The twins were basically sweet-seeking missiles. They'd just find candy somewhere else, but I had to admire her determination.

Bass from the DJ booth shook the floor, and Mom and Auntie Kim looked at each other and shrieked. Giving up on the twins, Auntie Kim grabbed Mom's arm and shouted, "This is the jam. We got to go."

With that, the two of them skated over to the floor, smooth as butter, to start some kind of rolling line dance, laughing the entire time.

"Your family is cute," Riley said as Grandmama moved out to meet them, posing as she rolled across the floor.

"Pretty sure my mom suggested this because the three of them used to go skating all the time and they just wanted to show off." I laughed, then took a sip of my drink.

"Grandma Florence has some sweet moves. I'd show them off, too, if I was her." Nadiya swayed to the music until Freya skated by in a leather bustier.

All three of us sat up a little straighter and slapped giant, fake smiles on our faces. She looked vaguely annoyed, which made the party even more enjoyable in my mind.

Riley nudged my side. "Sour grapes much?"

"Maybe she's mad because that costume says Madonna in the eighties and she just figured out it's the wrong decade."

I shrugged and waved at my little cousin to hand me some Fun Dip.

"Or she's just mad that people are loving your party," Nadiya said, waving at my cousin to hand her some candy, too.

"Good," Riley said, joining in on the wave for candy. "If she wanted to have a good time, maybe she could try being nice."

"I wouldn't hold your breath." I looked at the two of them, and we all started cackling. The twins looked at each other and rolled their eyes. Emptying their pockets into our hands, they stalked off toward the games.

"Your mom and aunt are good dancers. Like—"

"Sorry. Is that . . ." Nadiya's voice trailed off as we turned to watch Russ wedge himself through the Skate Deck door, with Chris following behind him.

"Russ must have invited him. I'm sure it'll be fine. It's just two Davies people," Riley said, sounding cautiously optimistic.

Russ and Chris stopped just inside, letting their eyes adjust to the change in light. My heartbeat picked up a full notch, and I wondered if maybe they would notice that no one else from Davies was here and turn around. Russ was one thing. At this point, it'd be mean not to invite the guy. But Chris was another. It wasn't that I didn't want him here per se; it was more that I didn't want to deal with everyone else knowing he was here.

My breath caught as they turned to face us. While Russ had opted for a bright blue sweat suit made of swishy material and a bucket hat, Chris was a different story. He'd gone full grunge, complete with long, baggy cutoff shorts, combat boots, a graphic T-shirt, and a plaid tied around his waist. His usually tidy hair was messy, framing either side of his face. I was used to seeing him clean-cut or in workout clothes, but this suited him. He looked, in a word, hot.

Russ cupped his hands around his mouth and leaned back, turning himself into a human megaphone as he yelled, "Happy birthday!"

So much for no one noticing that they were here. Half the rink turned around to see who was screaming. Even Freya and Christine, who'd been taking pictures by the sweet sixteen backdrop, stopped to look at them. Riley raised one eyebrow in an oh-well gesture, then pushed themselves off the bench and skated toward the two.

Nadiya looked at me. "Nothing going on, huh?"

"Seriously, I didn't invite him," I said under my breath. "You were there when Russ invited himself. I couldn't control who he told."

"Right." Nadiya pursed her lips to one side and stared at me as if a hard look was going to change my answer. I wrinkled my nose at her, and she sighed. "Fine. Let's go say hi."

Grabbing my wrist, she yanked me off the bench and back onto the insecurity of eight wheels before I had time to protest. Nadiya kept an iron grip on my wrist as we approached, only letting me go when we had enough momentum to guarantee that I couldn't stop before we reached them.

"Thanks for inviting us," Russ said. "Spencer said this was a no-presents party, so I made you a card. I hope you're having a good birthday." He held out an envelope with MEG WILLIAMS written in his tiny, neat handwriting.

"Thanks for coming." I tried to sound like I had actually invited them as I took the card. It really was a sweet gesture, especially from someone who'd known me for all of four seconds.

"Happy birthday." Chris smiled at me, and I was struck by that hundred-watt glow again. That thing was almost magnetic, and I felt myself grinning back at him like he had an actual gravitational pull.

"Thanks." I looked down at the floor, hoping to hide the heat that was flooding my face. If Chris or Russ asked, I'd be able to blame it on skating, but Nadiya and Riley would be able to spot my lie from fifty miles away.

I could feel Riley's eyes on me as they said, "Let's get you two some skates."

"We're gonna go say hi to Tabitha real quick," Nadiya said, leaning into my side and elbowing me in the rib cage before adding, "See you three out there?"

They nodded and started toward the skate checkout. As soon as they were out of whispering range, Nadiya turned to me. "If there is nothing going on, then why are you being weird?"

"I'm not being weird. Why do you think I'm being weird?"

"Since when do you act shy?"

"I'm not acting shy."

"You were talking to the floor. You used to do that when Trevor was around before you two dated."

Oh, shoot. She wasn't wrong about that . . .

But this was different. I was probably acting weird because I hadn't expected Chris to be here. And I wasn't used to him being in costume. I wasn't used to me being in costume either, for that matter. That was likely why I was acting shy. At least, I was pretty sure that was why.

"I was just checking my shirt. I'm not used to having my torso be two different temperatures." I shrugged. Not a total lie. It was kind of weird trying to adjust to only half my stomach being covered.

"Sure." Nadiya rolled her eyes. "Well, Cold Tummy, you better get used to it fast, or you're gonna have the whole Chris situation on display for literally all of Hirono to see. So unless you want your birthday party to turn into a bloodbath—"

"You are so dramatic."

"I'm just trying to make sure my bestie doesn't do anything stupid the day she is finally able to get a license. I didn't drive you around for six months for you to be murdered by Freya."

"If I get murdered, it won't be by her," I joked, hoping to make Nadiya ease up just a little. "What if I just don't get killed period?"

"I mean, obviously, that's ideal." Nadiya's stern face started to crack into a smile. "Now, I'm gonna say hi to Tabitha so I don't look like a liar."

"All right. Love you, friend." I waved at her as she started to skate away.

"Stop sucking up to me," Nadiya shot back, laughing over her shoulder. "And remember, your grandmother still wants to take pictures with you."

I shook my head and started skating toward where my family was waiting to take a picture. Then I noticed my mom's face—looking like she smelled something foul—and followed her glance to the photo backdrop.

There were Trevor and Jasmine, trying to long-arm a couple selfie where they're trying to kiss each other and take a picture under the banner that said HAPPY SWEET SIXTEEN, MEG!

My stomach dropped and my brain started to whirl. I had accepted that Jasmine and Trevor were together. I was even okay with it. After all, I wasn't going to get any less ambitious, and if Trevor wanted someone with fewer goals, then I wasn't the girl for him. But a couple selfie under my birthday banner?

My eyes started to sting, and my face got hot. Suddenly the lights came down and the DJ said, "All right, everyone clear the floor. It's time for partner skate."

With that, the opening bars of "All My Life" by K-Ci & JoJo started playing. Trevor dropped his arm and looked over at Jasmine, who squealed and grabbed his hand so they could rush to the floor. Meanwhile, I was alone with no boyfriend selfie or partner skate on my sixteenth birthday, just me and my never-dating-in-high-school-again plan and my let's-invite-everybody party, even though I was nobody's special somebody and—

Nope. Nope. Nopity. Nope. This was too much.

Out of the corner of my eye, I saw Riley and Russ waving at me. There was no way I was going over there when the likelihood that I would burst into rage tears was this high.

This was my party and I refused to be crying over a boy. And if I was going to fall apart, I certainly wasn't going to cry in front of anybody over it.

"Getting air." I fanned myself, my vision blurring as I ducked behind a strange carpeted half wall that led to an employees-only area. From here, I couldn't really see the skate floor, which meant that the only way people could see me is if they were coming from the front door.

Secure in my hiding spot, I crouched down and pressed my palms to my eyes, forcing myself to take deep breaths. Why was I acting this way? I'd chosen not to let some new temporary boyfriend distract me from school. I should be fine. Instead, it felt like ever since I'd gotten to Davies—no, Huntersville—things had been weird. I'd been weird.

This was so stupid that it would have been funny if it wasn't me. After a moment, I pulled my hands away, then unwrapped my plaid so I could use it to wipe off the mascara from under my eyes. Looking at the smudges on the edge of my shirt, I laughed. I didn't even want Trevor. If this were anyone else, I would tell them to hold their head up and—

"No."

The word sounded pitiful. Even as I said it, it was too late. I saw Chris accept a pair of skates from the person at the window and turn in my direction. For a second, I thought he might not see me; after all, this was a bizarre hiding spot. I threw my plaid over my shoulders, crouched, shut my eyes, and willed myself to be invisible. It was magical thinking, but if there was one person I didn't want to see me right now, it was him. Okay, well, it was Freya, then Trevor, then Jasmine, then him. But still.

"Hey, Williams. What are you doing?" I cracked one eye

open to find Chris standing in front of me, his impossibly brown eyes looking down at me.

"I'm just hanging out here for a minute."

"In an inaccessible corner that smells like old shoes?" Chris tilted his head to one side to study me, then added, "While crouching."

"It's a good stretch." Why had I opted to pretend I was invisible? What kind of nerd does that? I forced myself to stand up, then shook out one arm, then the other, just in case that made the statement more believable. "Ready to skate again."

"Uh-huh." Chris looked behind him and watched partner skate go by for a second. I leaned around him, trying to see what he was seeing, only to get an eyeful of Trevor and Jasmine holding hands and gracelessly knocking into one another as they tried to skate close together. I straightened and exhaled right as Chris turned around.

He looked at me like he could see my pride cracking into bits. My eyes were probably still red, and who knew what state my makeup was in. I was lying and he knew it. He was going to call me out for being a wimp who was hiding from her ex so she didn't have to watch partner skate. I pulled my arms through my plaid and then hugged myself, bracing for humiliation.

"Do you need a hug?"

"What?" I scowled at him. Chris wasn't laughing or anything. The hint of a smile that usually hung around the corners of his mouth was gone. If he was going to make a joke out of the situation, somehow, the absence of his usual playful demeanor made the whole thing feel worse. Like he was actually trying to hurt me.

I gritted my teeth. "Don't be an ass."

Chris's eyebrows shot up in surprise. "I'm not. Or, I'm not trying to be anyway."

I could feel my face mirror his surprised expression as he set his skates down. Taking a step closer, he lowered his voice so that there was no chance people passing by would hear. "It's fine if you don't want one. I just thought it would be shitty to watch your ex and his new girlfriend at your party."

"And making out under my birthday banner," I grumbled.

"That's classy." Chris laughed, then gestured to his own chest. "If it were me, I'd want a hug. So, seriously, do you want a hug?"

I was halfway to saying no thanks when I stopped. This feeling was awful, and I wanted to feel comforted and understood. In short, I did want a hug.

"Okay. But you better not make fun of me later."

"Wouldn't dream of it."

The slow smile returned, and he held his arms open. Something about that smile was calming. Like, even though it felt like he was trying to charm me, he also genuinely meant it. I took a step forward, and he wrapped his arms around me.

In my head, this was going to be a quick hug. A tap on the back and then we'd let go. But that was not this hug.

The way he held me was just right, not so tight that I couldn't breathe but with just enough security to feel like we were in our own world. Closing my eyes, I let the warmth of his body wash over me as I snuggled into his chest. His familiar scent wrapped around me. I could feel his heart beating through his shirt. It felt like all the tension in my body was melting away and being replaced with something else. A low hum started to course through me, an intoxicating rhythm that made me want more. More of his smell. More closeness. More of the feel of him. More of his touch.

I wasn't sure how long we'd been wrapped up like this, but I wasn't ready to let go. There was only him in this space and I had no desire to move away from him. My hazy mind became aware of the change in music as a voice came over the speaker.

Chris's grip loosened, and he cleared his throat. "They're calling you."

"Oh."

I took a step back, and he blinked at me, his face looking as fuzzy and surprised as I felt. My skin prickled in the absence of his warmth, and I held my breath, unsure of what to do next.

Then, from the loudspeaker: "Meg Williams, it's your day. Make your way to the center of the rink, please."

Something about the DJ's voice jogged my brain into action. I pointed to the skating rink and did my best to form words. "We should . . ."

"Yup." Chris blinked twice, then nodded hard, like he was kicking his head into gear. As he picked up his skates, I started to think. Really think.

What had just happened? That was a hug from a friend. It needed to be, because I told Nadiya nothing was going on. Really, I just needed a hug. It could have been from any friend. Not even a friend. An acquaintance, really. I'd act normal, and whatever that hug was would just go away. Or something.

Chris nodded toward the rink. "Shall we?"

Mentally committing to just pretending everything was the same as soon as I skated onto the rink, I followed him toward the knot of people waiting for me. Chris stopped to put on his skates right as we reached the edge, and I remembered something about the hug. Seizing on my last moment before I let it disappear from my memory, I said, "Thanks for being cool back there."

"No big deal." He shrugged. It still felt like a very big deal.

"And thanks for the hug. You were right. I do feel better."

Chris's smile spread wide, and I turned to skate onto the floor, determined to fight that smile's gravity and forget this ever happened. And I would have . . . except then I heard his voice. It was quiet and just for me.

"I'm here for a hug whenever you need me, Meg."

Chapter Ten

"WE ARE *NOT* GOING TO BE THE PONIES."

"Of course not." I nodded at Cherish, treasurer of the former Hirono photography club and now of the Huntersville club, in what I hoped was a reassuring way, then closed my locker door. So far the photography club had managed to stay out of the homecoming war. They hadn't made a peep when Davies freshmen leaked their version of the fight song, complete with rude lyrics, or when the Hirono seniors tried to move the homecoming game to our old stadium. But, apparently, the mascot situation had gone too far.

"I'm not even picky," said Cherish. "But this list is stupid. Ponies, Octopuses? Or is it Octopi? We can't have a mascot where we don't know what the plural is. And what even is a krakenstang? And why do people keep telling me to write it in?"

"It's a combination of the mascots, mustang and kraken. Ask Russ. He's very excited about it." I threw my head back in exasperation, then righted myself when I caught sight of Cherish's face. I was supposed to be instilling confidence in my fellow Hirono students, not making them nervous. Pointing to the VOTE NOW poster, I said, "We just need a mascot for this year. Next year, if we hate it, we can change it again."

"Is that possible? I thought mascots were kind of a forever thing."

"Not if we decide they aren't. If I'm president next year, I'll work to make the mascot something we all love." I smiled my best politician-trying-to-convince-someone-of-something smile.

Cherish hemmed for a minute. Luckily, I was in no hurry to get home. Hell, if I could sleep at school tonight, I might.

"Well, if you're not elected, I guess I'm only here for another year. It'll make a good story when I go to college."

"That's the spirit." My smile tightened. I had no intention of not being class president next year, but apparently Cherish had her doubts. Great. Even the photography club had concerns. Who was next? Theater? Foreign languages?

As Cherish turned to go, I caught sight of Russ handing out krakenstang leaflets like they were information on a sale at a nearby store. The krakenstang wasn't even officially on the ballot, but he'd gone around writing it on every mascot-vote poster like it was. It would have been irritating if Spencer hadn't started campaigning first, by encouraging everyone to vote for the squid. On the upside, everyone in the school was officially campaigning for a stupid mascot, so at least no one was vandalizing anything. Hooray for hatred bonding.

Voting officially ended at 4:15 today, at which point, Mr. Bednarik would move the ballot box inside the Leadership classroom and it would become open season on pranks again. But this time, I was ready. Except . . . I needed to tell Chris.

I hadn't exactly been avoiding him since my party. It's more that we conveniently didn't find ourselves in the same place now that I had a better understanding of the Huntersville hallway system. Did it mean that sometimes I had to go out in the sweltering heat and cut across the front of the school to get to gym class? Maybe . . . but it also meant that I didn't have to figure out how to act around him, so there was that benefit.

Taking a deep breath, I popped on my forest green, square-framed Della sunglasses and headed toward the parking lot. I didn't have his phone number, so my plan was just to stand near his car, figuring out what to say, until he finished practice. Nadiya had to work today, so I knew she wouldn't be there to observe my traitorous behavior. I didn't like lying to my friends, but this was temporary. As soon as Chris and I got things contained, I'd go back to normal.

Only, his car wasn't there. My stomach plummeted. I knew he was at school today. I'd seen him at lunch. The guy never left school early. It literally hadn't even occurred to me that he might not still be here. If it had—

"Hey, Williams."

"Ah!"

"Ah!"

The squeak that had accompanied my jumping out of my skin was possibly the least dignified sound I have ever made. I clutched the stitch in my chest and turned around just in time to see Chris looking startled as well.

"Why did you scream?" He was dressed for the weight room and clutching the strap of his baseball backpack as his cheeks turned red.

"Because you surprised me. Why did *you* yell?" I scowled at him and felt around my neck for my pulse so I could figure out just how badly my heart was racing.

"Because you scared me when you started screaming." Laugh lines appeared around the corners of his eyes, and he placed a hand over his chest, ostensibly to encourage his heart to relax.

The memory of his heartbeat and the feel of his chest pressed against my cheek invaded my mind. Did he think of the same thing? How it felt to have me listen to his heart, or how I fit in his arms . . .

Okay, no. I was *not* thinking about that right now. Or ever. I was going to be normal. He and I were now cordial nemeses, plain and simple. Be chill.

"Thanks again for coming to my party." There. I could be normal around him.

"I was definitely told that this was a 'party for everyone,' so, one, Russ clearly misunderstood the instructions, and two, thanks for letting us party crash."

I grinned up at him, enjoying how it felt to see him smile. After a long pause, he said, "So. What are you doing here? Did you drive?"

Was I staring? Something was clearly wrong with me. He was the same Chris he'd always been. But here I was, making up signs and feelings where they had no business being. And really, even if I didn't have a plan, why would he have a crush on me anyway? I was a proud member of the nerd squad. A three-time champion of Shot's Coffee House Quiz Night. I wore loafers unironically, for god's sake. He was Huntersville royalty, with a baseball championship and a guitar. Even if we weren't on opposite sides of the homecoming war and I wanted to date right now, he was absolutely out of my league. I gave my head a shake and refocused.

"Uh, no, I didn't drive. I still have to take my test. Anyway. I realized that I didn't have your number to text you, so then I was looking for you in the parking lot to—"

"Oh," Chris held out his hand. "Give me your phone."

"Why?"

"So I can give you my number." He laughed. "What did you think I was going to do? Take it and run off?"

"I don't know." I pulled my phone out of my pocket and unlocked it, then handed it over to him. Belatedly, I remembered all the photos I'd saved of me and my dad on my camera roll for this evening. I desperately did not want to explain that to anyone. I'd waited years for Hirono to forget the HUNTERSVILLE HERO KILLED BY DRUNK DRIVER TRAGICALLY LEAVES BEHIND A WIFE AND TWO YOUNG DAUGHTERS headline. I didn't want to start that process all over again.

"Don't go poking around in there."

Chris looked up from the phone and smirked. "I wasn't planning to, but now I want to know what's on there."

"Oh, about fifty dozen photos of Riley's cat."

"Hmmm . . . that doesn't sound true—"

"Okay, give it here before I regret this." I reached for the phone and Chris yanked it out of the way, causing me to stumble right past him. He held the phone high above his head while he tapped something. I braced myself to take a running jump at him.

"Don't you—"

"All right. All right." He held one hand out in front of him as a stop sign and extended the phone to me with the other. "I didn't look. See, here's your phone."

Tucking the phone safely in my pocket, I glared at him one more time for good measure. I cannot believe I was fully in fantasy mode about this guy two minutes ago. Must have been the heat getting to my brain.

"Really, you can trust me, Meg." Chris ran a hand down the back of his head. I wrinkled my nose, and he dropped his hand to his backpack strap. "So what is it you wanted to tell me?"

"Hirono has a prank planned for tonight. We're going to move your mascot and bring in ours." I tried to sound deadpan, to let him know that he still wasn't forgiven for holding my phone hostage.

"That doesn't sound that bad." Chris shrugged.

"We're putting the kraken at the bottom of the pool."

"Oh." Chris sighed and winced. "That is bad."

"At least the swim team will have to dig it out instead of maintenance." Chris tilted his head at me, looking like a complete skeptic as the silence stretched until I finally broke. "Okay, it isn't great, but don't call the cops or anything, because I'm going to be there tonight to make sure it doesn't spiral."

For a moment, Chris didn't say anything. Then his expression cracked into a smile. "I wouldn't call the cops. Like I said, you can trust me, Meg."

"Ugh, stop." I rolled my eyes and laughed at how corny his callback sounded.

I looked up, but this time Chris wasn't laughing with me. Instead, he took a step back, confidence rolling off him. "You're going to like me eventually, Williams."

With that, he strolled into the parking lot, leaving me wondering what exactly he meant. A moment ago, I was convinced he wasn't interested in me. Now I wasn't so sure. I started the slow walk up to where Grandmama would be parked and pulled my phone out.

As soon as I opened the screen, I saw what he'd done. My phone background was now a silly old picture of him giving a thumbs-up in a Krakens uniform.

At school, I could almost forget about Dad's death anniversary. Pretend my heart wasn't in about fifteen different pieces. Time made the pieces less like boulders and more like large rocks. Little bits of my memories of him had begun to wash away. Sometimes, I worried that those rocks would eventually become sand and disappear altogether. This year, I realized that I couldn't really recall the sound of his voice anymore. Like, I could hear it on old videos, but I couldn't just imagine the sound the way that I used to.

I wasn't about to tell Mom that, though. Instead, I'd pretend that I remembered everything about him. Not just the feel of his scratchy face when he didn't shave. Or the sound of hospital beeps and the feel of Mac's hand in mine while we waited to say goodbye. For Mom's sake, I'd just pretend we were all feeling the exact same pain, because for Mom, that pain never seemed to change.

My phone buzzed and I looked down to see Nadiya's name running across my screen.

> How you holding up?

> > We ate dinner in silence, then Mom took some Tylenol PM and went to bed at 6:15 . . . so pretty good

I smiled down at my phone, grateful that I didn't have to hide what was happening from Nadiya. Besides Mac, she was the only other person I really trusted with this kind of honesty. If I told anyone else the truth, they'd probably think I was awful. What kind of person wanted to avoid their mother on a day like today?

> I'm sorry. You sure ur up for this tonight?

> > Yeah. This was my idea

> But the timing wasn't. Spencer and Riley would understand if you need to stay in

> > I don't. I promise

I inched my door open and stuck my head out to make sure everyone had truly gone to their room. The crack under Mom's door was dark, which meant that she was already in bed. The light was on under Grandmama's, but I could also hear her snoring, which meant that she was dozing and not quite ready to give up on reading. I was officially clear to sneak out and commit a minor act of vandalism. I just had to finish one final task.

My phone buzzed again, but I waited until I was solidly in the kitchen with a slice of leftover birthday cake before looking at it, just in case Grandmama heard me tapping my reply or something.

> All right. Riley and I will wait for you on the corner of your street at 11:30

> If you change your mind, let me know and I'll make up an excuse

> I'm not changing my mind. I'm already dressed in my prank outfit

> Is it all black?

> You are such a nerd

I looked down at my outfit. My jeans and sneakers were black, but technically my hoodie was dark green. Only because my old Hirono hoodie was the darkest sweatshirt I owned. Still, it counted.

Holding up my phone, I snapped a quick picture of me, my hoodie, and my cake, then sent it off to Nadiya.

> Proud of it

I put my phone back in my pocket and exhaled, then looked back at the cake. Every year, I managed to squirrel away a piece, then I'd celebrate with Dad on his anniversary. It was my own little ritual. Mom couldn't really talk about him, so I talked with him. I'd tell him things about my year, look at photos, and remember bits about him that made me smile, then make a wish.

Setting my cake down on the counter, I found the birthday candles in the junk drawer and popped one on top of my slice. I lit it and prepared to make my wish. I was halfway through my usual, *Please let me get out of Huntersville,* when it occurred to me that this year, I didn't want that. Or, rather, I'd wished it enough times that either Dad and whatever god was listening were going to make it happen or they weren't.

As I watched the wax drip down the candle, I thought about tonight. Would he understand why I had to sneak out? Would anybody in this house recognize me right now when I barely recognized myself? Was that such a bad thing? Maybe I should take Mac's advice and wish to have some fun.

I smiled, made my wish, and blew out the candle.

Chapter Eleven

I LEANED AGAINST MY LOCKER AND GRINNED DOWN AT A photo of me, Nadiya, and Riley all wearing snorkels next to the kraken statue that used to be in front of the school.

"You are a legend."

I looked up to find Christine standing in front of me and blinked just to be sure that this wasn't some kind of sleep-deprived Hungry Girl delusion. Nope, still there. I leaned away from the lockers and tried to look innocent. If the authorities ever found my phone, they'd know exactly what I'd done. In fact, I was pretty sure that if Principal Domit tried even a little bit, she'd know who was behind the maze of kraken paraphernalia at the bottom of the pool.

"I'm sure I don't know what you're talking about."

I winked and she laughed.

"Right. Well, next time you 'don't' do a thing, invite me." Christine put the word *don't* in air quotes. With that, she waved in an oddly menacing way that I suspect she thought was friendly, then walked off.

I felt like a zombie. Rounding up all the Davies Kraken plaques, statues, and figurines was exhausting, but placing them in the pool was even more difficult. Not to mention corralling the attention of my classmates long enough to get things done without doing any serious damage to the property. Thank god half the chess club owned wet suits.

"I didn't think you were that devious." Spencer walked up and nudged me with his shoulder.

"Just 'cause I don't get into trouble doesn't mean I can't. I usually try to use my powers for good."

"Dude, the Davies swim team is pissed." Spencer's eyes were wide like he was waking up on Christmas morning. "Apparently, Coach is making them retrieve everything today."

"I hope they have fun swimming through the maze before they do." I propped myself up against the wall next to him.

"Having us build that tunnel out of their trophies was genius."

"Thanks. I wonder if I can put this on a college application?"

"If you can't get into an Ivy League with this, they don't deserve you." Spencer laughed as the warning bell sounded. "Anyway, watch your back. Basically, anyone who ever won anything or had a kraken art project on display is trying to figure out who planned this."

"Thanks." I leaned off the wall to get to Life Skills so I could finish my tragic-looking pajama set.

I walked down the hall grinning and waving at anyone who even remotely looked my way. By the time Nadiya, Riley, and I had gotten to school last night, half the Hirono junior class was there. (All wearing black—take that, Nadiya!) It was nerve-racking, trying to sneak around with sixty people all looking at you for instructions, but it was also fun. In all the years I'd watched Riley pull pranks, the one thing they'd never told me was how exhilarating and hilarious sneaking around for something harmless was.

Pulling open the classroom door, I found my project crate and took my seat at my usual sewing machine. The bell went off, and the chair next to me was pulled out. I looked over and nearly choked. Freya was staring right at me, an exquisitely tailored mod dress clutched between her press-on nails.

"Can I help you?" I admit, it wasn't my smoothest greeting, but I was surprised, and it was the first thing that came to mind.

"Did you do the pool prank?"

"I don't know what you're talking about." I wasn't about to take credit for this in front of Freya. I turned back to my seam ripping.

"I know you did. I saw Tabitha's pictures."

"Then I guess you don't need to ask me."

My heart started to pound, and blood rushed to my ears. I focused on keeping my hands steady. Whatever Freya wanted, she wasn't going to trick me into giving it to her.

"Fine. Don't tell me." Freya sounded like she was talking through a clenched jaw as she twisted the fabric of her dress in her hands, and I wondered where this was going. "It's not like anyone told me beforehand anyway."

"Whose fault is that? If people don't trust you, Freya, maybe you should ask yourself why."

I looked up at Freya and bit down on my bottom lip. Her

face wrinkled with surprise. It wasn't like me to just say things without thinking. I hadn't meant to say those words out loud, but I was tired, both of her and in general.

"I—" Freya started and then stopped. Her mouth opened and closed as she tried to think of a response. Despite the heat rushing to my cheeks, I didn't feel bad. I mean, sure. If I had planned to call someone out, I might have tried harder to sound less like Grandmama, but whatever. Maybe it was just the prank, but something had clearly gotten into me.

"You're in my chair." Nadiya's voice came from behind Freya, causing her to jump.

"I was just leaving." Freya's cheeks were an aggressive shade of pink as she stood up.

"Byeee." I drew out the *e* sound in the word for effect.

"What was that all about?" Nadiya asked, dropping into the recently vacated chair.

"Who knows?" I shrugged and tried to keep the happy dance I wanted to do on the inside. Nadiya may not have been right about no one wearing black, but she was right about this. Letting our classmates know where I stood was good for everyone.

Except for the swim team. And Freya. But I was just fine with that.

"All right. Here's the ballot box." Mr. Bednarik was almost bouncing in his five-toed running shoes as he set the box down on the table in the back room. "I'm counting on you two to keep each other honest. No switching votes."

"I don't think you have to worry about that. Williams is pretty honest."

I could feel Chris looking at me, but I was convinced that if we made eye contact, I'd crack up, and that wouldn't be fair to Warm Fuzzy.

"I know, I know." Mr. Bednarik chuckled as he walked to the door. "I'll be in the other room grading papers. When you two have a winner, you let me know."

"Sure thing." I nodded, proud of myself that I managed to pull it together enough not to laugh.

Mr. Bednarik opened the door, then stopped halfway through. Turning to face us again, he said, "And remember. You are sworn to secrecy until after the announcement on Saturday. Everyone is going to be so surprised."

With that, he bounced out of the room, and I looked at Chris. For two seconds, we just blinked at each other, silently communicating just how silly this all seemed, and then we both doubled over and cracked up.

"I think it's the shoes," Chris wheezed as he tried to stand up.

"The shoes are just a symptom."

"A symptom of what? A man who has spent a lot of time reading self-help books?"

I tried to pull myself together again, this time getting as far as propping myself upright before I dissolved into laughter once more. Taking a deep breath, I nudged him with my elbow, "Come on, we need to start counting, or we'll be here all night."

"Okay, but only because I know you have to be tired after the stunt you pulled."

My gaze jerked to the door to make sure it was fully closed before I looked at him. "Shhh. Mr. Bednarik will hear you."

"Over the sounds of his daily affirmations? Unlikely." Half of Chris's mouth tugged into a smile as he dropped his voice. Putting one hand on the table, he leaned toward me. "I will deny it if you repeat this, but I have to say, the trophy tower at the bottom of the pool was impressive. How'd you do that?"

His voice so close to me sent shivers down my spine, and my chest squeezed. I needed to put a little distance between us if I was going to survive this without turning into some sort of weird pile of feelings goo.

Using my best stern voice, I stepped toward the ballot box and said, "A little fishing line and a couple of former scouts. Now focus."

His smile faltered for a flicker of a second. If I hadn't known better, I would have thought he looked disappointed that I'd put us back on task. Then the look was gone. Replaced with a grin as he straightened. "Yes, ma'am."

Chris walked over to where he'd set his backpack and guitar in the corner and began rummaging around. This Chris, the one with the easy smile, made more sense to me. Really, even if he was disappointed, what was I going to do about it? Nothing. And even if I would have done something, I'd just sunk half of Davies's trophies to make the point that I didn't care about him or anyone at Davies. That sort of felt like a deal-breaker.

Returning with two pens and a piece of paper, he leaned over the desk and began writing the names of the potential mascots in columns so we could keep track of the count. He looked up at me and opened his mouth to say something, then looked back down and scrawled a sixth word on the paper: *krakenstang.*

"Ready when you are." He smiled like he'd just told a prize-winning joke.

"Krakenstang isn't on the ballot."

"Just humor me." I sighed heavily, and he held a pen out to me. "Please."

"Fine. But if we need more space for counting Mustang votes, I'm taking that column over."

"I wouldn't expect anything less." Chris nodded with reverence as I rolled my eyes.

I pulled the lid off the box and took out a handful of ballots. Chris mirrored my motions, and for a while, the two of us worked quietly next to one another.

"I think krakenstang might win," Chris said.

"What?" I blinked at him, trying to bring my mind around to the idea that we were talking again.

Chris nodded to the paper full of tick marks. "The kraken-stang. A lot of people wrote it in." His voice was so gentle that I almost didn't register the note of humor in it.

"No, that's—" I looked down at the paper. Sure enough, the

krakenstang column was full of tallies. I reached for my pile of counted ballots. "There is no way. I don't think I had that many."

"I don't think we needed that many. The other five mascots split the votes." Chris lifted one shoulder with an ambivalent shrug, then peeked over the edge of the box to see how many ballots were left. "We can count them, but unless all of them voted for squid, I think krakenstang won."

"That can't be right." I set my pile of votes down and flipped through his ballots. Lots of krakenstangs. I thrust his ballot stack back at him. "Don't make that face."

"What face?"

"You know what face." I looked at the remaining ballots. "We have to toss out the krakenstang count and pick the next-highest winner."

"Pick squid? No." Chris looked appalled. Tapping his fingers, he said, "One, an underwhelming number of people want to be squids, and two, that would be unethical."

"How is it unethical? Krakenstang isn't even on the ballot."

"Well, clearly it should have been, because the people have spoken."

I crossed my arms and leaned my hip on the table. "The people can't speak that way. We didn't give them the option to. We'll just have to throw out—"

"No." Chris's eyes went wide. "You sound like a tiny dictator."

"I am not a tiny dictator. I'm a president. And I'm not even short."

"You have on platform clogs."

"These are loafers, not clogs. And—" Chris's mouth twitched into a smile, and I shook my head. "No, I refuse to be derailed by a discussion on shoes. We can't have a krakenstang as a mascot. What do we even call something that stupid? We can't call it the krakenstang or we'll be laughed out of town."

"Jasper."

"Jasper the Krakenstang?" I lifted one eyebrow in case he was unclear on how profoundly stupid that sounded.

It had no effect on him. Instead, Chris nodded resolutely. "Yup. Jasper is the perfect name for imperfect things. Everyone loves a Jasper."

"Tell that to Jasper Heywood."

"Who is that?" Chris had the nerve to look at me like I was the ridiculous one now.

"The priest who translated the works of Seneca. The church was not a fan. Died in exile. So, not a well-liked Jasper."

"You spend way too much time on the internet." Chris scrunched his face as he shifted to mirror me. Planting both feet on the ground in a power stance, he crossed his arms. "We are leaving Jasper the Krakenstang. It's only right."

"It isn't named Jasper." I dropped my hands to my sides with a loud thump. "And it isn't our mascot."

Chris's jaw set and his eyes narrowed. "I'll compromise on a lot. But I'm not compromising on this. The people voted. Jasper stays."

"How about this? We let people see Jasper the Krakenstang at the game. If everyone in town laughs at the entire junior class, then we change the mascot—"

"Fine," Chris jumped in, his face relaxing, before I'd even finished the sentence.

"—to the mustang."

"Not fine." He snort-laughed. It should have been a dorky sound, but it was oddly adorable. "However, I will agree to take ponies off the list if people hate Jasper. Which they won't."

"I can live with that." I held out my hand. "Deal?"

Chris looked at my hand for a moment, then took it. His hand felt solid. The tips of his fingers were rough with calluses from playing the guitar. He nodded, then let go, which felt too soon.

"We should get these last few votes counted, so our numbers add up."

"Yup. Otherwise, Mr. Bednarik will be forced to grade all his papers, and nobody on the student council really wants his notes on our personal-reflection essay." I flexed my hand behind my back. It felt like I'd taken off a glove on a cold day. I gave my hand a shake and tucked it into my pocket so I didn't have to think about whatever that meant.

"I personally want to know how Warm Fuzzy feels about my fifth-grade Little League championship." Chris laughed as he finished putting check marks on the page.

"Oh, I'm sure he's writing that out for you right now." I reached for a stack of ballots and tucked them back into the box.

Chris put the last of the ballots away, along with the tally, and placed the lid back on the box. Watching him pick up his guitar case, I grinned as he turned to face me. "What?"

"Nothing." I tried to suppress my grin as I walked to the door.

"Why are you smiling like that?"

"Smiling like what?" I stopped and waited for him to get the door.

He put his hand on the handle but didn't open it. Instead, he looked down at me, scrutinizing my face. "Like you know something."

"Because I do." I grinned and nodded at him to get a move on. "The name of your band. The Wicked, isn't it?"

Chris's mouth dropped open, and it took no small amount of effort for me not to gloat. I walked through the door just in time to see him pull himself together. He turned to me and started to say something when Mr. Bednarik looked up.

"Do we have a winner?"

"We do. Jasper the Krakenstang."

"Oh." Mr. Bednarik pursed his lips and nodded. If I had to guess, he was probably trying to work out why Chris and I hadn't called for a revote. Hell, I was still trying to figure that out myself. "Well, what the school wants is what the school gets. Russ will be pleased."

"I thought the same thing," Chris said, using his best talking-to-a-teacher voice. A little part of me wanted to elbow him in the side for sucking up, but the other part of me thought it was kind of funny.

"I just hope people still like it when it goes on the uniforms," I said with a shrug, then turned toward the door, eager to get to the parking lot before Nadiya left Freshman Homework Help Club volunteer duty. "See you later, Mr. Bednarik."

"One more thing." Warm Fuzzy's voice stopped me in my tracks, and I turned back around. "I want to talk to you two about helping the sophomores by working concessions for the game. And, Chris, I have your essay."

Mentally, I sighed. I guess I wouldn't be beating Nadiya to the parking lot. But on the upside, seeing Chris's horror-stricken face at the mention of his essay was probably worth sticking around for another five minutes.

I opened the front door to the sound of absolutely nothing. When Mom was sad, she used music to drown out her thoughts. But when the grief got too bad, the house went silent. Before Mac left, the two of us would make enough noise that it felt like people were still alive in the house. But with Mac gone, it seemed like Dad's grave became our home. The silence was eerie even though I'd known it was coming.

Stopping by the kitchen, I found a granola bar on top of a note in Grandmama's perfect script.

Baby,
Gone to the church bid whist tournament. Left dinner in the fridge for you and your mama to heat up. Don't burn the house down.
Love,
G-ma

I tucked the note in my denim skirt pocket—it made me happy, and I figured that if Mom didn't leave her room tonight,

I could at least take it out and laugh at it later. For now, I'd get a start on my mountain of homework. If nothing else, my ambition meant I had enough homework to keep me busy and my mind off things for at least three weeks.

"Hey." The sound of Mom's voice made my heartbeat pick up. I hadn't expected to see her yet. Historically speaking, she only rejoined the world when one of us made her, usually anywhere between forty-eight hours and two weeks in.

"Hi, Mom."

"What are you up to?" Mom shuffled into the kitchen and stood on the other side of the L-shaped counter from me.

"Just grabbing a snack and then I'm gonna do my homework."

She looked exhausted. Had she always looked that way when she got up and I never noticed before? Then again, the combination of Mac leaving and Dad's anniversary was extra hard. Maybe this was a new level of grieving we weren't going to talk about. I toed the kitchen floor, trying not to feel frustrated with the situation, my body temperature rising with the effort. "How are you feeling?"

"Oh, you know." Mom shrugged.

The air grew thick with her unspoken words and the anger I was never going to voice. What did she think I knew? It wasn't like we'd had long discussions on how she was feeling. What I missed about Dad. Or the things I wished she'd tell me about him. That I had to guess his favorite color based on the pictures in the house. The more I thought about it, the weirder it seemed to have pictures you can't really talk about.

"All right, well. I'm gonna get that homework going." I turned to escape down the hallway and into my room before the weirdness hanging in the air swallowed me up. Why did this conversation feel so awkward? I used to be ecstatic when she would get up. Now I just wished she'd go back to her room so I could have the house to myself.

"Hey, Meg." Mom's voice sounded heavy, and I turned around. "Where did you go so late last night?"

My stomach dropped at the same time panic and heat started to course through me. A small part of my brain wondered if I should just tell her the truth. But there was no way I was doing that. Any other week, Mom might understand. Maybe even find it funny. But this week, my having fun and breaking rules? There was no world in which I was going to admit to being happy breaking rules when she expected me to be buried under a mountain of grief.

"I was just outside chatting with Nadiya."

"You were gone for longer than that." Mom's eyebrows knitted together, her shoulders slumping with the effort it took to speak.

"No." I shook my head and tried not to feel like a wretched person. I couldn't believe I was lying to my mom, or even remember the last time I'd done it. Then again, there was a first time for everything, including being happy without her permission. "Maybe the Tylenol you took to help you sleep through Dad's anniversary made you confused?"

For a moment, neither of us moved. I felt stuck to the kitchen floor like my lie had glued me there. At the mention of

Dad, what little color had been in Mom's face drained, leaving behind a gray mask. She closed her mouth and looked down at the ratty plaid she was wearing. When she spoke, her voice was soft. "Maybe . . ."

"All right. Hope you're up later. I'll heat some food for you." I had to get out of there before I said anything else mean but true. Mom nodded, looking like she might sink to the kitchen floor as soon as I left.

I walked to my room, taking measured steps even as my body screamed *Run*. Once I was safely inside, I closed the door, slowly twisting the handle and then releasing it to avoid even hinting at the idea that I would slam the door on her. Guilt threatened to swallow me whole. I never threw Dad in her face. That wasn't fair. But it also wasn't fair that she abdicated parenting for a week every year and now had suddenly decided to pop in for one disciplinary session after nine years of me watching over myself.

It felt like Mom was a sea of grief and I was standing on the edge of the ocean as the tide was coming in. I'd pull up my French worksheet, and grief would wash toward my toes with memories of my dad teaching me to ride a bike. Then I'd get up, move my beach umbrella and my towel, and try to settle in to work on my history essay. Only the waves would move again. This time with me, Mac, Dad, and Mom running through the sprinkler in the backyard during a heat wave. It was like the ocean of sadness was trying to swallow me whole without sound to ward it off.

The problem was that our house was too quiet. I'd spent

the last nine years learning to focus by tuning out the noise. I resented Mom for it, even. But now there was nothing to tune out, and I couldn't think of anything except my dad or how Mom looked when I mentioned him.

I picked up my phone and started searching through my apps for something to listen to. Ideally, something that wouldn't make me feel like the tide was chasing me. Something new . . .

Tapping up to the search bar, I checked to see if maybe I could find Chris's band, and almost dropped the phone when it came up. The band in the picture looked moody and dis-affected. I could make out Chris dressed in jeans and a striped shirt. He was trying not to smile, like the rest of his bandmates, but his telltale good humor was hanging around his lips.

My finger hovered over the Play button as I debated. What if his music sounded like crap? Then I'd have to see his face every day and know that he wrote bad songs and took them seriously. Would I even be able to look him in the eye? Or, what if the songs were about an ex? What if I knew them?

The muscles in my neck tensed, and I forced myself to take a deep breath. The whole point of listening to something was to relax and focus. If I hated it, I would just turn it off and pre-tend I never found the music. It wasn't like I was required to tell Chris his band was garbage even if he asked.

Taking a deep breath, I hit Play. A slow guitar lick floated out of the speakers as the first few seconds of the song started. This was what Chris sounded like.

I'd been afraid that his band would be awful, but as a bass and the vocalist joined him, I relaxed. It felt like the sound was sinking into my chest, the drum kick lining up with my heartbeat and carrying the singer's words through my veins. The song was about the usual—a breakup that wasn't staying broken up—but it was the guitar that mattered. In the middle of a messy heartbreak, the sound of Chris's guitar was soaring, pushing at the edges of the grief that had come over my house and threatened to pull me under.

I leaned back in my chair and closed my eyes, letting the feeling of the perfect song for the moment wash over me. The recording quality wasn't great. It didn't have the high-gloss polish of anything on the radio. But it didn't need it. The band was good. Like, really good.

When the song ended, I hit Rewind immediately, then tapped the Loop button. I knew there were other tracks on the EP, and I would get to them eventually. But right now, I just wanted this one.

Funny how I hadn't expected his music to be comforting to me, but it was. Not unlike how it felt to hug him. Maybe Chris would always have that effect on me if I let him. The idea that I would let him continue to comfort me was scary. But just as scary was how much I liked it.

Chapter Twelve

"STOP MESSING WITH YOUR TOP. IT'S MAKING ME NERVOUS." Nadiya adjusted the volume of the car radio with one hand and held on to her lip gloss with the other.

"Sorry." How had I let Mr. Bednarik talk me into working concessions with Chris? Worse, I wasn't sure what colors I was supposed to wear yet. As a result, I'd basically tried to wear them all, and now I looked like a walking rainbow. Like I should be stuck on the wall in a kindergarten classroom, not going to my first football game of the year.

I was just about to ask Nadiya to please not drive with her knees when she said, "Why are you being weird anyway?"

"I'm not being weird. I'm nervous because our class picked a stupid krakenstang as a mascot—which Chris has named Jasper, by the way—and now I'm gonna have to work concessions at halftime and hear all about it."

"You sure it's just about Jasper?" Nadiya looked over at me and raised an eyebrow.

"Eyes on the road. And don't call it Jasper. It's not staying." We turned in to the parking lot, and the tension in my chest released. Sure, I had a crush that was very likely unrequited and particularly off-limits, but at least my best friend wasn't going to run us off the road by fixing her makeup while driving.

"That wasn't an answer to my question."

"It's just the mascot. I swear."

I was not about to tell Nadiya that I'd been listening to Chris's band and that *maybe* the minor crush I seemed to have developed on him had somehow grown into a medium-sized crush. With any luck, I'd catch him doing something bizarre, like collecting lint, and it would go away.

"All right, then." Nadiya watched me for a moment, then reached for the door handle. "I can't believe Warm Fuzzy is making you help at halftime."

"Apparently not enough sophomores could figure out how to use the till, and the football booster club needs help."

"Well, the sophomore government should have to split the profits with us if they can't figure out how to read a manual." Nadiya huffed as she produced her school ID from the bottom of her purse for the security guard.

"If they make us do it again, I'll demand repayment. For now, being a good classmate serves us. Kelly's little sister is the class secretary, and Kelly is officially captain of the soccer team now, so it's worth it."

"You are like a vote-calculating machine. What will you do with this weird skill once you get to college?"

"I'm retiring from office once I'm out of here." I giggled as the security guard waved us through.

"There's Riley." Nadiya grabbed my arm and began the perilous descent down the metal stands. Unlike Hirono, which just had a football field that consisted of a bunch of random rusty bleachers around a multipurpose space, Davies had an actual stadium, complete with an announcer's booth and lights bright enough to signal to outer space. On the field, our team wore their black practice jerseys. I didn't know any of my classmates' numbers yet, but Russ was easy to spot because of his size. He seemed to be trying to learn the cheer squad dance in between running warm-up drills, completely oblivious to how hard the crowd was laughing.

We muscled our way into the mass of students to stand next to Riley. "Hey, you two. Ready to find out all the details about our school over the course of an extremely brutal and exploitative game?"

"You know it." Nadiya rolled her eyes, which made Riley and I laugh. Nadiya loved football. Even if we hadn't wanted to be here, she would have dragged us along. "What do you think they're going to do, announce everything at halftime or do a slow reveal over each quarter?"

"This has to be the silliest way to open a school," I said. "I can't believe they didn't just pick all this for us—"

"Shhh . . ." Nadiya shushed me. "I think we're about to find out."

The three of us watched as the team jogged to the locker room and Principal Domit strolled onto the field wearing a bright purple pantsuit.

"Guess we know what color the seniors picked," Riley grumbled.

"Hello, everyone!" Principal Domit shouted into the microphone like a wrestling announcer. "Welcome. I am so pleased to be here and to unveil the new Huntersville High mascot. Let's hear it for the purple and gray, the Huntersville High Krakenstangs."

"What is a krakenstang?" a freshman three rows up hollered.

"Gray? That is just sad," someone to the left of me groused.

I couldn't tell if I should hide or cheer. Some of my classmates were cackling, while others looked upset, and a good chunk of people seemed just plain confused. The one thing none of them were was silent. Principal Domit was still speaking, but I couldn't hear a word she said over the roar of the crowd.

By the time our team took the field in their new purple jerseys, I was fully dreading going up to the concessions, even if I could get myself a cookie to feel better. As the minutes on the clock ticked by, I started to sweat. Soon I'd have to walk all the way past four classes full of people wondering what the hell a krakenstang was. Thanks, Russ.

The game started and seemed to pass in a blur of cracking sounds, Russ running through people, and me ignoring everyone who tried to get my attention. I'd never focused so hard on something and retained so little. When the clock said four minutes left in the half, I gave myself a shake, hoping it would release some of my nervous energy, then turned to Riley and Nadiya. "I gotta go up. Save my seat?"

"Good luck," Riley called, looking as worried as I felt.

"You got this. Jasper is great," Nadiya teased.

"Jasper is not great," I called over my shoulder as I pushed toward the aisle. "And don't call it that."

Keeping my head down, I focused on getting up the metal

steps as quickly as I could without looking like I was physically sprinting away from my classmates. I'd managed to ignore my name being called at least three times, and I wanted to keep it that way for as long as possible. I knocked on the concession booth door and hoped that Mrs. Cabrini or Mr. Aggarwal would answer quickly.

The door wrenched open, and my face immediately started to warm up. Chris stood in the doorway, framed by the glow of the concession booth light like some sort of rock god in a movie.

"Hello, Williams." He grinned and stepped back from the entry, forcing me out of my mini-starstruck moment. He was still the same as before. And to be fair, I'd already known he was good at something. I just thought that something was baseball.

"Hi, Chavez. Thank you for getting the door." I stepped into the booth and looked around to get my bearings. Snacks were at one end; the other is where I assumed the new Huntersville High merch would go. "Where are Mrs. Cabrini and Mr. Aggarwal?"

"Break. They said they'd be back once halftime started." I walked over to the empty counter space and hoisted myself up to sit on it, then adjusted my skirt so it wasn't all hiked and wrinkled.

Chris closed the door, then turned to face me, a Cheshire-cat grin still glued to his face. He stuffed his hands in his pockets, then leaned forward and back as if he were waiting for me to say something. Finally, he cracked. "So . . ."

"Something you want to say?" It felt good to let my feet dangle against the cabinetry after standing for the first half of the game.

Chris paused and watched me. After a moment, he came to stand in front of me. "Are we not going to talk about how everyone loves Jasper?"

"Who loves Jasper? I didn't hear that from anyone!"

"I had six people come up here looking for a Jasper sweatshirt, and the local paper stopped by to say that they want to do an unveiling of it when the art is done. And I've only been here for, like, three minutes." Chris took his hands out of his pockets and crossed his arms with a smug smile. "Mrs. Cabrini said she wrote down the names of everyone who stopped by during the first half of the game, and it's like sixty people already."

"No way."

"Do you all have Krakenstang T-shirts yet?" We both jumped, then turned to look at the voice that had startled us. A blond freshman with pigtails, who had picked the least opportune time to prove Chris's point, stared at us, eyes wide, as she waited for an answer.

"It's called Jasper" and "Not yet," Chris and I said at the same time. He beamed at me, so I scowled at him.

"Oh. Okay." The freshman started to go, but then it dawned on me.

"Wait. He can take your name. Special deal—five dollars off for anyone who orders their Jasper gear tonight. Tell your friends."

Chris looked back at me, his eyes wide with surprise, then

a slow smile crept across his face. I raised one eyebrow and nodded at him to go help the freshman. I was grateful when he finally did, because that smile might have melted all my resolve to do nothing with this crush if he'd aimed it at me any longer.

"So you're on board with Jasper now?" Chris said as soon as the freshman turned to leave.

"I mean, I still think a krakenstang is stupid." I crossed my ankles, then leaned forward to rest on my palms. "But I'm a big enough person to admit when I'm wrong. Plus, we need money for homecoming."

Chris snorted, then slowly sauntered over to where I was sitting and leaned against the cabinet next to me. He was close enough that his hip brushed against my knee as he settled in, sending little sparks up and down my legs. "Leave it to you to see an upside to this. You really are good at governing."

"Thank you." I should probably have scooted over, but I couldn't. Our arms were close enough that I could feel the warmth from his skin on mine. "You're pretty good at it, too."

"Not as good as you."

"True." I paused, and Chris looked over at me. This time it was my turn to grin. "But that's okay. You're good at other things."

"Am I?" Somewhere the crowd cheered, reminding me that there was a world beyond us. One that I wasn't particularly interested in right now. I tilted my head toward him and waited for him to say more, but he just looked at me for a second, then down at the floor, giving his head a shake.

"I listened to your band." I bit down on my lip to keep from rambling as Chris's gaze jumped to meet mine. Unease crossed his face, and he went still. My heart started racing. I must have totally creeped him out. I wanted to tell him that his band was good, but I imagined doing it in a chill way. Not in a random, we-are-stuck-in-a-booth-and-you-can't-get-away-from-me way.

"Sorry, that's—"

"How did you . . ." He paused and ran a hand down the back of his head, then crossed one arm over his chest. Something was off. It was like all his usual swagger had melted into the floor. He winced as if whatever he was trying to say scared him. "What did you think?"

Was he nervous? My eyes popped open as it hit me. Me being a weirdo wasn't the problem. Chris of eminently-cooler-than-you status was worried about his band not being good enough for me. Me. Who unironically liked sweater sets. I couldn't help it, I laughed.

The sound made his face freeze in a grimace, and he leaned away from the counter to look at me, taking the warmth of his skin with him and leaving me suddenly cold. Inhaling a sharp breath, he said, "Actually, you don't have to tell me. I promise I'm not that guy who bugs you about listening to his shitty band or—"

"No. You're not shitty." I rushed to correct his misperception. The last thing I wanted was him to think I was laughing at him. Not when I'd listened to his songs on repeat all day. "You're really, really good."

"You don't have to say that." The muscles in Chris's jaw were still tight, but he leaned back against the counter again.

"Seriously. I'm laughing because it seems like a ridiculous question. And I'm not trying to be nice. You are talented." I looked over at him, watching his face to make sure he understood that I wasn't lying. "Like, okay, the recording quality needs work, but you're awesome."

At that, Chris laughed. "Yeah, our bassist is learning to mix. But we're saving up for a real recording session. Just gotta have something out there for now."

"Makes sense. So is that what you want to do?" Chris looked over at me like he didn't understand the question. "Be a musician, I mean. Since you're paying for studio time and all that."

"Maybe. My parents want me to study business, seeing as they built a whole business for the family. But I might minor in music or something." He lifted one shoulder as if being out of alignment with his family was no big deal, but his jaw clenched again.

Something about the way he tried to sound casual felt off to me, but I wasn't sure I knew him well enough to call it out. If he wasn't ready to talk about it, I'd leave it alone. His parents were probably right anyway. A business degree was the practical option. It was just . . .

"You could do it the other way around. Major in music and minor in business. After all, it never hurts a musician to have some business sense, and it's not like banking jobs or whatever your parents want you to do are going anywhere."

Chris turned to look at me, his eyes searching my face. His

gaze sent electricity through me. I should turn away, or back down from whatever this feeling was. After all, I'd told Nadiya nothing was going on and I'd sworn off dating for my own good. Only I couldn't look away. I wanted to stay right here.

His expression changed, as if something had clicked between us. Slowly, he leaned into me so our arms were touching. He was so close that I could smell him again, clean with a hint of spice. Being this close to him made me light-headed. His eyes jumped down to my mouth, and he licked his lips. My heart both stopped beating and started to knock around in my chest.

Oh my god. He was going to kiss me. My head started to go all buzzy, and the only thing I could think of was him. The feel of his skin against mine. The way our lips might fit. How he'd taste.

Chris looked me in the eyes again, and I held my breath. He leaned in just a little closer. "I really want—"

"Prepare for the flood!"

Chris jumped away from me, and I yelped, grabbing a stitch in my chest as Mr. Aggarwal charged through the concession stand door with Mrs. Cabrini right behind him—the two of them completely oblivious to the fact that they had interrupted something potentially important.

"Look alive, people. It's halftime and these slushies aren't going to pour themselves," Mrs. Cabrini said, bustling over to the register as a crush of people charged toward us.

Slowly, I slid off the counter and tried to regain my senses. Thank god they'd interrupted, or half the school would have seen us. I looked over at Chris. His cheeks pink, he was hyper-focused on pouring red slushies into paper cups so he could hand them out quickly.

Exhaling, I reached for the cookie tongs as the first students arrived. I could not kiss him. I'd promised Nadiya, and myself. Risking all our hard work over a boy was absurd. But that didn't stop me from being disappointed.

Chapter Thirteen

"IF THE SPACE WERE ANY BIGGER, YOU'D BE PARALLEL parking on a city block," Nadiya yelled at me through the open car window, which was excessive, seeing as I'd shut the music off so I could concentrate.

"Let me think." I cut the wheel so I was at a forty-five-degree angle, then inched backward while Nadiya huffed as she waited for me. Finally, I put the car in park.

"If you want to be ready for that driving test, you better have Grandmama and your mom practicing with you day and night, because I can't."

Nadiya practicing with me wasn't exactly 100 percent legal. Technically, she wasn't over twenty-five or related to me, so she shouldn't have been anywhere near me while I was driving at all. But I was desperate. Mom was still out of commission, and Grandmama was at some church fundraiser. And honestly, it was nine a.m. on a Saturday, and we were practicing in a nearly empty strip-mall parking lot. I dared anyone in Huntersville to care about the legality of that.

"You failed the test the first time. I suspect I'll be fine." I unclicked my seat belt and got out to switch places with her so she could reposition the car.

"Or you could learn from my mistakes." Nadiya sank into the driver's seat as I got into the passenger side. "Now, I'm just gonna have you do this from the other side, and then we can practice— Wait."

"What?"

"Is that Chris?"

"No. Where?" I sank lower in my seat.

"There."

Even across the parking lot, I recognized him. He was wearing jeans, a white T-shirt, and a red apron and lifting a box of flowers into a van.

"Oh." If I was lucky, maybe he wouldn't know what Nadiya's car looked like. "Let's keep practicing. I only have two more weeks to get ready."

Nadiya looked over at me and scowled. "What are you doing?"

"Nothing." I sat up and pushed my big, bug-eyed sunglasses off the top of my head and over my eyes.

She grinned, reaching for the key in the ignition and making my heart thump wildly in my chest. "If it's nothing, let's go say hi."

"It looks like he's working. Let's not bother him."

"It's not bothering when you're working for your parents. Trust me." She started the car, oblivious to the fact that I was basically sweating through my tank top. Thank god it was black.

I should have told her about the hug at the party and then

the tension between us when we were counting ballots. Not to mention the football game. But now was definitely not the time to confess to hiding a crush and being a mess about it.

"But—"

"Hey, Chris!" Nadiya leaned her head out the window and shouted from halfway down the parking lot. I'd never tried so hard to become one with the spilled coffee and other stains on her car mat as Chris looked around to see who was yelling.

"We really shouldn't—"

"Oh, it's fine. Plus, I heard his mom is thinking about starting a high school student internship program this summer. Don't you want in? It'd look great on our college apps." Spotting us barreling toward him, he waved, a big smile working its way across his face as Nadiya parked near his van. Looking over her shoulder at me, she smiled mischievously. "And let's face it, anything to get me out of the dentist's."

I waited until Nadiya was out of the car, then checked myself in the mirror. After smoothing a flyaway back into my ponytail, I forced myself to get out.

"Hey. What are you two doing here?" Chris asked, smiling between the two of us as if nothing had happened last night. Oh good. He was being normal, which meant all I had to do was act casual. I could totally do that.

"Helping her practice parking." Nadiya gestured in my direction. "Are you working?"

"Yeah. Three of our florists called in sick with the same flu, and we're booked for four weddings plus shipping two hundred and seventy-five bouquets today, so basically, the whole family is on deck."

"Wow, that's a lot of flowers." Nadiya peered toward the van.

"Yup." Chris's expression was flat, and I was grateful that my dark glasses let me watch him without obviously staring. "When do you take your driver's test, Meg?"

"Uhm." My brain stalled out as I tried to focus on anything other than the way his shirt cut just above the tone of his biceps. This was the most mundane question in the world, and yet it sent butterflies flapping around in my stomach.

"Two weeks," Nadiya jumped in, then looked at me, raising one eyebrow.

"You're gonna be fine. Someone gave Russ a license, and he runs over a curb like three times a week."

I tried to laugh, but it sounded like I'd been possessed by a cat who got stuck behind a dryer. Chris looked at me with a smile that was frozen in polite terror, Nadiya like I was a piece of malfunctioning tech.

Clearly, acting casual wasn't going well.

I cleared my throat. "So you—"

"Chris, can you help your—" A sturdy-looking woman in a crisp white button-up shirt and one of those expensive statement necklaces walked out of the door marked OFFICE, then stopped when she spotted us. "Oh, you have friends."

"Yep." Chris pressed his lips together and nodded like his mom had asked him to set the table while he was in the middle of a video game. Sighing, he turned to us. "This is my mom, Estella. Mom, this is Nadiya and Meg."

"Oh, Meg! The other class president." Estella looked at Chris and grinned as his cheeks turned pink. Facing me, she held out her hand. "Nice to meet you. I've heard so much about you."

"Nice to meet you, too." I shook her hand.

"And Nadiya—"

"Estella! You said—" An older man with salt-and-pepper hair strode out of the office, trailed by a sullen-looking middle schooler with glasses and a preschooler holding a plastic dinosaur.

"Seriously." Chris's eyes widened. Looking at his mom, he grumbled, "Is the entire family coming out?"

"I don't know what you mean." Estella blinked and smiled the same mischievous grin that Chris had. It was weird seeing it on someone else but kind of funny. Relief came over me. I might be feeling off around Chris, but I was still good at parents.

"Grandpa, my brother, Marcos, and my sister Angie." Chris listed everyone in age order.

"Nice to meet you. I'm Meg and this is Nadiya. We're on student council with Chris." I waved at everyone, all of whom waved back except for Angie, who walked over to her big brother and leaned against his leg in the shy way that little kids do when they want to be part of a conversation but aren't ready to speak yet.

"Do you girls want to come in?" Chris's grandfather asked. "We hear all about his friends from school, but we never get to meet anyone unless they're on the baseball team. We have sodas and—"

Chris, whose cheeks had transitioned from pink to red, cut him off: "No, Grandpa. Nadiya is helping Meg practice parking. And we need to get ready for the deliveries."

"Well, they can help," Estella said, waving in our general direction and picking up on the ribbing his grandfather was giving him. Nadiya and I exchanged glances as we tried to swallow our giggles. Something about watching someone with such a high cool factor get roasted by his mom made everything feel so much more, well, normal.

"Absolutely not." Chris gritted his teeth. "All of you go back inside."

"You never let us talk to anyone," said Marcos, shaking the hair out of his face and smiling the mischievous grin that was apparently a family trait. "I'm starting to think you're embarrassed. And I thought you were a nice brother."

"I despise all of you," Chris deadpanned. Running a hand over his little sister's head, he said, "Except for Angie. She loves me."

"Angie baby, do you think we should invite Chris's friends in?" Estella asked, lowering herself to the kid's eye level. Angie tucked the dinosaur under her chin and nodded at her mom.

"There! See? I could go get your father and Diana. I think the whole family could have fun getting to know your classmates and sharing stories about you."

"Okay, this has been sufficiently humiliating. Meg, Nadiya, see you on Monday." Chris reached out and wrapped his arm around his mother to herd her toward the curb.

"But, Chris, we have baby photos we can show them." His grandfather laughed as Chris pushed the flock back toward the office.

"We're done here. Meg, I'll text you later."

"You're such a nice young man," Estella said, laying it on thick. "Isn't he a nice young man? He used to be socially awkward, but he's really blossomed. So proud of this one."

"Inside. Now," Chris said, humiliation radiating off him as he looked between Nadiya, me, and his family.

"Baby pictures next time," I called. Estella burst into cackles at my joke.

"Nice to meet you!" Nadiya giggled as Marcos waved at us.

"Well, they're adorable," I said as soon as the office door closed.

"Super cute. Like a TV family or something." Nadiya nodded and reached for the driver's-side door. As soon as we were inside, she looked at me. "Want to tell me why Chris is going to text you?"

My head went blank as I searched for an excuse. The truth was, I didn't know why Chris would text me, unless it was about what happened—didn't happen, really—in the concession stand. I stalled by fussing with my seat belt so Nadiya couldn't see the panic on my face. "You know the windows are still open, right?"

"Don't deflect," Nadiya said, reaching for the window control console. "You're acting weird. He's acting weird. Why would he text you? What's going on?"

Shoot. Nadiya knew something was up, and no flat denial was going to shake her off. My brain turned over like a flipped coin trying to come up with something.

"We made a deal." I blurted out part of the truth. "He tells me if he hears about a prank. I tell him if I hear something."

"What!"

"Shh."

"I'll roll up the windows." Nadiya growled. "How could you do that?"

"It was after Warm Fuzzy made us write letters to the maintenance team. We thought it would help by giving each other time to come up with less damaging ways for the schools to express themselves."

Nadiya tilted her head at me like this was the stupidest thing she'd ever heard.

"Don't look like that. Did anything get seriously damaged by the pool maze?"

She blinked at me a few times. "Not really."

"Exactly." I pointed at her. "And has Davies done anything super bad to retaliate?"

Nadiya's mouth dropped open. "No . . ."

"And they won't as long as Chris and I can just keep tabs on the right people and convince them not to break stuff."

"But how does that even work?"

"I went to Spencer and Riley with the pool idea exactly ten seconds after the last Davies prank. That wasn't an accident."

"Oh my god."

Nadiya's jaw dropped open, and she looked at me so hard that I was starting to sweat again. I knew we didn't keep secrets, but surely she could understand why I kept this one. In fact, I'd better pray that she could.

I couldn't take the suspense anymore. "What are you thinking?"

"I can't believe you kept this from me. I'm low-key mad."
For a second, her expression was stony, then she smiled at me
like I was the eighth wonder of the world. "But also, you're an
evil genius. There's so much we can do with this!"

"Yeah, but we can't tell anyone. I wasn't supposed to tell
you." I smiled as relief flooded every cell in my body. She didn't
hate me.

"I mean, duh. What's their next prank? When is their next
prank?" She tapped my arm rapidly like she could somehow
speed up my mind with her excitement.

"I don't know." I pulled my phone out of her cup holder and
waved it at her. "We'll find out when he texts me."

I could hear Donna Summer blasting through the house before I got out of the car.

Grandmama's Lincoln was sitting in the driveway, washed,
waxed, and sparkling. She was clearly up to something.

"Hi, baby," Grandmama called from the living room. How
she managed to hear me come in over the music was a mystery
that scientists could spend decades on. I was halfway through
sliding off my shoes when she danced into the hallway shaking
her groove thing like it was 1979. "Guess who won money at
the church bid whist tournament?" Grandmama grinned but
didn't wait for me to answer; instead, she pointed at herself
and yelled, "Me!"

"Congratulations. I bet Mrs. Crowder was stunned." I tried

not to laugh. Something about gambling for God felt a little counterintuitive. Then again, if it didn't bother Grandmama, what business was it of mine?

"Oh, you shoulda seen her face." Grandmama cackled but didn't stop dancing. "Go get dressed. As soon as you get out of the shower, Grandma is taking everybody to lunch."

"Yes, ma'am." I shuffled down the hallway, bopping along to the music. It all made sense now. This was Grandmama's way of declaring this year's period of mourning over. Back to pretending we weren't sad about Dad until next year.

I opened my closet door and looked for my favorite pink sundress. It was perfect for celebrations, and it had pockets. I'd just pulled it off the hanger when my phone buzzed. Chris's name scrolled across the screen.

Dropping the dress on my desk chair, I scooped up the phone and bounced onto my bed, a cheesy grin on my face as I read the message.

Well that was embarrassing

I bit down, trying to get ahold of my smile before remembering that no one could see me.

Which part? Your grandpa trying to show us your baby photos? Or when your mom called you "a nice young man"?

Both.

> I bet it's the baby photos. You were a
> weird-looking kid, weren't you?

> I was adorable. It's the stories that go with the
> pictures that are the problem.

My fingers hovered over the phone for a second. Technically speaking, I wasn't flirting. I was just following up on a previous conversation. This wasn't a violation of my rules.

> I need evidence. Otherwise, I'm assuming
> it's the pictures.

> And I will ask your grandpa for stories, so you can
> prepare for that future humiliation now.

A moment later a picture of an extremely fat baby with a bowl cut appeared in our texts. In it, he was sobbing in front of a cake and covered in blue icing. I snorted. It was the most adorable ugly baby photo I'd seen since my cousins were little.

> You're cute in a messy baby way! Whats the story
> behind this one?

> It's still too traumatic to talk about. Ask my grandpa.

I could almost hear Chris's teasing voice as I read what came next.

It involved me being very surprised by the song "Happy Birthday" and the fact that our neighbor's dog wasn't a stuffed animal.

Now I have to know

Tell you in Leadership. I'm sure Russ would give up his seat for you.

Nadiya and Riley would NOT do that for you.

I'm working on Nadiya. She is gonna like me eventually.

My heart squeezed and I read the text again. Did he want my friends to like him? If he wanted Nadiya's approval, then it probably meant he liked me.

I started to type something back when my brain hit pause. Maybe I was jumping to conclusions? He could just want her to like him because he was class president and he needed votes next year, same as me. For all I knew, he could be flirting with everyone. Not that this was flirting. But . . .

I held my breath and decided to test the theory. Typing quickly, I closed one eye and hit Send.

Don't try and make friends with her on my account

I tossed the phone away from me and waited, part of me wishing that I could take the text back and the other part dying to know what the little dots that meant he was typing would say. I forced myself to get up and start to think about how I wanted to fix my hair when the screen flashed, and I dived back over to my bed. Taking a deep breath, I read his answer.

Too late.

"Eeee!" I squealed, dropped the phone by my side and flailed my feet around on the bed in a silent, completely graceless happy dance. When I picked the phone back up, I had another text from him.

I gotta go back to flower arranging, but we're planning a prank on Sunday night. Don't call the cops.

Smiling, I typed back the only thing I could think of.

You can trust me, Chris.

With that, I set the phone down and picked up my pink dress. Grandmama might be celebrating bid whist winnings, but I had something else to be happy about.

Chapter Fourteen

We have to go over there

No. We're doing no such thing

Just to see what it looks like

No one will even know we're there

I rolled my eyes at the phone. I'd purposely waited to tell Nadiya about the prank until late, because I knew she'd want to do something stupid like spy on them. Ignoring her text, I tried to focus on my French essay. I figured she'd eventually give up and realize what a trash idea it was.

I know you are there

Stop ignoring me

I WILL go without you

"Oh no you don't." I glowered at Nadiya's text, then hung my head. There was no talking her out of this. Either I was going or I would risk Nadiya doing something stupid and Chris finding out that I told her.

> Fine. What time are you gonna pick me up?

Five hours later, I was standing outside in my mom's black sweatshirt from the gym. When I asked for it, I was prepared to make up a story. I figured she would want details about why I needed it, but she just looked sad and handed it over. Somehow that made sneaking out again feel both worse and more justified. She should've wondered what I was doing, but she was either too sad or too uninterested to care.

Finally, Nadiya's car crept around the corner. Dashing to the passenger-side door, I slid in right as she said, "Are those rhinestones? And do they spell *strut*?"

"The only non-Hirono dark sweatshirt in the house is from my mom's gym."

"She goes to Strut? I thought that was a strip club." Nadiya laughed as we pulled away from the curb.

"It has a treadmill and a rack of weights in the window." Sometimes I wondered about my friend's powers of deduction.

"I don't know why you didn't just wear normal clothes. It's not like we're pulling the prank this time."

"To blend in. If anyone sees us from the parking lot, they'll just think that we're Davies students or whatever."

"Right. Or you just really wanted to wear sparkles."

"That too." I shrugged and we burst into giggles.

As soon as we were far enough away from my house, Nadiya turned her music back on and pulled out a pack of candy. Driving with her knee she started filling me in on the fight the Hungry Girls were having on multiple social platforms over Christine talking to Kimber's ex. All of it sounded stupid and juicy, and exactly like the kind of thing I didn't want to see on any of my socials but was delighted to hear about when Nadiya ran across it.

"So anyway, she then did that thing where she made everyone in the class a close friend and—"

Nadiya stopped talking and slowed down as we neared the school. Instinctively, we both reached to turn off the music as we watched three people huddled near one wall of the gym while a gaggle of other people crouched on the ground in front of the school.

"What is happening?" I watched as one person, wearing jeans and a dark shirt, ran at the building, jumped and latched onto the ledge of a high window. They hoisted themselves up until they could get their footing on the ledge. From there, they jumped for the roof.

Nadiya gasped, then immediately sighed as the person caught the roof and pulled themselves up. "Does Spiderman go to school here? What kind of parkour nonsense is this?"

"What are they doing up there?"

The person on top of the roof lowered a rope, and a second person began to climb with what looked like another rope strapped to their back. While a third, much bigger person, wearing all black, dragged something heavy toward the building.

"Parachuting into the building through a skylight? Is that Russ?"

"He's the only person I know who's that size." I shrugged. "And there's no need to parachute from sixteen feet up. I'm sure they're hanging a flag or—"

The sound of the car door opening stopped me mid-sentence. "We need to get a closer look."

"Nadiya, no."

"Don't worry. It'll be quick and we'll blend in." Nadiya waved her hand at my sweatshirt like that would make spying on Davies okay, which it totally did not.

"I don't think it's possible for us to blend in at this stage. There are only like a hundred and fifty people in the Davies junior class. They've all known each other for fifteen years—"

"You were the one who wore black because you thought we'd blend in." Nadiya crouched next to her car door.

"Yeah, from far away. I didn't mean to blend in if I was standing next to them."

"They can't see us. They're on the roof. Are you coming or not?"

"Fine," I hissed, and got out of the car as Nadiya began a crouched run toward the gym. "But we're looking for two seconds and then getting back in the car."

We crept up to a shrub by the entrance to the gym and watched as Russ started to wrap one of the extra ropes around the top of something covered in a blanket as a fourth person climbed to the top of the building. When the last climber reached the top of the building, the second climber approached to help them up over the ledge. Even if I hadn't been wearing a bedazzled sweatshirt, I would have been sweating buckets. The second climber was Chris. At this point, he'd appeared in enough of my dreams that I'd recognize his silhouette just about anywhere. Nadiya and I exchanged glances.

"We need to move," I whispered.

"Can't." Nadiya tilted her chin toward the building where Russ had finished tying the ropes around the blanket-clad thing. He backed up and took a run at the building, leaping all of six inches to catch the upper ledge of the window, his feet dangling just above the ground. The other three climbers watched, shouting different, conflicting tips at him.

"I don't think he's gonna make it up there. He's too big," Nadiya said in what she thought was a whisper but was actually just a breathy shout.

"Shh."

"Here, grab where I shine the—" A flashlight beamed on us, and we froze like burglars in a cartoon.

"Meg?"

"Oh no." Nadiya grabbed me and tried to cover me with her torso, tangling both of us in a mess of limbs and sticks.

"Ow, Nadiya." I fell over into the shrub, whose branches tangled in my hair and poked at my neck. "No. Stop—"

"We can see you," a second voice called from the roof, adding another flashlight beam on us. It crossed my mind that I might actually pass out or barf from humiliation.

"Hey, Prez!" Russ let go of the window ledge and landed with a thud. I pushed Nadiya off me and started to disentangle myself from the bush. Nadiya tried to curl herself into an even smaller ball. The tiny part of me that wasn't drowning in humiliation wanted to point out that it was hard to be inconspicuous since she was wearing lilac, when I realized that Russ was standing over me.

"Do you need help?"

There was no point in denying it was me or trying to make a run for the car now. All I could hope for was a comet that would literally fall from the sky and pummel me into the earth before I had to talk to anyone else. I waited a moment, but none appeared.

"No, I think I can—"

"I got you." Russ grabbed my arm and yanked me to my feet, the shrub's branches snapping in protest. He looked at me, and then down at Nadiya, who was curled in a ball and covering her ears. "Nadiya, do you need help, too?"

"Pretend you don't see me," she mumbled.

"But I do see you . . ." Russ's forehead wrinkled with confusion. "You know what, I'm just gonna help you up, too."

I eyed Nadiya's car, parked next to the side of the road, and considered making a break for it as the sound of blood pounded in my ears. Nadiya would understand. This truly was an every-girl-for-herself situation. Only she had the keys and—

The sound of feet hitting the pavement pulled my attention away from my potential escape. If I didn't make eye contact, I could still get out of this with a small shred of dignity. Don't look. Don't look.

"Meg, are you spying on me?"

I looked, then desperately wished I hadn't. Chris's expression hovered somewhere between surprised and vaguely amused. As if finding Hirono's president and vice president hiding in a bush was exactly what he'd hoped for.

A little voice in the back of my mind suggested that maybe this is what he thought would happen when he proposed that we share information on the pranks. Reaching deep into my well of righteous indignation, I bluffed.

"No. We were just driving and saw you." Noticing a twig stuck in my hair, I batted it away, then pulled my shoulders back.

"Driving from where to where?" A voice from the roof shouted, incredulous. Climber One looked over the ledge, and I realized it was Erin, the tumbler from the Davies cheer team. Explains how she was able to scale a building without rope . . .

"Practicing for her license," Nadiya called from behind the bush, jabbing at Russ's hand with a stick as he tried to pull her up. Finally making it to her feet, she glared up at the roof like it would intimidate Erin.

"At eleven-thirty-two?" Jackie called from the roof. She would be here, too, now that I thought about it. Davies didn't have a formal powerlifting team, but Jackie was in the gym a lot. If that thing was hard for Russ to lug, they also needed Jackie.

Chris raised his eyebrow and smirked like Jackie had a point. Even covered in bits of building dirt with disheveled hair, he was handsome. It was a little unfair, really.

"No—"

"We—"

Nadiya and I started to speak at the same time. She looked at me, signaling me to keep going. I tried again, hoping that if I rambled enough, a good excuse would come to me.

"We thought the parking lot would be empty. And we would have just kept driving, but then we saw you on the roof . . ." Looking around for an idea, I spotted one of those wall-mounted first-aid kits that you basically need a hatchet to get into. Turning to look at Chris, I said, "and that's dangerous. We're here for safety."

"Aw. Are you saying you care about me?" Chris batted his eyelashes and threw a hand over his heart.

I scowled at him. "There is a chasm of difference between not wanting you dead and caring."

"Burn!" Russ yelled, looking back and forth between me and Chris.

"Ouch." Chris staggered back in mock pain.

"Yeah, what she said," Nadiya jumped in. "Just driving by and saw you all. You should not be doing this. Vandalism is bad. Very bad. Shame on you."

"It's chalk," Erin called.

"And that's a Merry Mouse statue," Jackie yelled down at us like we were stupid.

Turning to look at it, we could make out the jaunty tilt of its little cap and its waving hand that used to greet visitors looking for a mediocre hamburger. Definitely the mascot of the old fast-food joint that closed down last year.

"We dressed it in Hirono colors," Russ said helpfully, as if that would explain how Nadiya and I had missed this.

"Oh." Nadiya coughed like the word had been stuck in her throat. Her eyes were wide as she shook her head slightly in the universal gesture for help-me-out-here.

"Well, that's silly." I jumped in and tried not to look at Chris, who was laughing. "Y'all are gonna hurt your backs. If you want to haul that thing up there, you probably need to belt it around the waist. Otherwise, the head is just gonna pop off—I mean, that's just basic physics, and . . ."

I trailed off as a few people who'd been in the front of the school came around the corner to see what the commotion was about. Nadiya wrapped her arm through mine and pulled me back a step.

"Exactly. We can do this prank better." She nodded. "And that's all we have to say. Let's go, Meg. No more giving them ideas."

"Right. Okay. Be safe," I rambled, then wished that I could dive back into the bush. *Be safe.* Was there a less cool way for me to exit this situation? Nadiya yanked me around, and we started our humiliated hurtle back toward the car.

"Thanks for the help, Prez!" Russ called without a hint of malice. He probably was grateful for the assist and completely unaware that this was a competition.

I looked back over my shoulder in time to catch Chris waving. "Night, Williams."

To anyone else, it might have sounded like Chris was taunting me. But he wasn't, and that was a problem.

Chapter Fifteen

I CLOSED MY LOCKER AND JUMPED WHEN I REALIZED FREYA was leaning on the one next to it, looking directly at me.

"So. I think we need to talk."

"Do we?" I tried to keep my tone flat as my mind whirled. I could not think of a single thing Freya and I had needed to talk about since that time we were assigned to be science partners freshman year.

"You know we do." Freya flipped her ponytail and looked at me like she wasn't going to put up with me playing stupid, which was irritating because her friends played stupid all the time . . . although maybe that wasn't playing.

"All right." I sighed and wished my locker wasn't so far away from the Leadership classroom. "What about?"

"I know that we are technically Huntersville High now, but that doesn't mean we can just give up our Hirono traditions."

"What have I given up?" I asked as we walked down the hallway. I knew I shouldn't have engaged with her, but I couldn't help it.

"Our pranks." Freya crossed her arms and looked over at me. "Going all in with Davies is just bad."

"I'm not going all in with them." I sighed and picked up the pace. It was unfortunate that Freya was taller than me, so she easily lengthened her stride to keep up.

"Why did you help them put Merry Mouse on top of the school dressed in Hirono colors?"

"What?" I'd been preoccupied with other things about that prank. Namely, what to do about Chris and how I was going to tell Nadiya. "I wasn't helping. Nadiya and I thought we could stop them."

"That's not what Jackie's video looked like."

"Well, Jackie's video didn't capture all the context," I growled. In truth, I hadn't even seen the video until yesterday around third period, when Riley pulled it up. Most of the comments were just people laughing at Nadiya for trying to harpoon Russ with a stick when he pulled her out of the bush.

"And yet they used your method to get Merry Mouse to the top of the school, where it waved at me this morning. Like I said, we may be one school officially, but that doesn't mean they can just disrespect us."

"Disrespect. Don't be dramatic. They didn't dye the toilet water green or something. Besides, Principal Domit said that as soon as they can get a crane out here, they'll take it down." I rolled my eyes, then spotted Riley standing at the edge of the hallway. I waved at them, and they started to walk over.

"I know you and Chris are a thing, but—"

"That's not true." I jerked my gaze away from Riley and

gave Freya my full attention, my heart pounding in my chest. "Who said we're a thing?"

"Ricki's little sister. You know, Ricki from the softball team?" Freya smiled like she'd caught me and was about to draw blood with her fangs. "She said she saw you two looking comfortable when she went to buy a Jasper sweatshirt."

"What does that even mean? And who is Ricki's sister?" Riley asked, popping up next to Freya. I'd never been so happy or terrified to see them in my life.

The problem was, Freya wasn't wrong. People were adjusting to the idea that we were one school, but that didn't mean they were ready to hold hands and skip in circles. Crossing the dating line too soon would be a disaster. Not that I was planning on dating Chris, or anyone. In fact, I planned not to do just that thing.

"Jennie. You know, the little blond freshman. Big into ponytails. She told me about the five-dollars-off deal." Freya shook her head.

"No idea who she is, but we weren't comfortable. I was literally sitting on a counter, and he was standing next to me."

"Sounds like Jennie doesn't understand the mechanics of comfort." Riley wrinkled their nose.

"The point is, someone's saying you two are in some kind of thing."

"Or Ricki's sister is bored and making things up," I hedged. "Ask anyone else who preordered Jasper gear if they saw it." If I'd known Ricki's little sister, whoever that was, was such a narc, I definitely wouldn't have given her a deal.

"Better yet, we could ask Ricki's sister," said Riley. "Maybe she isn't the one making things up?" They leaned forward and put their hands in their pockets. Their smile was all kinds of good-natured, but Freya picked up on the threat.

"Just know that you're not fooling me." Freya glared down at me.

I puffed up my chest with more bravado than I felt. "Good thing I don't need to fool anyone, then."

We stared at each other for a moment, until Mr. Bednarik threw open the classroom door. He clapped and rubbed his hands together in his usual eager manner. "Welcome, welcome! Come on in!"

Freya pursed her lips at me and squinted, then whirled around and smiled at Warm Fuzzy. "Thanks, Mr. B. I know some people aren't that excited to be here, but I sure am."

Riley and I glanced at each other, then busted up. We didn't need to exchange words to agree that that had to be the weakest sub-insult Freya had ever thrown at me. As we walked into the classroom, Riley said, "Even if seventy people saw you sitting in his lap, I got your back. Freya can kick rocks."

My brain froze as it tried to process what they'd said. Did that mean that Riley knew about the almost-kiss and didn't care? Or were they just reminding me that they were my friend?

For the span of one breath, I considered just asking them outright, then came to my senses. Why start a problem? Like everything with me and Chris, nothing technically had happened, so I may as well let nothing be the story.

"Thanks." I looped my arm through theirs, leaning on their

shoulder and hoping that my snuggle would convey what I couldn't bring myself to say: that I appreciated them standing by me, no matter what their reason was. I didn't want to hurt Riley. I just wasn't sure what was going on with me right now.

Chris was already in his regular seat, but the chair next to him was open. Memories of the football game washed over me. The way his eyes looked more like chestnut brown when he was close to me. The light casting shadows over his cheekbones.

He looked up and our eyes met, a question in his gaze. Warmth crept into my cheeks and spread through me. He'd said he would save a seat for me, and true to his word, he had. The question was, was I brave enough to sit in it? When I was away from him, it was so easy to say that I was done. That I would stick to the plan, avoid the social repercussions, and walk away. But looking at him now . . . it wasn't that easy.

Riley stepped forward, pulling me toward our chairs. I looked up and opened my mouth to tell them I needed to talk to Chris when Russ jostled us, knocking into Riley as he tried to squeeze past.

"Sorry, buddy," Russ called to Riley as he dropped into the chair next to Chris, oblivious to the link he'd just severed. Chris looked over at Russ and then glanced back at me. He was waiting for a sign: tell Russ to move or leave things as they were. Russ began rifling through his backpack, and Chris settled back into his chair.

Decision made: stick to the plan. I let Riley lead us over to our usual spots, my heart sinking with each step.

"All right. Big day today," said Warm Fuzzy. "We've got a lot to get done, so let's get kraken . . . stang." He laughed at his own pun while the rest of us groaned. "All right, all right. Today we're talking homecoming.

"Recap for those of you who aren't reading the biweekly recaps the other class secretaries are sending out." Mr. Bednarik eyed us as he dropped the reminder that these existed and I suspected that Riley likely hadn't sent a single one for us yet. "Freshmen will be managing the halftime show, sophomores Spirit Week, and you all will be handling the actual dance." He turned to the whiteboard. "So let's talk theme. What are people thinking?"

The air in the room shifted as we all looked from left to right, thinking the same things: Dances were stupid. Homecoming was extra stupid. It was silly and heteronormative and a popularity contest. We'd all had two years of putting way too much pressure on ourselves to make something special of the night when, in reality, we'd be in the cafeteria, the gym, or the courtyard with a DJ and an itchy outfit that our parents pushed us to wear, trying not to attach too much meaning to one night . . .

But also . . .

Homecoming was fun. All the magic I wanted to hate was there: Scouring thrift shops for the right dress. Laughing with Nadiya and Riley over hair and makeup. Trevor's dad driving us to dinner and seeing half of our class packed into the diner because they had the biggest tables and the most reasonably priced food. Swaying along to a slow song with Trevor's arms around my waist.

That thought hit pause on everything. Who was I going with? And how had I not considered this part of my focus-on-the-future plan yet?

"All right, people, same rules as before," Mr. Bednarik said. "Five ideas. No put-downs. Then we vote. Next week, we'll work out how to execute the theme, so don't get caught up in that now. Got it?"

Freya's hand shot up. Before he could formally call on her, she started speaking. "Moonlight masquerade."

"Enchanted evening," Amber jumped in without bothering with the hand-raising formality.

"Those two sound the same." Jasmine leaned around Trevor to better see Amber.

Amber shook her head. "They're totally different. One is, like, mysterious, and the other is more, like, magical."

"Riiight . . ." Jasmine drew out the *i* sound to hammer home her skepticism. "But how are they those things? They both sound like fairy tales to me."

"We are not doing fairy tales," Tori jumped in.

"Both can go on the board, and we'll work out the details," Mr. B said diplomatically.

"What about sixties mod?" Trevor said.

"No flower power, please," Amber replied, glaring at Jasmine as she shot the idea down.

"I don't mean flower power," Trevor said. "I mean color blocks and—"

"It's going on the board." Warm Fuzzy began scribbling. "What else?"

For the first time in maybe ever, I didn't have an idea. My brain was still hung up on the fact that I had no one to go with. Last year, I didn't even think about it. The year before that, Mac set me up with someone's cousin, Tim, who was in all of three pictures with me before we went to dance with our respective friend groups. It wasn't like Mac could set me up from college, could she?

"Cute countryside?" Tabitha suggested.

"Luxury," Freya jumped in again.

"Why does she get to have two?" Tori asked, looking between Freya and Mr. Bednarik like there was some kind of homecoming conspiracy happening.

"Fine. We can have six." Warm Fuzzy sighed and readjusted his glasses. "One more from someone who isn't Freya."

I could always just go with Riley and Nadiya. But what if they both had plans? They would tell me, right? Then again, my focus hadn't exactly been on them lately. Maybe I missed an update. Would I be a weird fifth wheel? For all I knew, I was coming up with a theme for a dance I wasn't going to.

"Dracula." Everyone in the room turned to look at Kyong like maybe she'd lost her mind. She shrugged. "What? It's a fairy tale, and red-and-black decor would be cool."

"Maybe we call it Gothic Storybook." Warm Fuzzy shuddered, then turned to the whiteboard, mumbling, "Don't want anyone to think biting is okay."

Instinctively, I glanced over at Chris to see if he'd heard what I'd heard. Clearly, something had happened that had made Mr. B skittish. Sure enough, he looked at me and smirked.

Turning back to us, Mr. Bednarik said, "All right, it's voting time. For the sake of expediency, split a piece of paper with your neighbor and write down your top two choices in case we need a tiebreaker."

The sounds of bags opening and paper tearing filled the classroom as we hurried to get our votes down. Nadiya passed me and Riley scraps of paper. I scribbled down my first vote.

1. Countryside

The second theme I wasn't so sure about. I looked up and saw Chris tapping the end of a pen against his chin as he thought. He looked at me and offered a small, quiet smile. The corners of my mouth lifted at the same time my heart squeezed. Turning my focus back to my paper, I wondered if his smile would always have that effect on me. Or if I would ever want it to not.

Nadiya put her hand in front of me and made the gimme-grabby motion to pass our votes to her. I scrambled.

2. Gothic Storybook

Looking down at my paper, Nadiya wrinkled her nose, then took them all up to Mr. Bednarik, who was already busy tallying votes. After a few moments, he said, "Well, team, it looks like the winner is Countryside, with twelve votes, plus two tiebreakers."

He looked relieved that it was not Gothic Storybook. "So next week, we break into teams and start figuring out decor, tickets, DJs, and all that good stuff."

As soon as Warm Fuzzy wrapped up, Nadiya looked over at me. "Meg, I'm so sorry, but I gotta go help my mom at her office. Can you get a ride?"

"No worries. I think Grandmama is hanging out with her friends from the senior center, so I can just chill in the library until Mom gets off work."

"Thanks. Apparently, my mom's receptionist got sick at lunch." Nadiya shrugged, then snatched up her backpack. "By the way, who are you going with?"

"Like, to the homecoming dance?" I asked, my stomach dropping.

"Didn't we already talk about this?" Riley asked.

"Yeah, but she was helping at concessions," Nadiya answered.

"Wait, who are you going with, Riley?" I tried not to sound surprised that this had been discussed without me. Not that I'd been talking to them about every choice I made. But still.

"Probably Tabitha unless she's changed her mind since we talked about it this summer." Riley shrugged and my heart sank. Were people really figuring this out in July? At this rate, who was left without a date?

"What about you, Nadiya?"

"Kelly, remember? She and I hung out last weekend." Nadiya began ambling toward the door. "So, what about you, Meg?"

"Oh god. I don't even know." I rolled my eyes as my chest tightened. "Who's left to go with? It sounds like everyone already has their dates figured out."

"You don't have a spreadsheet with pros and cons for every person listed?"

The three of us looked up to find Chris standing there. Nadiya's eyebrows shot up in surprise, and Riley did a double take, as if checking to make sure he really had just appeared out of nowhere to talk about homecoming. My heart slammed in my chest. I did not want to know if he'd figured this out already. For all I knew, he'd met some cool person at a show and had a date to this homecoming and every other dance in the county.

Chris just smiled at me like he'd always been part of the conversation, holding on to the straps of his backpack and waiting for me to answer the question.

Taking what I hoped would be a steadying breath, I said, "It may surprise you, but no. In fact, I'm not even sure who doesn't have a date at this point."

"You don't have a date, then?" Chris studied me and my heart stopped. The question wasn't exactly asking me to homecoming, but it felt like the same thing. Next to me, Nadiya froze, and Riley's eyes went wide.

"Well, not yet—"

"Meg's working it out." Nadiya looked at me with heavy meaning. "Phil Taylor doesn't have a date."

"Not Phil Taylor." Riley shook their head.

"Not an option." I glared at Nadiya. Was she trying to make me look desperate, or did she just not want me to go with Chris? I would rather stay home and rewatch *Murder, She Wrote* with Grandmama.

Chris's smile stretched as the three of us looked from one to the other. "What's wrong with Phil Taylor?"

"He bathes in body spray," I said.

"He eats paper," Riley said at the same time.

Chris leaned back and barked a laugh. "What?"

"Okay, the paper was one time, like, three years ago." Nadiya crossed her arms.

"That we know of." I pointed a finger at her.

"You don't want your date to eat the decorations?" Chris deadpanned. "I can't imagine why not."

"Whatever. I'm going to work." Nadiya put her hand on my arm and looked between me and Chris. With all the subtlety of an F-150 on a gravel road, she added, "Text me later."

"Text me, too." Riley wiggled their eyebrows, then followed Nadiya down the hallway, leaving me and Chris alone. For a moment, we just stood there, watching my friends wander away, me wondering when he was going to say something about homecoming and him saying absolutely nothing at all. I had to move this along or I was going to die of old age before he said whatever he'd come to say.

"All right, well, I'm going to the library until my mom picks me up." I waved, then turned to go.

"Soooooo." Chris stretched out the word until it felt like it had about fifteen syllables. I turned around and hugged my backpack straps in close to me as nerves shot through my body. This was it. He was going to ask me to homecoming, which would save me from Phil but would create other problems. I could live with that. It would sure beat watching my date try to snack on the walls or listening to Grandmama snore at eight-thirty. This time, I wasn't chickening out, no matter how much pig's blood Freya threatened to dump on me.

"Yes." I blinked up at him and tried to look calm and

collected. Like someone a future rock star would want in the documentary about their childhood.

"I gotta go to baseball practice, but we need to talk," Chris said. His usual smile was missing, and that made my smile falter. Maybe he wasn't asking me to homecoming. Just like everyone else, he'd already found a date, one who was going to look amazing in his documentary twenty years from now.

"About?"

He winced. "How do I say—"

"Spit it out. I'm a big girl." I tapped my foot, the sound of my platform clunking on the linoleum.

"Okay. You know that freshman—the one who wanted the Jasper sweatshirt that you gave the discount to?"

"Yes." I nodded as dread squeezed my throat. This was the second time she'd come up in one day, and I didn't even re-member her name.

"This sounds stupid—" Chris sighed, then said, more to himself than to me, "But you deserve to know, and—"

"Just tell me."

He squeezed his eyes closed and spoke quickly, like some-how that would make whatever he had to say easier. "Okay. She managed to tell a massive number of freshmen that the two of us are together. Which is not that big a deal, because fresh-men, but then you were also at the prank, and now everyone thinks you're the Bonnie to my Clyde."

He cracked one eye open, and I couldn't help it: I laughed, the sound echoing off the lockers around us. His face froze in a pained expression. "Is dating me that funny?"

"No. No." I shook my head so hard that my hair shook with

it. "It's just that Freya accused me of basically the same thing right before class. I mean, not with a creative metaphor, but you know."

"Ohokaygood." Chris exhaled the words together in one fast phrase. "Anyway, I figured I would tell you in case you didn't want people to think that . . . 'cause of the rivalry and all . . . not 'cause I care. It doesn't bother me at all one way or the other."

"Yeah. I don't think this rivalry goes away until we make it go away." I nodded, trying to parse his rambling. He was acting nervous again, so did that mean he did care? I wasn't sure. Then again, I wasn't sure about a lot lately. "We just need a plan. Ideally, one that doesn't end in violence."

Chris's laugh sounded ironic, like I missed some hidden meaning in his message. Clearing his throat, he said, "I have fall workout until four-thirtyish. If you're gonna be here, I could give you a ride home and we could work on it?"

I paused for a moment, doing the time math in my head. If I didn't text Mom, she wouldn't leave work until close to six, and who knew when Grandmama would be done gossiping and playing dominoes with her friends. This could work.

He must have taken my mental math for hesitation, because he added, "Assuming you're free. No pressure if you'd rather hang out with Phil or something."

I snorted. "No. I'm good. I don't think my mom or grandma will be home until six, so we could work on it at my house."

"Sounds good. Meet you in the parking lot?"

"See you then, Chavez." I waved at him.

"Looking forward to it, Williams." He waved over his shoulder, then hustled off toward the weight room.

I turned toward the library so he wouldn't see my face if he looked back. Otherwise, he'd know that I was looking forward to it, too.

Chapter Sixteen

WALKING OUT TO THE PARKING LOT, I TRIED NOT TO PANIC. When I invited Chris over, I hadn't thought about the state of my house. For all I knew, it could be a total mess. I just hoped Mom hadn't left anything weird out.

Spotting Chris standing by the old red Mercedes, I waved and then stopped. Why was I waving? It wasn't like he was on a ship sailing into port or something. I was the only other person in the parking lot. He could see me. I blamed it on Warm Fuzzy's goofy factor rubbing off on me. I wasn't nervous. And my nonexistent nerves were 100 percent not related to the concession stand and the almost-kiss, or the fact that he hadn't yet asked me to homecoming, or that I was bringing him to my house when my mom wasn't home.

Nope. None of that.

"Hey," I said as I reached the car.

"Hey." His cheeks were a little flushed and his hair was all over his head from the workout. I'd never seen him this disheveled, and it was, in a word, adorable.

I looked away to make sure I wasn't staring at him for too long. "This is a beautiful car."

"Thanks. It starts like something in a serial killer movie, so prepare for that."

"It's fitting for the life-of-crime image we're cultivating." I laughed and walked around to the other side of the car, and he followed me. "Oh, you don't have to open car doors. Those I can do myself."

He grinned. "I have to open this one. Old cars don't have automatic locks." Leaning past me, he fitted a key into the lock, then turned and yanked the door open. "After you."

I lowered myself into the car as gracefully as anyone in a denim skirt could, which was to say not that gracefully, since the car was low to the ground. Swinging my legs in, I looked up, intending to tell Chris that he could close the door, and caught his expression. It was intense. Like someone had turned the volume up on his usual expression so that it was strategically designed to mess with my head. All I could think was *hot.*

"All right, closing the door now."

"Huh?" I blinked up at him, willing my brain to reengage.

He pointed to the strap of my bag, which was hanging out of the door. "Do you not carry your own bag now either?"

"Oh no, I can manage that." I pulled the strap in as he laughed and then closed the door with a heavy thud.

A few seconds later, he got in and hit the gas pedal twice. Right as he was about to stomp on it a third time, he twisted the key in the ignition. The engine chugged for a second and then growled to life.

"It does low-key sound like we're in a street-racing movie." I giggled.

"I know, right? Plus, the stomping on the gas to start it. Big serial killer vibes." Chris grinned, then drove toward the exit. Hitting the road, he asked, "Which way?"

"Make a right."

We drove in silence for a second, and then he said, "I'm glad we're going to your house. It means my grandpa can't break out the baby pictures."

"If you think my grandmama would do anything different, you're going to be very disappointed. The saving grace for me is that she's playing dominoes, so she won't get the chance."

Chris laughed. "I'll still take your grandma over my brother and three sisters running into the room every fifteen minutes to check on us."

"Mac would never." I shook my head and caught his eye. "Mac is my sister. She's a sophomore at Berkeley."

"Is it just the two of you?"

"Next left." I nodded, absently running my fingers against the car interior. "Well, and my mom, but I very much doubt she would admit to checking in. She'd probably just hover outside with a stethoscope or something."

"At least she pretends to leave you alone." Chris's laugh sounded forced as he checked his mirror before turning. "My parents don't even pretend. Saying they're overinvolved would be unfair to overinvolved parents. They would check in every fifteen minutes. Which you probably figured out the other day."

"Your family is cute. And your mom is funny." I grinned over at him. "Left at the light."

"They are cute unless you live with them. Trust me." Chris's tone was flat, but the corners of his mouth turned up as he flipped on his blinker. The sound of the blinker was loud, and I realized there was no music on. I wasn't sure what I'd expected, but with him being a musician, silence wasn't it. But this was nice. Nothing in my life was ever quiet unless it was the unwelcome weight of sadness. Silence with him didn't feel uncomfortable. It felt like there were no expectations. Like me being in the car with him was enough.

"It's the gray one just there."

Chris parked on the street in front of the house and jumped out. I reached for the door handle and pushed hard. It was heavy. In fact, the car could best be described as a beautiful beast. It probably weighed a ton. Chris caught hold of the edge of the door and pulled.

"Really, I can get my own car door."

"I still have to lock it, so I may as well help." He smiled and held out a hand. Tingles ran up and down my arm as he helped me out of the car. I waited for him to lock the door and wondered if I'd ever get used to the feeling of his hand in mine.

"Hang on." I dashed up the walkway to open my front door. Cracking it open, I stuck my head in to see if I needed to make a mad dash into the living room in order to snatch a bra off the couch. Spotting nothing horrifying, I pushed the door open and stepped in, then started taking my shoes off.

"Did you just check to make sure there was nothing weird out?" Chris smirked at me from the front steps.

"Maybe." I chuckled. "Come in."

Chris toed his shoes off, set his bag down, then looked around. "You have a really nice house."

"Thanks. My mom will be delighted to hear that." I leaned toward the kitchen just to see if Grandmama happened to have left me a good snack. She hadn't. Turning toward Chris, I sighed. "Sadly, Grandmama didn't leave us any good snacks, so if you're hungry, there's basically string cheese or granola bars."

Chris shrugged and started toward the kitchen. "If you have the ingredients, I can make us cookies."

"You bake?"

"I'm the eldest of five kids. If I couldn't feed myself, I wouldn't be here." He laughed and walked over to the cabinets near the stove. "Where's your baking stuff?"

I pointed to one of the taller cupboards, and he opened both doors wide, pulling things down. "The bad news: no chocolate chips."

"The good news?"

"If you've got butter and an egg, we've got sugar cookies." He grinned and it seemed to light up the entire kitchen.

"You are serious about making cookies."

"I don't joke about cookies."

"I knew deep down you were an okay guy," I teased, and he made a funny face at me as I walked over to the fridge and fished out a stick of butter and an egg. "Here you go."

"Any chance you have two sticks of butter?" he asked

absently, fussing with the stove. "If not, no worries, I can make it work. We'd just make a half recipe, and that requires some math."

"I'll find us more butter. This is not a homework session." Reaching back into the fridge, I pulled out more butter, then turned around to find him staring intently at the counter, a cute little furrow in his brow.

"Baking sheet?" I guessed.

"Yes, and measuring stuff? Also, would anyone be upset if I used the stand mixer?"

"It's really my grandmama's. Have at it. As long as we clean up, she won't care."

"We'll clean up and stay on her good side." He nodded as I handed him a set of measuring cups with the little measuring spoons attached. Opening the bag of sugar, he began measuring. "Other house rules I should be aware of?"

"No boys in the bedroom with the door closed," I joked.

"Like that's ever stopped me from doing anything." Chris snort-laughed as my jaw dropped.

Unaware of what it sounded like he was suggesting, he chuckled and continued to measure while I tried to work out exactly what to say. Was he implying that if he wanted to be making out with me right now, he would be? Or just that in general, people made out with him regardless of house rules? Both?

As Chris looked up and saw my face, his laughter became a cough and his cheeks turned pink. "Not that we—"

"No. I know—" An explanation could only make this worse.

The last thing I needed to hear was some version of *I would never kiss you because . . .*

"Not that I wouldn't—"

"Maybe let's—"

"Uhh . . ." Chris stopped, started to reach for the back of his head, then realized he was still holding a measuring cup covered in sugar. "So do you have a bowl I can microwave the butter in for a second?"

For three full heartbeats, I just looked at him; then I started cackling. I mean, I laughed so hard that it echoed around the house. When I finally stopped wheezing and looked at Chris, he seemed so confused that I just started laughing all over again.

"What?" he asked as I tried to take big gulps of air to get ahold of my giggles.

"It's just, that was the least smooth transition in the history of the world. Could you be more awkward?"

"Apparently not," he mumbled.

"Because usually you're pretty cool, but—"

"Okay. We're moving on. Where is a microwave-safe dish for the butter?" Chris's cheeks moved from pink to just plain red.

"Fine. I'll give you this one. But don't think that I won't mention it again to get my way." I put the butter in a bowl in the microwave for fifteen seconds. "Shall we focus on the reason we're here, or did you have something else you wanted to say?"

"No. I'm not saying anything else." Chris shook his head

and took the bowl from me. Clearing his throat, he started to measure out vanilla. "So what are we going to do about the homecoming war? There's gotta be a way to end this for good."

"I feel like we need one massive prank to end them all. Something that can't be topped, so we *have* to let it go."

"Like what? Cling-wrap everyone's cars? TP Principal Domit's house? A food fight?"

I perked up. "That could work."

"What?" Chris looked at me for a second, then turned his attention to attaching the plastic mixer guard so the ingredients wouldn't spray everywhere.

"A food fight."

"No, that would be super messy." Chris switched the mixer on and looked at me.

"Not if we do it in the courtyard where Davies eats. We just offer to hose it down afterward." I shrugged. "I mean, I don't love the idea of trying to get ketchup out of my hair, but . . ."

"How would we even do that? I just walk over and throw a sandwich at you?" Chris laughed.

"I mean, don't throw it like a speedball or anything, but yeah." I nodded. The more I thought about it, the more the idea started to come together. Chris looked at me like I was losing my marbles. "Okay, hear me out. We make it big and public, so everyone sees. We'll probably get sent to Principal Domit's office, maybe even get detention, but if it gets everyone to have fun and get along . . ."

Chris pursed his lips as he listened. "It might work . . ."

"We could wait until close to the end of lunch, so people will have less stuff to throw. That way, most people are just watching. Plus, if both of us do it, it's everyone's prank, not just Davies or Hirono." The more I thought about it, the more I liked the idea. "Think of it as a primal scream for the whole school."

"Hmmm . . ." Chris switched the mixer off. "You really think a food fight will work?"

"If it doesn't, I don't know what would. A giant pillow fight?"

"That feels like someone is gonna put rocks in their case and take out someone's teeth," he said under his breath. He grabbed a spoonful of dough and popped it into his mouth. "Maybe a food fight is the best way to go."

"It is the best idea." I nodded, getting more excited as a little voice in my head started yelling that this was so not something I would usually do. I'd never intentionally gotten in trouble in my life. Detention was absolutely not part of my plan. Ignoring that voice, I said, "And since we know it's coming, we can wear something that won't get ruined."

"That wasn't exactly my first concern, but sure." Chris offered me a spoonful of dough. I took it, deciding to ignore that there was a raw egg in there. Waiting until after I'd crunched down on its sugary goodness, he asked, "Should we have a signal or something?"

"Better than that: What if I just walk up to you and cover you in food?"

"Why am I being covered in food first?"

"Someone has to be? And do you really want to be the guy with a baseball arm just chucking things at girls?"

"When you put it like that . . ." Chris frowned and started rolling the cookie dough into little balls that he set on a silicone baking mat. "So if I agree to this, your plan is just to cover me in food and then I, what? Dump my food on you and we call it a day?"

"Pretty much. As long as we cause a scene doing it, we should be good."

"Has anyone ever told you that you might be an evil genius?"

"It happens more often than you know." I smirked, remembered Nadiya, then tried to push away the guilt. Sure, I had my no-dating rule, and I didn't like to lie to Nadiya either, but hanging out with Chris was fun.

"You should go into PR or something after college." He half smiled. "When do we do this?"

"Soon. If we get detention, we don't want them to kick us out of homecoming or anything."

Chris looked pensive for a second, then said, "So maybe Thursday?"

"I can be ready by Thursday."

"All right. I can't believe I'm letting you talk me into this."

"It's for our own good." I grinned and snatched up a bit of dough from the cookie sheet.

"I guess if we are gonna let the Davies-Hirono rivalry go, we should let it go out in style."

"Exactly. And this is why you are the perfect other president for this job."

"I knew you'd like me eventually." Chris grinned and re-placed the cookie I'd taken.

"Don't push your luck." I picked up the dough he'd just put down and took a bite out of it.

"I feel like this plan is gonna work," Chris said as we walked into the living room. Both of us had filled up on enough cookie dough that we weren't really hungry, but he insisted that we plate the cookies nicely for Mom and Grandmama. He set the plate down on the coffee table.

"Me too." I tucked myself into a corner of the couch with my feet underneath me and watched him wander around the room. All afternoon, I'd found ways to work homecoming into the conversation, and not once had he mentioned his plans. Worse, he hadn't mentioned including me in them. I bit down on my lip and willed myself to be brave.

Holding my breath and trying to look neutral, I finally said, "So, what are you doing for homecoming?"

"I'm still figuring it out. I have a gig in San Francisco, so I may not go at all." Chris stopped looking at a family photo to study me, his eyes narrowing as if he could see the question I was really asking. I looked down at the bracelet I was wearing. Gold with a little heart charm at the end. I'd seen it a thousand times, but it was suddenly so much more interesting than sur-viving his X-ray eye contact.

"Oh. That's . . ." I searched for a word that didn't sound like *distressing* or *disappointing* or *I want to throw myself in a dumpster if Phil truly is my only option* and settled on "fun, too."

"Kind of." Chris laughed to himself, and I couldn't figure out what to do with that answer. It was like the two of us were trying to say something in different languages and the code we needed to understand one another was missing.

Or maybe I was reading too much into it. This was probably a sign that we weren't meant to be, and I should just let the prank be the end. Stick to the plan, work in peace, and get outta town after graduation. No distractions. I took a deep breath to reassure myself. It was a good thing he was busy that night.

He leaned down to look at a picture of the family, all wearing shiny aviator glasses and sitting on the curb outside the house. Then another of Dad and Mac in round glasses after her dance recital. Pointing to the picture, he said, "Your dad was a sunglasses person, too?"

I stopped fussing with my bracelet and looked at him. Of course he knew about my dad. It was googleable and all that. I just hadn't expected him to pick up on that detail.

"It was kind of a thing for us when he was alive," I answered slowly. It felt deeply personal to tell anyone this. Like I was showing someone a cut underneath a Band-Aid. "Some people take family photos in matching pajamas. My dad liked us to wear matching glasses. He thought sunglasses made for the perfect California Christmas card photo. He'd spend an inordinate amount of time looking for just the right ones that also came in kids' sizes."

Chris grinned at the picture as if the people in the photo

had told him that story, then looked back at me. "It is very California. It's nice that you share that."

"Thanks." I tried not to feel flat as I said it, but he must have picked up on my tone. Walking over to the couch, he dropped into the middle of it, so my knees were nearly touching his thigh.

"Why does it sound like it's not nice?" His eyes searched my face. "If you don't mind my asking. You don't have to tell me if you don't want to. We can change the subject. I'm pretty good at that."

I snickered at the callback. The words *It's not a big deal* were halfway out of my mouth when I stopped. His gaze had given way to something gentle. It made me wonder . . .

I'd been keeping the truth from everyone lately. What would happen if I told him? Would he think I was a monster? There's this thing that happens when people know you've lost someone. They expect you to be in a perpetual state of either grief or confusion, constantly monitor you for cracks in your armor, so you have to pretend you're fine. Then there's the judgment for experiencing joy without him. Every prize, award, or first-place ribbon—hell, even a participation trophy—has to come with an acknowledgment of who I lost; otherwise it was like I didn't really win at all.

It had been so long since I'd tried to explain this to anyone. Admitting that one of the hardest parts of his dying was living in a town where I couldn't exist without his memory casting a shadow. That I didn't get to choose how, when, where, or even if I grieved or celebrated him. Not even in my own home.

Worse, I wasn't high-achieving to honor his memory; I was working this hard to get away from it.

"It's not the sunglasses that aren't nice. It's this place. The house, the town. All of it. It's like living in a memorial to him without actually doing anything to remember him or say goodbye. My mom doesn't know how to feel sad, so she tries not to feel anything negative at all. We have reminders of him everywhere, but we can't talk about him or she gets upset. Everything we do is centered on trying to pretend that it's fine that he isn't here anymore. It's weird, and it's why I gotta get outta here. Just one college scholarship and two more years, then I'm gone."

I exhaled the truth as fast as I could, then watched him, trepidation building in my chest. Chris tilted his head to look at me. Really look at me. As if I were a word problem on a math test and he wasn't sure that he understood the question. My throat felt tight, and my mind started to race. Was there a way out of this? Could I say, "Just kidding! Everything's great, I love it here!" and undo this?

"You know what? It's silly. Forget I said—"

"No. It's not silly. It makes sense. Huntersville is small." Chris shook his head. "I don't know what it's like to lose someone like that. But I do know what it's like to live with a shadow and want out. I imagine it's hard not to be able to grieve in your own way or in your own time. I'm sorry."

I watched him carefully. Trying to guard the space in my heart that wanted to open up and make room for him. He wasn't fidgeting or avoiding looking at me, or any of the usual things people did when they weren't sure what to do with someone else's grief. Instead, he was just there, quietly making room for whatever I wanted to feel or say next.

"Thank you." I smiled at him, then looked down at my hands and tried to get my bearings. This feeling. The feeling of being near him and seen by him was both dizzying and reassuring.

It was also getting uncomfortable. I'd been sitting on my feet long enough that pins and needles were starting to kick in. Instead of delicately, casually sliding my feet out from under me, as I imagined myself doing to regain circulation, I listed sideways. In an almost out-of-body experience, my entire being attempted to right itself in about fifteen horrifying ways. My arms went out to catch each edge of the couch so I wouldn't fall onto the coffee table, while my legs flailed around as if I were attempting my first trapeze lesson. One of Chris's hands shot up to block his face, ostensibly so I wouldn't accidentally break his nose with my foot. The other reached over and anchored my knees back toward him, effectively halting my momentum so I didn't roll off the couch entirely.

Guiding my legs across his lap, he laughed. "What just happened?"

"I'm so sorry!" Pushing myself upright, I nestled firmly into the couch and mentally committed to never moving again as a fresh wave of humiliation washed over me. "My feet were going numb, and I didn't want to stand up . . ."

My brain disconnected from my mouth as I regained sensation in my legs. They were still resting across his lap. But it was his hand that caught my attention. Or, rather, his thumb absently tracing the curve of my calf. The touch was gentle, barely above a whisper, but the sensation was doing wild things to me.

"So you tried to kick me in the face?" Chris raised his eyebrows, his laugh low and rich. His hand was still there, wreaking havoc on my nervous system and my ability to mentally process anything other than his touch. "If you didn't want to talk anymore, you could've just told me."

My laugh sounded breathy, and I looked at my lap to give my brain time to think. "The kicking was just a side effect of the whole not-standing-up thing."

I looked back at him and . . . holy temptation. That was a mistake. I thought I'd gotten used to the way he looked at me, as if he was paying attention. But this was different. Almost as if his eye contact had its own gravitational pull.

If his gaze got any hotter, I would melt. He bit down on his bottom lip, want rolling off him in waves. Fighting the temptation to crawl into his lap seemed like a pointless battle that I was losing. I wanted—no, needed—more than just his hand on my ankle.

The sound of the garage door rumbling rocketed through the house like a shot. Squeaking, I yanked my legs out of his lap and back under myself, careful to leave a few inches between us. If trying not to get caught in a minimally compromising position were an Olympic sport, I would have cleared the initial time trial without issue. Chris blinked at me in surprise for a moment, then turned to look out the front window as the headlights from Mom's car flashed into the driveway. Think. Think. Think. What were we supposed to be talking about?

"So, about school." My voice sounded strange and bright.

He laughed and reached for a cookie. "Very smooth."

"You're one to talk." I glared at him.

"Meg, baby, are you home?" Mom's voice was about twelve times louder than usual as she came through the kitchen. Her sneaky way of warning me that I'd better not be in my bedroom with the door closed.

"In here," I called, narrowing my eyes at Chris, who took a bite out of his cookie, which had exactly zero impact on his smirk.

"Whose car is—" My mom rounded the corner and grinned. "Well, hello. Meg, I didn't know you were having a friend over."

"Hi, Ms. Williams." Chris shifted his cookie to his left hand and brushed the crumbs off his jeans as he got up and extended his hand. "Chris Chavez. I'm the other class president."

"Ohhh." Mom managed to draw the word out as she appraised Chris. After a moment of sizing him up, she grinned, and I almost melted into the floor. Whatever her internal checklist of boys-I-will-let-in-my-house was, he must have passed it. "Nice to meet you, Chris. I see you made cookies. What else did you two get up to?"

Mom asked the question as if it were normal, but I knew better. It was one thing for Mac to say he was cute; it was another thing for Mom to see him. I would never hear the end of this. She hadn't liked Trevor much, so she generally avoided saying anything about him other than that his socks looked crusty every time he took his shoes off.

"Just talked about student council stuff mostly. Want a cookie?" Chris walked over to the coffee table to grab the plate, and Mom gave me a big, dorky thumbs-up. I shook my head at her right as Chris straightened up and my mom dropped the gesture. He looked from me to her with confusion.

"That is so sweet of you. Your parents raised you well. Thank you." Mom picked up a cookie and then grew serious. "So, Chris, tell me about yourself."

"No, Mom." I bounced off the couch. "He's going home."

"I don't have to go. I can—" Chris started to protest as I snatched the plate of cookies from him.

"Trust me." I shook my head. "She's going to give you the third degree."

"I hardly think it's the third degree." Mom's smile was so large she was on the verge of an evil cackle. "There's a new person in my house and—"

"Bye, Chris." I shoved him toward the door, feeling flustered as his mouth fell open with surprise.

"Umm. I—"

"Want to stay for dinner?" Mom was outright gleeful over her planned humiliation.

"No dinner." I nudged him again and he staggered toward the hallway, where his shoes were.

"Oh. Okay." He picked up one shoe and turned to face my mom. "Thank you for the invitation. Maybe another time."

"Yes. Did Meg go over the rules? And show you the photos

from our family trip to San Diego? Because if not, we could always do that and—"

"Other shoe," I squeaked, and shot a look at my mom: unless she wanted to wake up with a horse's head in her bed, she'd better pipe down. Chris smiled from me to my mom and then put his other shoe on as if this whole thing were funny.

"She did go over the rules, and I'd love to see the pictures from San Diego next time."

If it was possible to dribble into a puddle of humiliation and leak off into my room, I would have done it. Instead, I wrenched the door open and pushed him through it. "See you tomorrow."

"All right. Nice to meet you, Ms. Williams." He waved. "Good night."

"Nice to meet you, too, young man."

"Okay, bye." As soon as I closed the door, I looked at my mom, who was leaning toward the living room to wave at him through the front window.

"Mom. 'Young man'?" I threw my hands in the air. "Are you trying to humiliate me?"

"He's cute." Mom shrugged. "I wondered whose car was out there. It's a cool car, by the way."

"Well, it starts like a serial killer movie."

"What? Who's a serial killer?" Mom called, still giggling.

"Me, if you embarrass me again," I practically growled as I made my way to my bedroom.

"Wait until I tell Grandmama."

"Not Grandmama. Not Mac either." I closed my bedroom

door and dropped onto my bed, throwing my elbow over my eyes so I could think, and not just about strangling my mom.

My cheeks felt hot as memories of the way he'd looked at me coursed through my mind. The phantom feel of his fingers tracing small circles on my skin sent shivers through my body all over again.

Then there was our conversation. Something scratched at the back of my mind. He'd said he knew what it was like to live with a shadow and need to get away. But how?

Exhaling, I sat up and looked at my phone. I couldn't just text him about it. Not after my mom basically tried to destroy my social life with stories of me getting seasick in San Diego. Instead, I was going to spend the rest of my night wrapped in the memory of him and wishing I knew more.

Chapter Seventeen

IT WAS THURSDAY, AND WITH TWO MINUTES TO GO, I WAS losing my nerve. I kept catching my legs shaking, and I hadn't touched my lunch. And not just because my nachos had extra fake cheese on them. Through the glass windows, I could see Chris sitting on one of the metal tables outside with the rest of the Davies class, holding court like I wasn't about to throw my food at him. We'd avoided each other all morning, so I had no idea what he planned to do.

"Earth to Meg." Riley waved their hand in front of my face, and I blinked up to see Christine and Freya standing next to us.

"Do you have a minute? We've been talking, and we're cool with Jasper, but—"

"*You're* cool with Jasper," Freya grumbled, and Christine rolled her eyes. Something about the sound of Freya's voice talking trash about Jasper grated on me like an old metal nail file. If I was going to stop conversations like this one, it was going to be today.

"Whatever," Christine continued. "What I was trying to say is that we want to talk to you and—"

"Actually, would it be cool if we do this later? I need to take care of something before lunch ends." I stood up, taking my nachos with me. Nadiya and Riley exchanged surprised glances.

"Oh. Okay." Christine sounded irritated as she took a step back to let me get by.

"Great. Thanks."

Riley started to pick up their lunch, and I shook my head infinitesimally. I needed to keep my friends far away from looking guilty if this was going to work. Pulling my shoulders back, I waved at people as I walked toward the lunch tables, trying to draw their attention outside.

Crossing into the sunshine, I marched up to Chris, who was listening to Tori talk. Glancing up to see who was blocking his sunlight, he flinched slightly. "Hey, Meg. Are you—"

"Stop pushing us around."

"What are you talking about?"

"This is for Hirono."

You know how in movies the girl slips and everyone sees her coffee spill in slo-mo? Well, dumping my tray of nachos on Chris's head was nothing like that. It felt like someone else had taken hold of my body until I felt the crunch of chips in Chris's hair and saw his mouth open in shock as nacho cheese began running down his face and onto his black T-shirt.

Next to him, Tori squealed and tried to jump off the table to get out of the way as I twisted the tray on his head. Around us, a volley of *oh*s and other shouts filled the courtyard.

"That's it." Chris grinned, ducking out from under my arm and knocking the tray off his head. Snatching his Gatorade off the table, he wrapped a cheese-covered arm around my shoulders.

"Not my—" I shrieked and tried to cover my hair as orange-flavored liquid ran down my head and the front of my navy-blue sweater.

"Not cool, fam," Russ yelled, jumping out of the way of the splashing drink. In that moment, I realized two things. First was that I'd made a mistake bringing only one thing to throw. Second was that Russ had a half-eaten sandwich in his hands. I darted over to him.

"Sorry."

A gang of Hirono students were running out of the cafeteria, shouting and pointing as I turned and flung turkey at Chris. It hit him square in the chest right as he reached up and emptied a bag of barbecue chips over me.

From somewhere a fry flew past my face, and I watched Tabitha wind up with the full force of a varsity softball pitcher to launch a vending machine pastry at Amber, who stumbled back from the force before grabbing her salad and roaring at Jasmine.

Chris grinned as I hit him with a tomato, and a quiet kid wearing a lot of eyeliner screamed, "Food fight!"

Then chaos.

There were so many guys in black T-shirts that after a while, I wasn't sure what I was throwing or who I was throwing it at. I snatched a half-finished bottle of orange juice and tried to find Chris, when arms wrapped around me and my feet left the ground.

"Put me down." I flailed and tried to see who was squeezing me like a python strangling the life out of its prey. "Russ. No, I'm—"

"Prez, you have to stop this," Russ shouted as he carried me toward the opposite corner of the lunch area, shaking his ketchup-covered head. Setting me down, he held my hands to my sides and bent to look me in the eye. "This is unacceptable. I'm very surprised by your behavior."

He sounded like a parent, and guilt flooded me. Behind him, Principal Domit was holding a megaphone, her pointy-toed kitten heels sliding on ranch dressing as she strode into the center of the mess. Her entire body was practically vibrating with anger as she started yelling, causing everyone to freeze.

"I want all of you—and I mean all of you—in the gym." A hush fell over the group as she looked around. Spotting me, she picked up her megaphone again. "Except Meg Williams and Chris Chavez. You two report to my office. Now."

Chris reached over and tried to untangle another chip from my hair, the plastic garbage bag he was sitting on squelching with the motion. "Sorry about the chips."

"No talking," Warm Fuzzy said, disappointment dripping off each word.

"Sorry," I said for the zillionth time. Chris grinned and dropped the chip onto the bag between us. Unlike me, he didn't look the least bit worried about what we'd done. Meanwhile, my stomach had officially done its seventy-fifth backflip as we waited for our parents to arrive.

"Megan Denise Williams." Mom's voice echoed through the hallway. As soon as she saw me, her jaw dropped and she froze. Chris stopped trying to dislodge the chips from my hair and looked down at his hands. Glaring at me, she crossed her arms. "What is wrong with you?"

"I—"

"Don't answer that. Look at you two. What do you have to say for yourselves?"

I paused, unsure of whether she wanted me to try to answer this one or if it was rhetorical as well. Chris took a deep breath. "We—"

"Young man, don't try me." Mom glared at him, and Chris shrank back. Walking up to Mr. Bednarik, she shook her hair over her shoulder and said, "I assume we are waiting for this heathen's parents."

"Well, I wouldn't call them heathens." Warm Fuzzy frowned. "More like good kids who got carried away—"

"Don't make excuses for them. They know better." Mom cut him off, too, then turned around to glare at us all over again as Mr. and Mrs. Chavez rounded the corner.

An extremely stern-looking man with Chris's build and a salt-and-pepper goatee strode into the room, followed by Chris's mom, who may as well have had steam coming out of her ears, she was so obviously pissed off. "Christopher, you better have a good reason for all this."

"It was—" Chris tried again.

"They don't have one. I already asked," Mom said, building up speed on what was sure to be one of her most biting lectures. "Look at you two, just sitting here. Smelly. Covered in food."

"I don't understand this," Estella said. "Chris, you know we're meeting with the Flower Growers Association this afternoon. Your grandfather is on the way there now. What is this about?" Her forehead wrinkled.

"We didn't—"

"On Tuesday, you two were getting along just fine," Mom interrupted again. "In my house making cookies. The kitchen was spotless." She curled her lip. "Now you're trying to tell me—"

"Hi. Thank you for coming," said Principal Domit, walking from her office wearing bright green gym sneakers. My heart sank. Hopefully, her other shoes weren't ruined for good.

Mom threw me one last nasty look and then straightened, instantly transforming into Professional Mom. Extending her hand to Principal Domit, she said, "Hello. Kendra Williams. I'm Meg's mother and I'm sorry we're meeting under these circumstances. Believe it or not, Meg hasn't done anything like this before."

"Nice to meet you. Estella, Ray, good to see you again. Of course, I know we all wish it were for other reasons. Typically, we would have this discussion in my office, but given the"—Principal Domit paused to search for a polite word, then continued—"state of these two, I think it may be better if we just keep them on their trash bags."

"Understood." Ray's nod was curt.

Principal Domit closed the door, then turned back to face us. Gesturing to Warm Fuzzy, she said, "As I'm sure you know, this year has been a challenging one for Huntersville High. However, most of our classes have started to settle into the new way of things, with the exception of our junior class, which is truly a shame."

Estella sighed loudly, shooting fiery looks at Chris. Principal Domit waited for a second to see if more outbursts were coming, then said, "Mr. Bednarik tells me that the two of them have been trying to bring their classes together. Clearly, the pressure was too much today. Now, I know that these two were not the only students involved in the fight this afternoon; however, my understanding is that they did start it. And while I cannot possibly give the entire junior class detention, I think a week for these two is fair."

"Generous, even," Ray said through his teeth. "Are you sure you don't want to extend that time frame?"

I stayed still and tried not to get my hopes up. We expected detention. I could live with a week or two. I doubted colleges would even care about that.

"Even if she doesn't give you more, Megan," said Mom, "I can tell you now that taking your driver's test is off the table. You aren't driving anywhere."

The knot that had been untangling in my stomach tightened. That wasn't fair. It wasn't even like I had a car, so what was the point of withholding driving other than to make her own life harder? "Mom! What if there's an emergency and—"

"Then you can walk to the hospital, because you aren't getting that thing until after November." She held up a finger as I opened my mouth to talk again. "I don't know what has gotten into you lately. Frankly, be grateful I don't believe in spankings. Your scrawny backside just better pray your grandmama has evolved to see it that way, too."

"Kendra is right," Estella piped up. "If Principal Domit is fine with a week, that's her business, but you, Chris, and your car aren't going anywhere anytime soon." She propped a hand on her hip and tilted her chin at Chris, daring him to say anything.

All the fight appeared to drain out of him. He looked down at his hands. "Yes, ma'am."

"That's what I thought." Ray nodded.

"May I make a suggestion, and you can do with it what you will," Mom said, her eyes practically closed, she was squinting at me so hard. "I know you can't give everyone detention, but you can give them community service hours. I have about a hundred and fifty senior citizens in the county who could use some yard work, help with forms, groceries delivered, boxes moved to storage, and the like."

"Oh, that is good, too!" Estella said, her smile somewhere between vindictive and joyful. "He'll take that. Twenty hours ought to teach you the value of hard work, not to waste food or disrespect the maintenance staff, and—"

"That is a wonderful idea," Principal Domit cut in. "I'll talk to our vice principal about how to make that announcement and manage the hours. Kendra, perhaps I can reach out to the county social services office to start arranging work hours in the next few weeks?" The principal smiled, but without any of the hint of evil that Estella had. "Also, Mr. Bednarik has agreed to supervise their detention and make sure that they are helpful, productive members of our school community."

"Thank you, Mr. Bednarik." Ray inclined his head toward Warm Fuzzy, who looked oddly distressed by the entire scene. "There's plenty of gum to be scraped off lockers, I'm sure."

"In the interim," said the principal, "given their state, I think it is better if these two go home and get cleaned up."

"Thank you for your time, Principal Domit." Mom waved for me to stand up, then looked me over, her shame so palpable that it started to cling to me like the ranch dressing I was already wearing. "Could I trouble you for a second trash bag, so she doesn't get this all over my car?"

"We should just stick you in the bed of the truck." Estella shook her head.

Mr. Bednarik handed Mom a trash bag. She ripped a hole at the end. "Put this on. And you will be hosing off outside before you step foot in my house. You smell."

With that, she picked up my backpack. I caught Chris's eye. He looked at me for the briefest second, half a smile crossing his face before he returned his gaze to the floor. That small smile said a thousand things, namely that we'd pulled it off. The homecoming war was officially done for good.

Chapter Eighteen

WHEN RAY SUGGESTED GUM SCRAPING, I DON'T THINK HE counted on just how averse to manual labor and punishment Warm Fuzzy really was. Handing both of us a spool of giant white ribbon, he looked meaningfully at the scissors in his hand, then said, "I'm counting on the two of you to talk out your differences, understand?"

"Thank you, Mr. Bednarik." I took the scissors from him, doing my best to be solemn.

"I'm going to check on how the freshmen are doing with the posters for Wacky Hair Wednesday and then on Russ, Tori, and the rest of the Countryside photo wall team, but I'll be back. And when I get back, you will have finished helping the sophomores with the sashes and crowns." Mr. Bednarik tried to sound stern but then relented. "And it's okay to ask for help or say you need more time. Just, no violence, please."

Chris tried valiantly to press a grin into a straight line and nodded. "Yes, sir."

We waited until he was gone, then looked at one another and started laughing.

"Should I measure you for your sash," I said, "or do you want me to just take my best guess?"

"Stop." Chris's cheeks turned pink. "I don't need one."

We'd been sentenced to helping the freshmen and sophomores pull together Spirit Week and homecoming game festivities on top of our homecoming dance assignments (me, DJ research, and Chris, finding a photographer). This was funny only because Chris had been nominated for homecoming court, which effectively meant that he was planning his own coronation.

"Right," I teased. "You try telling Alexa and the rest of the sophomore class that the junior homecoming prince doesn't want to wear a sash and see what she says." I set the ribbon down and picked up one of the dollar-store crowns in front of me. "She did tell me that she thinks you are a 'legend with dreamy hair.'"

Chris coughed out a nervous laugh and shook his head like I was being ridiculous. "I think both of us are legends right now. It's not just me."

"And yet all she said to me was 'You have good aim.'" I shrugged. "Just saying, if anyone wanted to kill off sashes, I think she'd be most receptive to the homecoming prince—"

"I didn't win anything yet." Chris toed the ground with his sneaker, looking like he would rather run into a dense forest and hide for a week than keep talking about anyone thinking he was cute, let alone a whole group of people voting for him.

"Fine. But I'm putting extra glitter on this crown just in case."

"You wouldn't do that." His eyes went wide as I pulled some spray glue and multicolored glitter from the craft bin. "That amount of glitter is chaotic evil."

"You'll be wearing it for weeks." I grinned, then walked over to the plastic sheet Mr. Bednarik had laid out for us to craft with (after he conveniently reminded us that it was not for moving or hiding bodies, which was dark but also funny).

I aimed a faux-innocent smile at Chris as I sprayed glue, then unscrewed the top of the glitter and dumped it all over.

"Okay, that is enough glitter for all of Las Vegas." Chris reached for the sticky crown. I tried to move it out of his way, my shoulder colliding with his chest and knocking us both against a cabinet. Sliding to the floor, I took the crown with me, doing my best to keep the glittered monstrosity out of his reach and over the plastic as he sank down next to me.

Chris leaned over my knees trying to get to the crown, pulling his torso even with mine. I could feel his laugh vibrating against my thigh as he turned to look at me, both of us realizing at the same time how close we were. My breath caught in my throat, and he licked his lips. Slowly, he leaned away from me and back onto the cabinets, still holding my gaze.

My thoughts spun in a thousand directions. There was no reason I couldn't kiss him anymore. Our classes were getting along. Not a single fight at last weekend's football game or even a whisper of a prank. The only thing stopping us was my overthinking brain. I didn't want to overthink anymore. I just wanted to have fun.

Setting the crown down, I angled myself toward him. "You

know, I'm glad I smashed nacho cheese in your hair. The school is finally getting along, so we don't have to be enemies anymore."

"I was never your enemy." Chris looked down at his shoes and then turned back to me, his eyes serious as he searched my face just as he did that night in the concession stand.

Slowly, I reached for his face with my glitter hand. I cupped his chin, running a finger across his cheekbone and leaving behind a streak of bright pink glitter. Chris closed his eyes at my touch, then registered what was actually happening and jerked them open.

"You are evil!" He laughed, pushing my glitter-covered hand away from him as I started to giggle. He wiped a hand across the glitter on his face, then reached for me. "I look like a disco ball."

I squealed and tried to back away, but he wrapped his arms around me, keeping me by his side so I couldn't stand up. Not that I wanted to. My heart thudded inside my chest. Finally, he was going to kiss me. Chris ran his thumb across my cheek and slowly leaned into me. Stopping just before he reached my lips, I felt him whisper, "Your phone is ringing."

"What?"

He pulled away, a devious smile creeping across his face. Pointing toward the pocket of my skirt, he repeated, "Your phone is ringing."

"Oh." Now that I thought about it, I could feel my phone vibrating against my hip, which was conveniently sandwiched next to his. I fumbled for my pocket and tried to force my brain to function. Next to me, Chris was shaking with silent laughter. An unknown number flashed across my screen and then went to voice mail.

"Why are you laughing?" I grumbled.

"Your face." Chris giggled. "Turnabout is fair play."

"Is it, though?" I wrinkled my nose and leaned back against the cabinet, trying to figure out how best to pick up where we left off, when the little red message icon appeared.

Who leaves voice mails, and why would they interrupt me now, when I was this close to finally kissing him?

I pressed Play and held the phone up to my ear as the message started.

"Hey, Meg. It's Sharon from the Monterey Flea Market." As soon as she said her name, I sat up straighter, pressing the phone closer to my ear. Chris's posture became tense as he watched me.

"Listen, kiddo, vendors are setting up, and I got a gal two stalls down who seems to have the Tabby Brichmans for fifty dollars. I didn't want to ask too many questions just in case she got suspicious and jacked up the price. Market opens tomorrow, but I think most people are gonna be here setting up tonight and no one is gonna say no to foot traffic that wanders in early. So yeah, get down here tonight if you can. Talk to you soon, kiddo."

It took a minute for my brain to kick in after the message ended. Pushing myself off the floor, I turned to Chris. "I gotta go. Can you let Warm Fuzzy know I'll make up the hours later?"

Chris's forehead wrinkled. "Is everything okay?"

"Yeah. I just gotta get home." I looked down at my phone.

It was 3:24. The second bus left in six minutes. I snatched up my bag and started for the door. If I hurried, I could catch it.

"What's going on?" Chris asked, pulling himself up.

"Long story. I've been looking for a pair of sunglasses, and they're at the Monterey Flea Market right now. If I can get there fast enough—" Chris's expression forced me to pause. "What?"

"How are you getting there? It's, like, an hour and a half away."

"The last bus will get me close to my house and then . . . Shit."

I stopped as my brain connected the dots he'd already put together. What happened next? I didn't have a license. And I didn't have a car. Was I going to add grand theft auto to my new delinquent lifestyle? Tears prickled behind my eyes, and I shook my head. I wasn't about to cry and give up before I'd even started. "I'll figure that part out. Maybe try and bribe my grandma or maybe Dr. Huq will let Nadiya leave work early, or—"

"I can take you," Chris said, standing up and brushing at the glitter on his face.

"You don't have a car right now."

"Yeah, but I know where I can get us one. It just has to be back before nine-thirty." He shrugged, then reached for his backpack. "I'll text you. We should run for the buses."

Fifteen warring thoughts ran through my head, and I searched Chris's face for any sign of hesitation. We were basically grounded. Neither of us should be driving anywhere.

Skipping out on detention was likely to get us more detention. Why was Chris willing to risk getting in serious trouble over this? If I were a good friend, I'd keep him out of my trouble.

But I wasn't a good friend. I was desperate. I shrugged. "Let's go."

Chapter Nineteen

I WAS STILL BREATHING HARD AS I DUMPED THE CONTENTS of an old purse on the floor and snatched up a loose dollar bill. If jogging home from the bus stop had made me this winded, I really needed to work on my cardiovascular capacity. Clearly, running the mile in gym class wasn't cutting it.

Reaching for another purse, I made a mental note to email Mr. Bednarik an apology from the road just so he knew that I was responsible for encouraging Chris to leave. It might not get me out of extra detention, but hopefully, it would help Chris out.

I was busy mumbling a list of people I would also need to apologize to when someone knocked on the front door.

"It's unlocked!" I yelled, then prayed that it was actually Chris on the other side and not a cannibal or something.

"Meg?" Chris's voice called down the hall.

I crawled to my open door and stuck my head out. "In here."

"Am I allowed in your room?" Chris asked as he walked down the hall and came to stand in my doorway.

"As long as you don't close the door."

Chris laughed and dropped his head to his chest. "Are you ever going to let me live that down?"

"Unlikely." I giggled, then started digging around under my bed for the bin that held my winter coats. I was forever leaving change in the pockets of my jackets.

"Everything okay?"

"Yup. Just looking for change. I don't know how much those Tabbys are gonna end up being, and I want to make sure I have the cash on hand for them."

"Right." Chris rocked on the edge of his sneakers for a minute, then leaned against the door. "It's just, you didn't really explain what's happening."

"Oh." I nodded slowly, buying time to try to sort out how to explain myself. "You kind of figured it out the other day. My dad collected sunglasses. He had this pair of blue Tabby Brichmans that he loved. I'm not sure what happened to them after the accident. Most likely they were in the glove box when the car was towed. Anyway, I've been looking for a pair like them.

"It's silly, I know. It's not like I think that this is the same pair, or that it will bring him back or anything like that. It just seems like, if I can find them, all this will . . ." I focused on organizing my change. I could feel his gaze on me, but I was too scared to look at him until I found the words I needed.

If Chris was going to go get these things with me, I needed to make sure he understood that this wasn't macabre or a casual hobby. This was completing a ritual. A kind of celebration and a final act of mourning. It was goodbye without ever having said the words.

"All this will . . ." His voice was gentle as he prompted me to finish my thought.

If I could be brave, he'd understand. I closed my eyes and exhaled. "All this will make sense."

Chris put a hand on my arm. His touch was warm and reassuring, managing to convey an embrace with one small gesture. When I looked up, his rich brown eyes were sparkling.

"What do you want help with so we can leave?"

Every inch of me relaxed. Those words felt like home, and he didn't even know it. Chris looked around the room, the slow smile I'd grown to love spreading across his face.

"Want me to put things away so your mom doesn't think you were abducted or something?"

My laugh sounded shaky but felt good just the same. "I'll leave a note on the fridge. Grandmama forgets to check her texts, so that will cover both of them and explain why my room looks like a tornado hit it."

"We should get going so we don't get stuck in rush hour." Chris stepped over a pile of shoes I'd thrown to get at the bottom of the closet.

While he made his way out of the house, I dashed into the kitchen and scribbled a note that I stuck to the fridge. I said a small prayer that Mom wouldn't be too pissed when I got home, then ran out of the house. I'd just finished locking up when Chris's car engine coughed and growled to life.

"You are gonna have to use your phone to navigate. Obviously, this thing isn't set up for GPS or anything. I do have a cassette player, so there is that." Chris chuckled at his own vintage car joke. "Box of tapes in the back seat."

I pulled the box off the floor, then leaned back into the leather seat, randomly taking out tapes, all of which featured people who had an astronomical amount of hair product and giant shoulder pads. I looked over at Chris as he flipped on a blinker and pulled away from the curb.

Sensing my question, he said, "They're my grandfather's tapes, so your options are basically R&B broken-heart songs, smooth jazz hits about marriage, and early nineties Spanish pop music, which may not be as interesting to you, since you're taking French."

"Just because I don't speak the language doesn't mean I can't enjoy them. Are they also love songs?"

"What do you think?" Chris looked over at me, smirking. "The guy started a flower shop and has a recurring order at Mandie's for their chocolates."

"Aw, your grandpa is a romantic." I put my hands over my heart and sighed. "That's so cute."

"It's really not. Trust me."

"I've heard your music. You are totally a romantic, too, aren't you?" Chris eyed me, the corners of his mouth turned up even as he tried to suppress a smile. "Oh my god, you are!"

"I am not." He looked back at the road, but the smile was still fighting to make its way onto his face.

"You are probably like that guy from the movie who stands in someone's front yard with a boom box."

"I don't know what movie that is." Chris laughed. "And I don't have a boom box. I have a Bluetooth speaker that I take with me if I need it to do practical things, like play music in the gym."

"Deny it if you want, but I know the truth." I fished out a tape with a guy in a wet shirt looking wistful and standing in the ocean. "What about this one?"

Chris looked at the tape briefly before merging onto the freeway. "Jon Secada? That one is sad, actually. The title is basically 'another day without seeing you.'"

"Sounds crushing. We're doing it."

"Guessing you don't think of yourself as a romantic." Chris chuckled, then sighed. "All right, but if we're both crying by the time we get there, that's on you."

"Only a romantic would cry over a song." I smiled at him, then stuck the tape in the deck as the light turned.

"Take this left." I was practically howling instructions over the stereo at Chris, who was singing every word to a Whitney Houston song I didn't know. We'd made pretty decent time, all things considered.

"Oh wow," Chris said as we slowed, forcing me to look up from the map I was trying to figure out. "That's beautiful."

The ocean spread out before us on the other side of the road. I turned off the stereo as he rolled down his window, the smell of salt and the sound of waves following us downtown.

"I always like the ocean. It's like being at the edge of the world. Like an adventure is out there." He said this quietly, as if this thought were mostly for himself and I was just lucky enough to hear it.

"Please don't sell your voice to a sea witch and become a merman just to find out what's down there."

"The sea witch is a feminist icon, and they killed her for being a savvy small-business woman," Chris deadpanned.

"Ooh. Hot take. I feel like those are fighting words in some corners of the internet. The map says there should be parking just down there."

"I stand by it." Chris grinned, then leaned toward the steering wheel as we passed a parking spot. Throwing one arm over my seat, he turned and began backing the car into a spot just outside the massive fairgrounds.

My pulse quickened. We were doing this. If everything went right, I was maybe fifteen minutes away from the Tabbys. It almost didn't feel real.

"Is it weird that I feel nervous?" I got out of the car and stood on the sidewalk, shaking my hands and hoping the jitters would leave my system. Chris finished locking the car up and then leaned on the top of it.

He looked at me, the wind pushing his hair around in every direction. "You've been looking for these for a long time. I think it'd be weirder if you weren't."

"I low-key feel like I might pass out. Or barf. Or both."

"Just—maybe put your hair back." He smiled over at me, then walked around to the front of the car. "I mean, if you're gonna barf."

"I don't know about this. What if it's a scam? Ugh." I moaned, then pressed a hand to the side of my face. I was definitely flushed. "I might have dragged us out here and maybe got us in more trouble for nothing."

"It's not a scam. The worst that happens is that they aren't real. We both sit in the car, listen to Jon Secada again, cry a little, and go home." I managed a weak laugh as he lifted one shoulder in a matter-of-fact way. Looking me up and down, he held an arm out and motioned for me to come to him. "Come here."

Slowly, I ambled around to the front of the car, forcing myself to breathe normally so I wouldn't hyperventilate. When I was within arm's reach, Chris grabbed both of my shoulders. Bending slightly to look me in the eyes, he said, "You aren't going to barf, and Sharon isn't scamming you. If she were, she wouldn't have waited for years to try to take you for fifty dollars."

"Technically, I have seventy-two dollars on me."

Chris laughed and pulled me into him, wrapping me up in a hug. In a soft voice, he said, "We've come this far. I'm right here with you. You've got this."

I leaned into him, resting my head on the comfortable spot just below his collarbone, letting the warmth of his words and the solidness of his form reassure me. He was right: I'd been dreaming about this for years. Laying the groundwork for everything to come together. The only part I hadn't planned on was him. But having him here was so much better than trying to do this on my own.

"Thanks," I mumbled, nestling myself closer to him. "For all of this, I mean. Not just calming me down but driving me here and coming with me. It means a lot."

I took a deep breath, memorizing the way he smelled and

how I felt wrapped up in him. We stood in the moment for a little longer than was strictly necessary, but just as long as I needed, and then he loosened his embrace. "Ready?"

I nodded, hoping the motion would shake away the last of my fear. "Let's go."

Pulling me close to his side, Chris draped one arm around my shoulders and began steering us toward the row of brown buildings that encircled the fairgrounds where the flea market would be.

My pulse fluttered as we walked toward the entrance, and I focused on the feeling of being tucked under Chris's arm. Around us, vendors walked between the parking lot and the stalls they were setting up. As soon as we cleared the entrance, Chris stopped. "How do we do this? Just wander until we see sunglasses?"

"I think it's easiest if we find Sharon. She's white, probably in her late sixties, long gray hair, and usually wearing tie-dye with too many necklaces. Trust me, you'll know when you see her."

"All right." Chris dropped his arm from my shoulder as we entered the crowded aisles between stalls. I tried not to notice its absence. I was being ridiculous. A few months ago, I didn't need him. Didn't really know him or his music. I'd certainly lived without his reassuring touch. Being this attached was silly, and I knew better than to be this reliant on him or anyone from Huntersville.

Still, knowing all of that didn't stop me from wanting him nearby.

I'd just started to make a right turn toward another aisle when Chris grabbed my hand, pulling me back to look where he was pointing. "Is that Sharon? Under the pink umbrella."

My eyes followed where he was pointing until I spotted her, wearing a bright yellow T-shirt that said STOP STUPID, a brown safari hat, and about twenty-three beaded necklaces.

"That's her." I smiled even as my stomach twisted. Grabbing Chris's hand, I tugged him toward Sharon, waving until she noticed me.

"Hi, kiddo! You made it up here." Sharon spread her arms out wide for a hug. She smelled like lavender and the kind of soap you buy in the vending machine at the laundromat. Taking a step back, she looked at me. "Did you grow?"

"Not since the seventh grade." I laughed.

"Well, your aura is taller, then."

Behind me, Chris giggled, then turned it into a cough when Sharon looked over at him and raised an eyebrow. "Who's the hair product?"

"This is Chris. He's co-president of my class with me. He gave me a ride."

"We all need rides." Sharon looked him up and down, then nodded as if indifferent to him. Chris tilted his head slightly but didn't say anything. "Meg, let's get you those glasses. Don't you two look at the same time, but you see the lady in the poorly cut jeans and the white sweater, like, four tents down? Ah, what did I just say?"

Chris and I both snapped our heads forward at the same time, then exchanged a glance to negotiate who would look first. I tried to peek over my shoulder surreptitiously and spotted her. In her defense, her jeans weren't really any worse than Sharon's. In fact, if Sharon weren't so committed to her hippie vibe, they probably would have been friends.

I turned back around and nodded at Sharon to continue.

"That's Careen Knowles. Don't be fooled by her grandmotherly ways. She is a shark, but she doesn't know sunglasses well enough to know anything other than that those Tabbys aren't made of cheap plastic. She's got what you're looking for in her junk tray."

"Got it." I put my hand in the pocket of my skirt just to make sure my money was all in one place.

"Be slick about it, though." Sharon nodded toward the stall and dropped her voice. "She's doing her price stickers now, so if she gets a whiff that you're interested or connected to me, she may try to knock it up."

"All right." I twisted my hands together, then shook them out again. "I'm gonna wander over. Chris, you stay here. She'll be able to smell a newbie."

Chris's brow furrowed. "Okay. Is there a sign that I should come over or something?" I smirked at him, and he shrugged, looking flustered. "I don't know. I've never been to a flea market before."

Sharon snorted. "Don't worry, Meg. By the time you get back, I'll have schooled him on the basics."

"Thanks, Sharon." I sighed and shifted from one foot to the other a few times to get the jitters out. "Wish me luck."

Each step I took toward Careen's stall felt like walking

in wet cement. By the time I reached her tent, I'd probably sweated through my sweater. Smiling in a noncommittal way, I clocked the Tabbys immediately but pretended to pick up a few other items and set them down while she wrote *0.99* over and over again on sticker dots.

"Looking for something special?" Careen's voice was sweet, but her green eyes were hawkish.

Picking up the Tabbys, I tried to sound blasé. "How much are these?"

"A hundred dollars."

"A hundred dollars?" Incredulity replaced my faux-casual expression. So much for being sneaky. Careen had clearly figured me out.

"I could come down to ninety." She shrugged as if she didn't care, but I'd done this dance before, too.

"How about—"

"Babe, let's go." Chris appeared at my side, wrinkling his nose at the Tabbys.

What was he doing? I'd told him to stay with Sharon. Did he think that my putting my hand on my hip and looking irritated at Careen was a code after all?

"But I'm—"

"There's a sunglasses place in town. You don't need used ones."

"But these are cute." I wide-eyed him. Careen was watching us intently, and I didn't want to blow my cover. Shaking my head at Chris, I tried again. "Reusing objects is good for the environment."

He shrugged. "They look scratched. If you're just gonna

throw them out in a week and buy new ones, you may as well not waste money."

"For the little environmentalist," Careen said, looking between the two of us, "I'll give them to you for sixty dollars."

"Not worth it. Let's—"

"Call it fifty and you got yourself a deal." I stared at Careen hard and held my breath.

Careen looked from me to Chris, who seemed downright bored with the entire exchange. "Fine. Fifty dollars it is. I've got a case somewhere you can take so you don't have to hear your boyfriend grouse about the glasses getting scratched."

I chuckled. Surprise flickered across Chris's face, then his expression went blank again. Fishing a few crumpled bills out of my pocket, I handed them to her as she handed me the case. "Thanks."

"You kids have a good night." Careen grinned as she flattened out my bills.

"Let's go," Chris said, wrapping his hand in mine. I had just enough time to catch Sharon smiling at us before Chris quickened his pace. He still looked bored.

"We got the glasses," I whispered, trying to crack his hard exterior.

He smiled almost imperceptibly, then dropped behind me, placing a hand on the small of my back to guide me through the crowded entry gate and into the parking lot. The closer we got to the car, the more he started to relax, his smile growing with every step. At the car, he turned to face me. "We did it!"

Without thinking, I bounced over to him and threw my

arms around his neck. Chris stumbled backward from the force, then wrapped his arms around me, picking me up and rocking me back and forth. I squeaked in a completely un-dignified manner as my toes left the ground. Even after he set me down, I was tempted to stay wrapped up in him, feeling his hands around my waist. Sighing, I forced myself to let go.

"I can't believe that worked," Chris said, taking a step back from me and adjusting the front of my sweater, which had gotten bunched up during our hug.

"What worked?" I asked, but my mind was busy replaying the feel of his fingers brushing against the cotton of my T-shirt. Chris shrugged and put his hands in his pockets, effectively keeping them to himself and bringing my attention back to the glasses and the fact that he was talking.

"Sharon said Careen figured you out. She told me I smelled like money and looked like someone who doesn't do vintage."

"I mean . . ." I tilted my head back and forth, half smiling.

"Shh." Chris shook his head, bemused. "She told me to go be a pushy boyfriend and that would make Careen come down and speed up the bargaining. But then we had to get out of there because Sharon didn't want Careen to know she was involved. Something about a peace treaty after a 1996 Matchbox Twenty concert. . . . Anyway, Sharon was right."

"I totally owe her a favor."

"Her?" Chris pointed to his chest with both hands. "I had to do the acting."

"I already made you a glitter crown. That is thanks enough."

"Is it, though?" Chris chortled, then ran a hand over the place where I had smeared glitter on his cheek.

"Fine." I blamed the sunglasses for the giddy, heady feeling I had and not the memory of being so close to kissing him. "I do have an extra twenty-two dollars for gas. Or I owe you about seventy-five hot chocolates from the student store."

"Or, hear me out. Maybe we don't leave yet? We're just gonna sit in traffic, so why not hang out here for a while?"

"Don't you have to be back by nine-thirty?"

"It's six-fifteen. We could leave by seven-thirty and be fine."

"Hmmm . . ." I waffled. Mom still hadn't texted me, so she either wasn't home or wasn't worried yet. Still, we were bound to get into even worse trouble if we were gone much longer.

"Come on. I know a good place for snacks." Chris held a hand out to me, his smile sweet and sincere. He batted his long eyelashes, and my resolve melted. I took his hand, and this time, neither of us let go.

"Okay, you were right." I sighed, popped another bite of the sticky, sweet cinnamon roll in my mouth, and moaned. "This is delicious."

"And to think you almost missed it, worrying about us getting more grounded." Chris laughed, then snagged another forkful of pastry.

"I'll just tell my mom to try one, and then she'll understand."

After wandering downtown to grab the cinnamon roll, he insisted that we sit on a bench and watch the sunset. Which I agreed to only after he promised to set a timer on his phone so that we wouldn't miss our window to get on the road. He laughed at me but obliged, seeing as I was still new to this whole relaxing, rule-breaking thing.

I looked down at the cinnamon roll he was holding, then back at his face, bathed in orange from the sunset. I'd never noticed it before, but in this light, I could see flecks of gold in his eyes. Somewhere in the background, a sea lion barked, and a few gulls squawked in return. My memory floated back to the night at my house. Just like today, we'd had sugary baked goods. At the start of the school year, I never would have guessed that I'd be breaking rules with him. Or that he was a romantic with a sweet tooth.

Thinking back on everything I didn't know and couldn't have predicted made me smile. Then I remembered my unanswered question.

"Hey, can I ask you something?"

"Sure," Chris said, his eyes still on the orange and pink streaks running across the sky.

"At my house, you said you knew what it was to try to outrun a shadow. What did you mean?"

"Nothing, really. It's stupid. Not like you and the glasses. That is legit." If I hadn't spent the last few weeks with him, I might not have noticed that his usual joy seemed hollow. Like he'd put on a Chris Chavez suit and was wearing a shell of himself. But now that I knew him, I couldn't just sit with this version of him.

"How do you know what I'll think if you don't tell me?" I nudged him with my shoulder, and he looked down at me, the forced smile slowly transforming into something serious. His eyes traced my face. Turning to look back at the sunset, he was so still that I thought maybe he'd forgotten I was there, but then he sighed.

"You've met my parents. They're very loving and extremely intense. The only thing they love more than their children is setting them up for achievement. In fact, I think they might love our winning more than they love us."

"That's . . ." I paused, trying to find the right word. Mom might be messy sometimes, but she never asked me to be anything other than me on most days. "A lot."

Chris exhaled a laugh that was rooted more in irony than in humor. "It is. They took my grandfather's little flower shop and turned it into an empire. They love to say stuff like 'We're building this for you kids.' But they never actually asked if I wanted the business."

"Oh." The force of what he was trying to explain hit me like a floodlight. Someone had set up a life for him, and he didn't want it. He wanted out just as badly as I did, even if his reasons were completely his own. "I get why they want you to go to business school now."

"Yeah. They have big plans to open locations in other states, so then their kids can create an interstate conglomerate and corner the ethical flower market." Chris's voice grew small. "Now you get why it's stupid. I'm a cliché. Who whines about having a family that works hard, loves them, and sets them up for financial stability?"

Frown lines appeared around the corners of his mouth, and I felt my heart crack in places. He looked lost without his usual confidence. It was unnerving. I wanted to lie and say it would be fine. To prop him up, as he'd done for me. But that felt wrong. I'd told a lot of little lies lately, but this wasn't a problem I could solve by pretending it would be okay. All I had to offer was my understanding, meager as it felt.

"Anything sounds stupid if you list the flip side," I said. "The truth is, the things they've built come with strings, and they're strangling you. You can't live like that. No one can." I leaned into his shoulder, so he looked down at me. "Are you going to tell them the truth?"

"Are you going to tell your mom the truth?" His words stung, even though his tone was gentle. A sad smile pulled across his face, and he exhaled, his shoulders sagging. "Not unless I have to. They won't take it well. My sister Diana tried that last year, and they basically forced her into fifty-seven job shadows. Pretty sure they were disappointed when she didn't fail chemistry and decide being a doctor wasn't for her."

"So when will you tell them? We can't avoid it forever."

"I know." Chris perked up a bit. "But I've got a plan. Get into USC. It's got a good business school and a good music school. Then I don't have to tell my parents what my major is until I graduate or something."

"Reasonable." I laughed. This was a highly developed plan that I did not see coming. For all his layers of cool, Chris was a planner like me. He just hid it better. "Not saying you need a different plan, 'cause you have a good one. But as someone who identifies as a professional life planner, I'd like to suggest that if USC doesn't work out, you could take a gap year and just see what it's like to play in dive bars. The worst that happens is you sleep on couches, realize you aren't cut out for the grind of being a musician, and come home. At least you'll know."

Chris looked over at me, half a smile tugging at the right side of his mouth. "Count on you to plan out my future, since yours is sorted."

"It's a skill." I smiled back and ignored the fact that I felt like my life was anything but sorted since coming to Huntersville. He didn't need to know that right now. I'd figure it out eventually. Instead, I turned to watch the sun continue to set in earnest. The cold air rushing off the water made me shiver, and I tucked my hands between my knees. Chris's eyes were on me, and I wanted to point out that he was missing the sunset. Another ten minutes and it'd be gone, taking the magic it layered over today with it.

"You're getting cold." Chris jumped up. Fishing the keys out of his pocket, he dashed off toward where he'd parked and came back a minute later holding a giant old-man sweater. Throwing one side of the sweater over himself, he plopped back down on the bench.

"Was that in your trunk?"

"Yes. Along with more tapes and a weird number of my grandpa's fedoras that I don't want to know about." Chris held open a flap of cable knit. "Here."

Sliding under his outstretched arm, I fitted myself next to

him, enjoying the deliciousness of his body heat against my cold skin. Resting my head on his shoulder, I reached over and pulled the other end of the sweater, and him, closer to me. Chris sighed and shifted so I could snuggle just a little deeper under his arm, a comfortable quiet settling over us.

The last of the orange and gold had officially left the sky, leaving behind pink and purple streaks. Part of me never wanted to move from this spot. This place was so easy. Everything felt simple here on this stretch of beach, far away from the real world and our carefully created truce. Here, there was no hiding our friendship, or whatever this was. No one to question our loyalty or threaten to destroy our hard work.

The other part of me knew that at any minute, his phone would chime, signaling the end of everything. I took a deep breath and tried to soften the blow of reality by speaking first.

"Why is your grandpa storing his hat collection in your car?" Chris looked down at me, his forehead wrinkled with surprise. Suddenly all the dots clicked together. "Wait. Is that not your car?"

"No. It's my grandfather's second car. He's had it since 1978. I drive it for him on Tuesdays and Thursdays so it doesn't stop running." Chris smirked. "Have you never seen my car? It's a Honda that my sister Gina dented when she tried to ride her bike with her eyes closed in the driveway."

"What?" I sat up so I could look at him properly.

"It was stupid, but Gina's nine, so I see how—"

"No. I mean, that explains why I couldn't figure out if you

were at school sometimes. . . ." If this wasn't his car, then how did he get it today? My pulse spiked as I imagined his sweet little old grandpa standing in the garage and panicking over his missing car. "Your grandfather knows you have it, right? He hasn't reported it stolen or anything."

"He's covering for me. Kind of. I mean, he didn't technically say he would, but I'm sure he figured it out. . . ." Whatever my face looked like must have scared Chris, because he rushed to explain. "I texted him that this was for a special occasion. I drive it for those, too."

"Why is this a special occasion?"

"Because my parents have the keys to my car and it's not a cool car anyway." Chris shook his head.

"Why do we need to be cool? We're three times younger than everyone else at the flea market." I laughed.

"Do you really not know?" Chris leaned away from me slightly to study my face. "I feel like I've been hinting at this for weeks . . ."

"Hinting at what?"

"Everyone knows you're into vintage stuff, and I have access to a vintage car, so . . ." Chris lifted one shoulder and shook his head slowly. "Opening doors, working together, your party, the food fight, making cookies."

"Oh." It felt like the bench beneath me disappeared and I was in free fall as the puzzle pieces came together. A thousand little grand gestures. This moment sitting on a bench, even. Chris never wanted to be at war, or in trouble. He certainly didn't want to be grounded. He wanted me.

"I didn't realize. I mean, I realized part of it, obviously." Words tumbled out of my mouth before I could arrange them in any order that made sense. "But I just thought that was standard. And—"

"I didn't think I was subtle, but to avoid any remaining confusion, I'm just gonna say it plainly." Half of a smile crossed his face. His voice was low and quiet but unafraid. Like he was offering me something precious and cared for. "I really like you. And I want to kiss you."

"Now?" My breathing stopped even as my mind whirled.

"Right now." He held my gaze, his voice barely above a whisper. "If you'll let me."

I nodded.

"Kinda need to hear you say it," Chris teased, and part of me melted.

"Please, just kiss me."

The other half of his smile caught up to the first as he leaned in, his lips brushing mine, gently at first. I ran my hand up the plane of his chest and around his neck, enjoying the feel of the silky hair at the edge of his haircut on my fingertips. His mouth tilted into a smile before he deepened the kiss. He tasted like cinnamon, sugar, and something else. Something wilder and more unknown. It made me dizzy, and I wanted more.

The sweater we'd wrapped around us pulled tight as his hand went to my hip, the tips of his fingers grazing the skin where my shirt had crept up. His skin against mine sent shivers all through me, and the only thing I could think about was him. The way he tasted, the feel of his chest rising and falling, his hands on me.

Slowly, Chris pulled away from me and smiled. The cold sea air rushed to fill the spaces where he had been moments before.

"What . . ." I started as Chris untangled himself from the poor stretched-out sweater and reached into his pocket for his phone. I heard chimes and realized the alarm I'd insisted he set had finally gone off.

"Alarms ruin everything," Chris mumbled, looking as dazed as I felt. Tapping the Stop button, he bit down on his bottom lip, closed his eyes, and took two deep breaths. When he turned back to me, he looked less foggy. "We should go home."

"I guess." He stood up and offered me his hand. I started to reach for it, then hesitated. If I stood up, the night was over, and I wasn't ready to let this moment go.

As if reading my mind, he smiled at me. "You know you can kiss me anytime, right? There are benches all over Huntersville."

I laughed and took his hand, twining my fingers through his as we made our way back toward the car by the light of the low moon. Leaning into his shoulder, I grinned up at him, remembering our car ride. "So I guess I was right about you being a romantic, then?"

He smiled down at me. "Only when it comes to you."

Chapter Twenty

I EASED THE FRONT DOOR OPEN AND TRIED TO SLIP INSIDE without making a sound. Taking off my shoes, I slunk past the darkened living room, then almost ate it as the light flipped on.

"Megan Denise Williams, where the hell have you been?" Mom was sitting on the couch, looking livid.

"I left a note." I pointed in the direction of the kitchen.

"Which had no details. And then you conveniently turned off your phone location." Mom crossed her arms. "You know damn well you were grounded. What has gotten into you? You are not acting like yourself lately."

My cheeks got hot as she listed out all the things I'd done. As if I'd intentionally upset her. I fished the Tabbys case out of my bag and walked into the room, hoping that she would understand. "I found the Tabbys, Mom. Sharon from the Monterey Flea Market called me this afternoon to tell me where they were, so I just had to get down there."

I held the glasses out to her. She looked at them for a moment but didn't touch them. Shaking her head, she continued:

"So you're telling me that you cut out of detention early, scared poor Mr. Bednarik half to death—"

"But they are—"

"Ungrounded yourself and missed curfew to get some sunglasses in Monterey?"

"I'm fifteen minutes late. It's not even ten-thirty."

Mom held up a hand to be sure I wouldn't interrupt her again, and I felt my pulse spike. I had tried so hard to make her life easier. She even joked about me being a rule follower. Until now, I'd never missed curfew. That should have been worth a bit of grace. But it didn't matter. Keeping unpleasant feelings away from her was the only thing that mattered to Mom.

"And it took you six hours instead of three to get there and back? Young lady, I thought you were dead."

"I feel like I'm dead in this house."

Mom's eyes narrowed. "Excuse me?"

"Just because you can't say goodbye to him doesn't mean that I won't." My words felt hard and sharp, and my hands were shaking. I knew that bringing up Dad would make this whole conversation so much worse, but I'd changed. I couldn't stick to my plan anymore.

"Goodbye to whom? Your driver's license? Or that boy who dropped you off?" Mom's tone matched mine, although her words didn't cut the way mine did, and we both knew it.

"You don't recognize these, do you?"

"No." Mom shook her head. "How is that relevant right now?"

"Of course you don't. Dad was wearing them when he left

the house. You don't even recognize his favorite things. It's like you can feel me trying to move on and say goodbye to him, and the second I find something to help myself, you freak out." Mom's jaw dropped, but I was done with this argument. Done with pretending to feel bad or good on the cycle that she chose. "This place is a shrine, but the only thing preserved is your grief. I can't live like this. I have to get the hell out of here."

Mom blinked at me a few times, her expression broken. I shook my head and walked down the hall toward my bedroom. "Meg . . ."

I didn't bother turning around. What was left to say? Instead, I closed the door and picked up my headphones.

"I'm so glad you're finally helping out," Grandmama said as she flipped on her blinker and we turned into the church parking lot.

"I'm doing community service, Grandmama. I don't think that counts as helping out."

"Well, Mrs. Crowder doesn't know that." She sounded practically gleeful as she shut off the car.

She hadn't said anything about my disappearing or my fight with Mom, although I was sure she knew about it. Even if she hadn't been in the room, the walls in our house are tissue paper thin, so we probably woke her up. Plus, she was a little too upbeat for me to believe that she was excited only about rubbing Mrs. Crowder's nose in my presence.

Hoisting myself out of the car, I took one last look at my

phone, hoping Nadiya had responded to my *Call me* text, and came up with nothing. Silly as it sounded, after fighting with Mom, I wanted to tell someone about Chris and finding the glasses who would actually be happy for me.

I was just about to put my phone away when Chris's name popped up. A smile spread across my face before I even had a hope of stopping it. Glancing up to make sure Grandmama was still talking to Deaconess Kilm, I opened the message.

> You going to homecoming with Phil Taylor or not?

I snickered and slowed my walking pace to a shuffle so I could answer.

> Staying home to watch Grandmama's murder show marathon has more appeal than Phil

> Or maybe I'll join a band and skip it like you

Almost immediately, the little dots that said he was typing came up.

> Or I could find a sub and you could go with me.

> Unless you want to watch murder shows . . .

> I won't eat dinner napkins, if that helps.

Butterflies filled my stomach and my mind flooded with plans for us. Sure, it was last minute, but I could probably find a dress. Dinner reservations might be harder to come by, but maybe we could just invite people over and make food. And, obviously, he had access to flowers. Not that it mattered. I would have gone in the ripped-up jeans I was wearing now if he wanted.

I tapped the phone in my hand, trying to think of how to say yes without sounding like I was trying to organize our whole lives together in a single hour.

"You coming, slowpoke?" Grandmama's voice rang out around the parking lot. Pulling the goofy smile off my face so she wouldn't suspect anything, I hurried to catch up.

"Hi, y'all! I brought my grandbaby to help with the clothing drive." Grandmama put a hand on my shoulder, cueing me to wave at the group of roughly a dozen older people surrounded by boxes and empty clothing racks. "She looks small, but she's pretty strong."

I grinned. I'd failed the stupid PE strength test every year since the fourth grade. Apparently, lying in the rec center part of the house of the Lord wasn't a sin. Or at least it wasn't when it made Mrs. Crowder's face look like she was sucking on a lemon.

After waving hello to a few of her friends, Grandmama put me to work hanging up a box of dresses on an empty clothes rack. I wondered what kind of suit Chris would wear and if there was a chance we could coordinate, even though it was too late to get a tux.

"Here, honey. Can you add this one to the rack?" Mrs. Crowder's voice interrupted my thoughts as she waved a fluffy avocado monstrosity in front of me.

"Sure." I took the dress from her and realized that it was one of those weird off-the-shoulder formal dresses that were popular in movies from the seventies. Popping it on a hanger, I held it up in front of me and snapped a picture. Still holding the dress, I texted it to Chris.

> Would you go to homecoming with me if I wore this?

"What are you doing?" Mrs. Crowder asked, nosing over to try to look at my phone. "Who are you sending that picture to?"

I popped my phone into my pocket before she had a chance to read anything.

"Just trying to figure out what to wear for homecoming."

"Oh. Well, that sounds fun." She did not sound like she thought it was fun. "Who are you going with?"

I wrinkled my nose. I got why Grandmama didn't like her. She was incapable of minding her own business. I opened my mouth to try to politely tell her to buzz off, when Grandmama cut in.

"She's been out with a nice boy, but I don't think he's asked her yet," Grandmama called from where she was hanging up shirts and eavesdropping. "Meg, has he asked you?"

"I'm working on it, Grandmama." Ugh. An entire day with these two was going to be very long.

"Well, don't work too much longer, or you'll work right past the dance," Mrs. Crowder said. Grandmama threw her a dirty look, and I took that as my cue to go reorganize the racks on the other side of the gym.

Picking up a box that was much heavier than it looked, I swayed over toward the rack of blazers, then dropped the box with a thud. A few people browsing the clothing displays jumped and then turned to look at me.

"Sorry." I waved around, turned back to the box, then did a double take. "Freya?"

"Oh." Freya's expression froze somewhere between terror and distaste. She was holding a billowy yellow skirt and a massive belt. She blinked at me for a moment and then regained her composure.

"Hi." This was awkward. I looked around, wishing that I had just pretended not to see her so I didn't have to make small talk. "Are you volunteering, too?"

"No." Freya laughed, the sound bitter and cold. "I thought you, of all people, had figured it out. Given how much vintage shopping you do."

Tension stretched between us as I tried to put together what she was saying. Bits and pieces started rearranging themselves in my mind. How good she was at sewing. Her being weird about vacations. The dress that looked just like hers . . .

"Oh." I blinked, feeling foolish. She was right, I should have figured it out sooner. But also . . . "You made everything? You are an exceptional tailor." Freya shrugged, looking pleased. "Why would you lie about that?"

"Because at one point everything about me was true. God, you don't know me at all." Freya rolled her eyes. "Typical you. Liked by everyone, friends with no one. Class presidents are supposed to know people, not use them."

"Who am I using? And it isn't my fault that I don't know you." I crossed my arms and let every ounce of irritation I was feeling show on my face. "I'm not obligated to try to be besties with someone who's mean to me."

"My mom left my dad and me when I was in ninth grade. She took her money with her." Freya's face went paler than usual except for her cheeks and the tips of her ears, which turned pink.

"I still don't understand. Why not just be normal like the rest of us?"

"Think about who my friends are. Does it seem like they'd want to hang out with someone who spent her summer in Encino at her grandmother's apartment complex pool?"

"I guess not." I hesitated, thinking about the Hungry Girls. How competitive and cold they were with one another. It was a bond built on exclusivity. At least with Riley and Nadiya, our little band of misfits lifted each other up until we were strong enough to stand on our own. They had my back, and I had theirs. What Freya called friendship must have been lonely.

A pang of sympathy ran through me, and I checked it. Freya was lonely because she couldn't figure out how to be less awful. The thinly veiled insults, the bullying, the weird comments about diversity that were so broad I couldn't even figure out what category of problematic to put them in. My pity wouldn't fix any of that.

"Why not make new friends?"

"With who? You and your friends?" Freya snorted as if

I were being unreasonable. A cold smile crossed her face. "You've made it clear you'd rather eat glass than talk to me."

I held my breath. That stung because she wasn't wrong. I'd been so busy trying to avoid her or outsmart her that I hadn't ever actually stopped to think about her. Little bits of unwanted memories floated toward me. Her looking disappointed not to be invited to the prank. Trying to warn me about Trevor in Life Skills. The way the Hungry Girls treated each other, that probably was her twisted attempt at friendship.

I shook the memories away. "You aren't exactly kind to me."

"I know." Freya looked at her shoes. Exhaling, she turned to face me again. "And I'll back off the whole rivalry thing if you don't tell anyone about this. If you haven't figured it out we're broke, that means no one else will."

My eyebrows shot up. I didn't know what I had expected from her. Maybe an apology. Or a promise to try to be a kinder person. Something. Instead, she was offering an uneasy truce. My silence in exchange for hers. It didn't sit well with me, but then again, maybe it didn't need to. This was Freya's demon, and she was running from it, just as I was running from mine. Suddenly, I wasn't so sure that either of us could avoid them.

"This doesn't absolve you of the things you've said about me or my friends."

"I'm not asking it to," Freya scoffed. Turning toward the exit, she tucked the yellow skirt under her arm. "See you on Monday, Meg."

My mind and heart tangled as I watched her go. Freya

wasn't a threat or a friend. She was confused and trying to protect herself. I could relate to that.

"Meg. You listening?"

"Hmm?" I was not, in fact, listening to Grandmama. Since leaving the church sale, I'd been thinking things over. Everything in my life was topsy-turvy, and I wasn't sure what to do about it. In nine years, I'd never lashed out at Mom or confronted Freya. Never gotten detention. Or snuck out. I certainly hadn't lied to teachers, my family, or my friends.

I'd also never had fun like this. Mom, my teachers, even Freya would be happier if I'd just stuck with my plan, kept my head down, and got out. But I couldn't make myself, and that scared me. If I wasn't going to follow the rules and I wasn't going to stick to the plan, then what was I going to do?

"Never mind." Grandmama looked over at me as we passed the final stop sign before our block. "You're awfully quiet. Want to talk about something?"

"No. I'm just tired," I half truthed. I was tired. But I also didn't know how to talk about what I was feeling. In the Williams house, we danced our feelings, or made jokes out of them. What we didn't do was feel them.

"All right. Well, if you get some rest and you find you want to say something, I'm here," she said, pulling into her spot in the driveway.

"Thanks, Grandmama." As I opened the door my phone

started buzzing. "You go ahead. I'm gonna talk to Nadiya outside." I waved my phone at her so she could see it really was Nadiya calling.

Grandmama watched me for a moment, her eyes narrowing. I smiled at her and she relaxed. "Okay, baby. But don't stay out here too long. I'm gonna get lunch going."

"All right." I nodded and then walked away from the front window before answering.

"Hey. I'm on break." Nadiya's face popped up on my phone, tucked into the supply closet of her mom's office. Dropping her voice to a whisper, she said, "Cryptic text much? Is this about the hedges for homecoming, because Riley said they'd deal with them."

"No." I looked over my shoulder and then walked a little farther away from the house. "I have something to tell you, but you gotta promise not to freak out."

"Cross my heart. Does this have something to do with you disappearing from Friday detention, because Warm Fuzzy was nearly in tears, according to Jennie." I arched an eyebrow and Nadiya filled in the requisite information. "Ricki's little sister."

"Jennie really needs to mind her own business." I rolled my eyes. "But yes. Kind of."

"Oh my god." Nadiya's eyes lit up. "You didn't murder Chris and hide his body, did you?"

"Umm." I winced, trying to think of the best way to break the news to her. "I mean, Chris was there. But he is very much not dead."

Nadiya readjusted her crouch and waved at me to hurry up. "Tell me everything. Now."

I took a deep breath and felt my throat close as if trying to protect me from having to tell my friend the truth. But Nadiya wasn't just a friend; she was one of my best friends. I had to tell her eventually. Squeezing my eyes half shut, I exhaled the whole story in what felt like one long breath, trying not to flinch as Nadiya's face passed surprised, rounded on shocked, and landed on full-blown disbelief with each new detail.

"What?" Nadiya shrieked, then looked up at the supply closet door. Dropping her voice again, she said, "You said you weren't interested in him. Swore up and down it was nothing."

"It just happened."

"Breaking news just happens. The writing has been on the wall for weeks. The texting, you being all shy about seeing him at work, him just hanging around your locker. How did I miss this? Since when do you keep things from me!" Nadiya was smiling, but there was a layer of hurt under her voice.

Echoes of Mom's accusations came back to me uninvited. I wasn't acting like myself. Or, rather, I wasn't acting like the me before Huntersville. It wasn't my intention to shut Nadiya out. She'd been asking me what was up for ages, and I just didn't know what was wrong with me. Everything seemed to change so fast. I never meant to let it go this far. To hide things and lie to her for this long. In that way, I'd treated my friends the same way Freya treated hers, and I hadn't even noticed. . . .

But this was different, it had to be, because I had planned

to tell her at some point, hadn't I? My words felt caught in my throat, and I swallowed hard as Nadiya waited. "I'm sorry."

"I swear, you tell me what you're gonna do only after you do it these days. I blame Chris and the whole Davies-Hirono-Huntersville transition." Nadiya sighed and every part of me felt like I'd been shocked. Maybe this wasn't that different from what Freya had done. The thought jabbed at my heart. Was that who I was becoming? Someone who lied to hold on to their place in the world?

Nadiya paused and looked up at the door again. "Shoot. I gotta go. Mom's looking for me. Finish talking about this later?"

She'd already hung up by the time I said, "Okay."

My mind spun. This whole thing had started with the school merger and Chris. All this time, I'd been going back and forth over what to do and how to do it, when the right decision was always there in front of me. Huntersville was always temporary. Me and my friends were supposed to get out of here, and I'd almost derailed that. I was fighting with my mom for the first time ever. Hell, I'd even upset Warm Fuzzy, a man who truly believed world peace could be achieved with one more hug. It was as if when Hirono went away, I just attached myself to the first things that came along—the homecoming war and Chris.

I started to walk back toward the house when my phone buzzed with a text from him. My heart sank as I opened it and saw a picture of an avocado-green fedora with a burnt-orange feather stuck in it.

I'd say that my grandfather has a matching hat in the trunk, so our pictures will look amazing

Tears pricked at the back of my eyes, and I closed the text. I wasn't going to homecoming with him, avocado-green matching outfits or not. My birthday wish was for fun, but dreams weren't real life. It was time to let it go. I needed to stick to my plan, and Chris and Huntersville were not part of it.

Chapter Twenty-One

GRANDMAMA WAS A TERRIBLE ACCOMPLICE. MY PLAN HAD been to arrive just before the bell so I didn't have to explain anything to Nadiya until things with Chris were sorted out. I'd hide in the library at lunch, then find Chris after school and tell him that I was sorry but we were done. Then I'd catch a ride home with Nadiya, and everything would be in the past.

This would suck, but it was just one kiss.

Of course, like everything else in my world lately, nothing was going to plan. I looked down at my phone. Still fifteen minutes before school started. I decided to stop by the library and pretend to look at books, then I closed my locker door and jumped.

"Good morning." Chris stood in front of me, his usual smile in place.

He rocked forward like he might try to kiss me, and my pulse started to race. If he kissed me again, I might lose my nerve. I pushed my hair behind my ear and looked down so he couldn't read my expression. Instead, I watched his sneakers.

"So good news is, I found a sub. Now I just need to know, are we making this seventies green thing happen or what? You didn't answer my text."

He laughed and my heart started to thrash around in my chest.

Gritting my teeth, I forced myself to look him in the eye. "We need to talk."

"Did I do something?" His smile faltered, but he picked it back up again. "We don't have to wear that color green."

"It's not that." I tried to laugh, and it came out shaky. "I can't go to homecoming with you."

All traces of the joke had left his voice when he asked, "Are you still grounded?" Also gone was his smile, and seeing him without it felt like I'd chipped off a piece of my heart.

"No." I shook my head, and my throat squeezed with the words I was struggling to say. This was for the best. It would hurt now. But both of us would be better off without the other. We'd both be free. No more pressure, or rivalry, or sneaking around. I took a deep breath. "Look, I shouldn't have gotten carried away and dragged you into my nonsense. You've been so nice to me, and I made a mistake."

"What do you mean, 'mistake'?" Chris's features hardened. "Like kissing me was a mistake, or—"

"No. That wasn't a mistake. Or, it was, but not like that. You make it sound bad."

"Because it is bad."

"I just have to restore some order, you know? My mom's upset, Nadiya said she doesn't know me anymore, even Freya is acting weird. Better to keep everything in its container. Not let my foods touch. Does that make sense?" I laughed at my nervous, rambling analogy, but Chris did not. He looked stunned.

"So you're what? Breaking up with me because you can't control everything? No, that doesn't make sense." His disappointment hung thick in the air between us, so strong I could almost taste it. "I can't believe you're shutting me out."

"Not like that. I thought about it on Sunday, and everything feels precarious. We just got everyone calmed down. I don't want to keep rocking the boat. And—"

"At least be honest." Chris's voice was flat and quiet. "You are scared, and you can't control everything or how people react to us, so you're ending it before you can even find out where it goes."

I froze. He was right. I was afraid, but he just wasn't getting it yet. If I put everything back the way it was, things would calm down. My plan could still work.

But putting him back hurt. This wasn't how I wanted this to go. In my head, he'd understand. I'd say the words and he'd get it, because he got the rest of me. This was supposed to be sad but easy.

"You're right." My voice was small, but he asked for honesty, and I could at least give him that. "But if I stick to the plan, maybe things will get less scary."

"At least give us a chance. We could figure this out together." Chris's voice held a note of pleading, and the little bit of my heart that I'd chipped cracked completely.

My throat closed up, and tears burned in my eyes. My friendship with Nadiya. Getting out of town. Maintaining a relationship with my mom. Even earning back Warm Fuzzy's trust. Setting us aside was the way to make sure those things happened.

"I can't."

"Fine." Chris closed his eyes and swallowed hard. He took a deep breath, then opened his eyes. Standing up straighter, he smiled down at me. "Take care of yourself, Williams."

He stepped around me and then walked down the hall.

The tears I'd been fighting started to roll down my face. It felt as if I'd shattered my own glass heart and handed him the shards, making him bleed, when neither of us was supposed to get hurt.

I'd followed the plan. It was supposed to make things better. So why did I feel so awful?

Chapter Twenty-Two

"SORRY, SORRY," RILEY SINGSONGED AS THEY SQUEEZED into a spot in the stands that wasn't really big enough for two, let alone three of us, forcing our classmates to smush against one another to make room.

"Maybe we should just go a few rows back," I said, ducking around someone's bag of popcorn.

"Nope, it's homecoming and we need to be front and center for the action when we crush Jackson." Nadiya shoved me forward, using her peak "football fan" voice.

Nadiya hopped up and wiggled around in her bulky Huntersville sweatshirt and her purple pants until there was room for me. I hesitated. I was done crying—or at least I was done spontaneously crying—but that didn't mean that I wanted front-row seats to watch Chris potentially be crowned homecoming prince. Not that I told Nadiya and Riley that. As far as they were concerned, I'd had some kind of mental blip that made me do something totally unlike me and now Chris and I were done.

"Get up here." Riley reached down and linked their arm through my purple sweater–clad arm and pulled me up to the bench. That sweater was the most school spirit I could manage under the circumstances and looked downright puny next to Riley, who'd spray-painted their hair a bright purple and decked themselves out in purple and gray sparkles.

The whistle blew and I did my best to smile at my classmates without looking around. I was fine as long as I didn't see him, so my plan was to just not look, maybe even leave to get a snack when the homecoming court was announced. While Nadiya leaned across me to explain to Riley what was happening in detail, I tried to focus on how even-keeled my life had been over the last week.

Mom and I hadn't talked about our fight, which was strange. But the important thing was that we weren't fighting anymore. She'd even said she would reschedule my driver's test. I'd apologized to Mr. Bednarik, who mostly just seemed happy that Chris and I had decided to work together on something. Freya continued to avoid me, which was all I ever really wanted from her. The dance decorations had gone up in the gym without any big mishaps, and the student council had even managed to get Davies-Hirono pairs to work in the student store without erupting into violence.

I'd gotten what I wanted, and it should have made me happy, but it mostly made me numb.

A buzzer went off and the marching band started playing "Seven Nation Army" at halftime, making my classmates jump around and jostling me out of my thoughts. Principal

Domit walked out onto the field in her purple suit, and my chest squeezed.

"I'm going to go to the bathroom."

I tried to step off the bleachers, and Nadiya grabbed my hand. "There's no way you're getting out."

The crowd around us had swelled, locking us into the stands as Principal Domit began calling out the freshman homecoming court and its winners. My body temperature rose, and I started to sweat.

"Look at Russ." Riley giggled and pointed to the huddle of students waiting in the corner for their turn to walk onto the field. He was doing a strange little dance that looked like a combination of what the cheer team and the band were doing.

I forced myself to laugh as Russ hopped from one foot to the next. His body shifted, and my breath caught. There, chatting with Christine, Spencer, and Tori and looking happy, was Chris. Everything about him was what I imagined he'd look like, and none of it felt right. I was supposed to be cheering him on. Later, Chris and I would joke about him being down there at the dance. Laughing at him covered in the sparkles I'd dumped all over everything before we'd kissed.

But none of that was happening now. I'd ended things because I thought it would make everyone happy. And everyone was happy. Except for me. My bottom lip trembled and I pressed it into a flat line.

"Wait, what is happening right now?" Nadiya looked over at me.

"Nothing."

Except for the fact that Chris was probably making best friends with Tori, Spencer, and Christine. Which meant soon he'd hang out with Freya, who was probably at her least evil. Then he'd start hanging out with all of them and I'd have to see him happy with them and—

"It doesn't look like nothing." Riley eyed Nadiya as if they were having a full-blown telepathic conversation, then turned to watch as Principal Domit began calling out the junior class court.

Nadiya's eyes followed as Chris marched onto the field, smiling and waving and being just fine without me. "I thought you said this was a mutual thing that both of you were just getting out of your systems?"

"Not exactly." The bits of my heart that I managed to tape together started to come loose, and I looked down at my shoes, taking big deep breaths so I could calm down.

"Did he break up with you?" Riley shrieked, causing a freshman in front of us to turn around.

"No. I don't know why I'm reacting this way. Nadiya even said it, I never used to do stuff like this, so then I ended it with him. I mean, I used to tell you two everything, and then I met Chris and the whole school-merge thing happened, and suddenly, I'm grounded and fighting with Mom, and Freya said something true, but I still don't like her and—"

"What does Freya have to do with this? And how did you get 'break up with him' out of what I said?" Nadiya looked at me as if I'd lost my mind. "That is not what I was saying. I meant that you should tell me before you do stuff like this. Because that's how friendship works. You silly cow."

"Okay, maybe we don't need to name-call." Riley wrapped their arm around me, shielding my tears from the view of people around us. "Also, I love you both, but neither of you is making sense."

"And your junior class prince is Chris Chavez." He stepped forward, all easy smiles until Principal Domit picked up the glitter crown. His smile flickered. To everyone else, it looked like he was avoiding massive amounts of glitter in his hair and not the memory behind it.

A sob shook my body.

"Are you okay?" a freshman in front of us asked.

"Mind your own business, Jennie," Nadiya snapped, then reached for me. "Okay, we have to get out of here."

"But you'll miss the game," I blubbered into my sleeve. "And we're trapped. And you love football and now I'm messing that up, too."

"This is pitiful." Nadiya looked repulsed.

"She's hit the nonsense stage." Riley stepped off the bench and elbowed their way through the crowd. "For once in your life, let Nadiya and me handle something for you."

On the ride home, Riley and Nadiya made me retell the whole messy story, which took forever, because I'd never told Riley about the deal I made with Chris around the pranks, so they had a ton of questions. Then there was Nadiya interrupting to add details and poking at some of my weirder choices.

By the time we got to my house, I was still sniffling, so they found me some sweats and a shower cap for Riley so the purple dye didn't get everywhere, then we settled into the couch for me to try to explain the reason behind the whole trip to Monterey, the fight with Mom, and how Freya said her friends were mean—leaving out the part about her lying, since it wasn't mine to tell. This part was equally slow, but that was because I kept crying and not because they were interrupting. In fact, they were blessedly quiet, except for the occasional pile-on hug.

"Okay, so that's a lot," Riley said, snuggling close to me and handing me another tissue.

"I'd cry, too." Nadiya snuggled into my other side so the two of them sandwiched me in. "Do you want to talk through anything now or maybe later?"

"I mean . . ." I sniffed, debating whether I'd rather stretch out the pain or just rip the bandage off.

"Later wasn't actually an option." Riley laughed. "That was just Nadiya's attempt at being subtle."

"Hey. I'm very subtle." Nadiya leaned forward to make a rude face at Riley, and the three of us giggled.

Dabbing at what was left of my mascara, I sighed. "Okay. Where do you want to start?"

"Magical solutions," Riley said.

"Hiding shit," Nadiya said at the same time.

"Oh no." My voice trembled.

"No, no. Don't cry again," said Nadiya. "We're just gonna pick one, and I'll go first, because Riley has that soothing, camp-counselor energy, so it's better if they go last."

"Said no one about me ever." Riley laughed until Nadiya cut them a look. Clearing their throat, they said, "Continue."

"Thank you, Riley." Nadiya angled her body slightly so she could hold my hand and look at me. "Meg. I'm sitting here feeling all bad about what I said, and I just keep wondering why you would hide having a crush on Chris from us?"

"With the whole rivalry thing, I just wanted to do right by everyone."

"I get the part about everyone else, but we are your friends. Why hide from us?" Nadiya's eyes were gentle, though her words stung. "What I was trying to say on the call is that you don't have to make all your decisions by yourself. I admit, I was hurt you didn't tell me." She shook her head. "But only because I thought we were better friends than that. In my mind, you two are my unconditional friends, and I thought you knew that."

"I do know that."

"Do you, though? Because you tied a lot of strings to our friendship that Riley and I sure didn't put there. We love you, even if we don't always get you." Nadiya smiled at me, then laughed. "Not that we don't get wanting Chris. He is genuinely a very good-looking person."

"Why are you shutting us out?" Riley asked, bringing the conversation back in focus.

I took a shuddering breath. "I don't know. Maybe because I was comfortable at Hirono? It was predictable and we had a plan. Suddenly, we're at Huntersville and everything was just off. And the stupid homecoming war made that harder. Like, even though I couldn't find my footing, at least it was fun. But then things spun out and I didn't know what to do to get back to that Hirono-plan feeling and everything was confusing. I just thought if I shut out all the noise, I could figure it out, and I accidentally shut you two out, too."

"Okay, I get wanting to figure it out." Nadiya wrapped an arm around me and squeezed. "But like, you know plans can change. It's okay to want something different from what we wanted when we were twelve."

"Technically, I came up with the plan when we were elevenish." I sniffed, leaning my head on her shoulder.

"New rule," said Riley. "Let's modify or abandon any plans we made before the ninth grade." They giggled.

"Okay, Riley. What was your thing about magic?" I immediately regretted asking when Riley sat up and looked at me, their usual mischievous expression replaced by something serious.

"I want to start by saying that you can decide what to do with this. But it's about the sunglasses."

"Ooh." I moaned like a cow.

"Don't be dramatic. It's not that bad." Riley grinned and twisted the hem of their sweatshirt in their fingers. "It's just that you seemed to think the sunglasses were going to fix something. An object can't force change. People do. In my experience, if you want your family to change, or accept you changing, that starts with you telling them how you feel."

Somewhere in the back of my mind, the little bit of strength

I'd managed to cobble together crumbled. Riley was right. The sunglasses were important because they seemed like an easy fix for grief. I'd been mad at Mom for never moving on, but in a way, I'd trapped myself in the same cycle.

I covered my face with the sleeve of my sweatshirt as a fresh wave of sadness rocked my body.

"Come on now." Riley squeezed my other hand. "You just have to give your mom a chance to change with you."

Using the edge of my sweatshirt to wipe my eyes, I sniffed. "You said it wasn't that bad. As if changing years of precedent was easy."

"Can't be any harder than combing the state looking for used sunglasses that you can afford," Nadiya said, as if counting up the miles we'd put on her car checking out thrift stores.

"I guess not." I sighed, and Nadiya and Riley both piled a hug on me.

"That's our girl," Nadiya cooed.

"Look at you, growing emotionally," Riley needled before peeling themselves off me.

Sitting up, I looked at the pair of them. "What are we gonna waste gas on, if we aren't looking for sunglasses?"

"Oh, we can still do that," Nadiya said. "We're just going to do it like normal people, not people who think that the glasses will grant us three wishes."

I laughed, and this time, it felt like I meant it. "Thank you. I haven't been a hundred percent open, but I am grateful for you two, and I know I'm super lucky to have friends who love me and will be honest with me. Not like Freya."

"Nothing like her. Please don't ever think we're like the Hungry Girls again. That's maybe the most insulting part of this whole story." Nadiya laughed as headlights flashed in our driveway.

"We love you. And don't you forget it." Riley leaned back to peek out the window. "Your mom's home, which means we should go. You obviously have stuff you need to talk about."

The look they gave me was so loaded that I almost laughed. At least no one would accuse my friends of being understated. I walked them to the front door and gave them each a hug right as Mom and Grandmama stepped in.

"Well, hello. I thought y'all would be at the game," Grandmama said. "We didn't know you were here, or we wouldn't have gone to dinner and not brought you anything."

"No worries. We're on our way out. Good to see you both." Nadiya gave Grandmama a hug as Riley slipped on their shoes.

"Drive safe, you two," Mom called as soon as they finished up their goodbyes, then shut the door. She and Grandmama both turned to face me, and immediately their expressions changed.

"What's wrong, baby?" and "Are you hurt? Is everything okay?" Grandmama and Mom asked in a chorus, their faces etched with concern.

"Yes and no." I twisted the ball of my socked foot on the floor. "I'm physically fine, but we need to talk. . . ." Mom's face relaxed and I almost felt bad adding, "About Dad."

"Okay." Mom's voice sounded as if she'd had the wind knocked out of her.

"Maybe you two go in the living room," Grandmama said, eyeing me. "Keke, I'm gonna get you a sweatshirt like Meg has on and your slippers. I know you feel better with those." This was her way of giving us space without actually committing to not listening in.

I walked back into the living room and tucked myself into my corner of the couch as Mom dropped down on the other end. I took a deep breath. Part of me wished I could go back and undo everything. But I'd tried that, and it didn't work. Instead, it made everything worse, and I ended up crying at a football game like a fifties song cliché.

No, if I was going to be happy, I had to be honest but kind. And if our fight had taught me anything, it's that doing that was so much harder than it seemed.

"I want to talk about what I said the other day. Because part of it is kind of true. But I don't think it has to be."

"Water under the bridge, Meggy Bear. I know it can be tricky when a memory of your father takes hold." Mom patted my knee as if her pardon was enough to end the conversation. I wished it was, but I couldn't pretend that was a normal parent-child fight. It was me letting her know that I'd changed and so had my relationship with her, and with Dad in a way.

"That's not what I meant. I mean, Dad still has a hold on the house. Maybe you haven't been aware of it, but when Mac or I bring him up, you won't talk about him; you make jokes or turn on music."

"Uh-huh." Mom grew still. Somehow the fact that she wasn't moving made this so much harder.

"Then, once a year, the whole house shuts down. The music is gone, but we still don't talk about him." My throat started to close as I thought about what I didn't want to say. "The truth is, I can't remember some things about him without your help. I can only remember small things, and I wish I knew him or could get to know him through you."

Mom's face was frozen in pain, and part of me wanted to stop. To leave the rest of the hard stuff for another day. But Riley was right: I had to give her a chance. And if I was really serious about it, I had to give her the whole truth.

"It's part of why I want to get out of this town. I don't want to live with his shadow. I need to stand in his sunlight. To celebrate his life. But I can't say goodbye to him if you won't. At least, not while I'm here." I took a deep breath as my body shook. Luckily, I'd cried so hard with Nadiya and Riley that there weren't many tears left to actually cry out.

Mom was nowhere near as fortunate. Massive, soggy tears rolled down her face. "I hadn't realized that you felt that way."

"I never said it to you, so I didn't give you a chance to know." I laughed and reached for Mom's hand. "It sounds silly, but it feels like crying is unacceptable and feelings outside the 'Day of Silence' aren't allowed. We follow the rules, and everything just barely holds together. 'No surprise grieving' was a rule up there with 'no boys in the bedrooms' and 'no shoes in the house.'"

"Oh, that is not what I wanted for you. I fully thought my kids would break a few rules. Although I never thought about how I would react when you did." Mom chuckled through her sniffles. "I wanted you girls to be able to feel happy, not weighted down by losing him. My plan was to focus on the positives, then we'd be okay. I didn't want you two to feel like you were missing anything."

"I think you might have taken the plan too far." I winced. "I've done that recently, too."

"I was never good at moderation. Your dad was the rule follower. The one to look up directions or figure out dinners for the week. That guy loved a plan. He had our wedding scheduled out in five-minute increments." Mom laughed and swiped at her tears with the back of her hand. "I see a lot of him in you. In both of you, actually. It's hard to lose someone like that. I know I don't need to tell you that, but it's true. And I can recognize that maybe I haven't done the best job processing my grief."

"Yeah, not so great. Although I think I've heard music from every concert you two ever went to by now." I giggled.

"Not the same as grieving." Mom laughed, then grew serious. "If you're amenable to it, I think it'd be good for both of us to get some counseling. Clearly, there are some skills around processing negative emotions that I need to develop, and it'd probably be good for you to talk to someone, too."

"I'd like that. I'm very pro letting go of the no-sad-feelings rule." I smiled, then crawled across the couch to hug her. Mom wrapped her arms around me and sighed. If hugs could communicate, this one tried to say everything from "I'm sorry" to "I love you" all at once.

Finally, she relaxed her grip on me, and I leaned back just as she said, "Although it didn't seem like you were taking the no-boys rule seriously. Is he why you were sneaking out? What happened to him?"

"Not really. I snuck out to put the Davies Kraken at the bottom of the pool."

"Okay, that's funnier than the food fight. But don't do it again either." Mom's chest shook with laughter.

"I won't. Trust me."

When she quieted, I looked down at my socks and hoped that I'd officially run out of tears. "Chris is gone. I messed that up."

"Messed that up how? He was just here—"

"Sorry. It took me a moment to change." Grandmama's timing was impeccable as she rounded the corner to the living room in her lilac velour sweat suit and held a hoodie and some pink slippers for Mom. "Here, Keke, put these on. Now, did I hear you mention that boy?"

Mom and I exchanged glances. Grandmama was so not-sneaky that it was almost hilarious. "Well, Meg was about to tell me why she isn't going to homecoming with Chris."

"Oh, really." Grandmama raised an eyebrow and dropped into the armchair across from us. "Tell me more."

I hung my head and tried to think without their eyes on me. This was something I wasn't proud of, but if I'd come this far on honesty, I may as well lay all my flaws out for them. I looked up, took a deep breath, and started the whole messy story for a second time that night.

"Yikes," Mom said, patting my knee, as I finished up with his flinching at the glitter crown.

"Yeah. And that's why I'm home and possibly never dating again for real this time."

"I don't think it's that bad," Grandmama said, shaking her head. "You didn't bleach his favorite suit or anything. You can fix this." Mom and I exchanged concerned glances but didn't say anything. What was Grandmama up to when we weren't around?

"Not anytime soon. You didn't see his face when I basically stomped on his heart in steel-toed boots."

"I think there's still hope." Grandmama shrugged, as if she undid breakups all the time, and I wondered what exactly was happening at the senior center.

"Grandmama's right," Mom said, looking at me. "Assuming he didn't fire the sub he hired, which would just be bad form in the music world, you could still go to homecoming together."

"Like how? I just show up at his house with chocolates tomorrow and hope he's there?"

"You said this boy is a romantic? It's gotta be bigger." Mom chuckled. "Although I don't think you can get a billboard or arrange a flash mob in the next twelve hours."

The three of us grew quiet as we each tried to figure out a grand gesture worthy of a guy who was basically one giant walking act of adoration. It had to be something personal. Something he would think was funny, or cool, or—

My brain hit the brakes as it dawned on me. "Actually, I might have an idea."

"What is it?" Mom leaned forward, getting excited.

"I'll tell you, but first, I need to text Russ." I tapped my pockets for my phone, then looked at Grandmama. "Also, I might need to get into the church."

"Okay. I'll call the deaconess. But what are you—"

"And I need to talk to Grandpa Chavez." I grinned. "Or at least his chocolatier."

Chapter Twenty-Three

"OBVIOUSLY, I'M NOT WORRIED, BUT JUST IN CASE, WE'LL wait around the corner." Russ, dressed in his tux, clutched the steering wheel of his truck at exactly ten and two. He looked at the back row of seats, where Riley and Nadiya were sitting. "If things don't work out, we can eat the chocolates together."

"If this doesn't work out, y'all are still going to the dance and I'll eat the chocolates with my grandma." I laughed even though my nerves were actively trying to strangle me. Pulling on the truck door handle, I jumped down and said, "Seriously. If you don't hear from me in ten minutes, go to Debbie's without me."

"Good luck." Riley waved, the sparkles on their purple jacket catching the light.

"We love you unconditionally," Nadiya teased, throwing her hands over the neckline of her white jumpsuit.

"Bye." I rolled my eyes and tried to adjust the itchy neckline of the avocado dress I'd fished out of the unsold-items bin at the church rec center. Thanks to Mr. Aggarwal and Life

Skills, I'd done a passable job making the thing fit me, but it still looked desperately seventies even after I cut it short.

Taking a deep breath, I turned on the little Bluetooth speaker hanging from my wrist and started the walk up Chris's driveway. Originally, I was just going to stand outside his house playing music, but after seeing the massive thing, I revised the plan. I had no idea which window was his, and I desperately did not want to be playing sappy music outside one of his little sisters' windows. Instead, I rang the doorbell.

God, I hoped he came to the door and didn't have his mom slam it in my face. My pulse felt as if it was ricocheting around my body as the sound of running footsteps approached the door. I had just enough time to take a deep breath when the door cracked open about three inches and a little tiny face poked out.

"Hi."

"Hi, Angie. Is Chris home?" I bent down slightly and hoped she recognized me under all the layers of green.

"Uh-huh." Angie nodded but didn't make any moves to call him. After a moment of blinking at one another, she added, "You look pretty."

"Thank you." I shifted the box of chocolates from one hand to the other and hoped the heat and stress coming off me wasn't melting them. "Can you get your brother for me?"

"He's watching—"

"Angie." As Chris's voice bounced down the hallway, her eyes got wide. "What did we say about answering the door on your own?"

"Okay, bye," Angie whispered and closed the door abruptly.

I stood there looking at the door, still crouched as if a pre-schooler was on the other side, then panicked. What if she didn't tell Chris I was there? What if she did but he decided to ignore me? Should I ring the bell again and force him to tell me to go away? Maybe I should just go around the corner, make Russ take me home, and start eating the chocolates now.

Standing up straight, I held my breath and then turned to go. This was a dorky idea, and Angie's inability to answer the door was probably a blessing in disguise.

The sound of the door opening made me freeze midstep. "Meg?"

All my careful planning flew out of my mind as I turned around. Chris was standing in the doorway looking rumpled in a pair of shorts, a T-shirt, and white socks, one of which was pulled up a little higher than the other. His hair wasn't care-fully combed, so the long parts at the top were sort of falling everywhere. Want and heartache shot through me. I'd never seen him look truly messy before, and all I wanted to do was reach out and run my hand through his hair and hug him and his wrinkled T-shirt. I missed him.

"What are you doing here?"

The sound of his voice, hoarse as if he hadn't used it in a while, pulled my attention back to the moment. He looked me up and down, frowning.

"I'm here to ask you to homecoming." I waved the choco-lates at him, feeling deeply uncool as the speaker around my wrist bounced, reminding me that I was supposed to play music before I asked him to the dance. I tried to start again. "I'm trying to be romantic. I was going to play Jon Secada in your front yard, but based on your face, that feels like a no." This was not going how I thought it would. I shook my head and tried to calm down. "I'm messing this up. Maybe we just talk instead?"

"You broke up with me." Chris rested his hand on the door and took a step back. "I missed my gig and now I'm missing the *Murder, She Wrote* marathon. Not really a lot to talk about there."

"I know. I know. And I'm new to grand gestures. Obviously, I'm botching this one. . . ." Chris raised an eyebrow, and I cut off my digression. "Just give me a chance. Which I didn't give you, so I know I don't exactly deserve it."

"Okay. Go on." Chris leaned against the doorjamb and crossed his arms, his features still tense, as if he was considering closing the door at any moment.

"Right." I adjusted the neck of my dress, then set the chocolates and speaker down as I tried to quiet my nerves. I'd practiced some version of this speech about fifteen times, but now that I was looking at him, it felt inadequate.

"I owe you an apology. You were right. I was afraid. I'm still afraid, actually." I laughed, the sound nervous and stretched. Chris tilted his head like he was trying to understand where this was going.

"Anyway. I try not to get my hopes up. I don't get excited about things I can't control. That's risky. And loving what you can't control is a recipe for heartbreak. Instead, I have a plan and I execute the plan and that makes me happy enough. Or it did."

Chris shifted his weight, and I paused in case he wanted to ask a question. Instead, he uncrossed his arms, his forehead wrinkling, and I couldn't tell if it was because he wanted to go back into the house or if he wanted to hear more.

"The thing is, I'm happy with you. It's a wild and incandescent kind of happiness. I can't predict it. You don't come with a checklist. It's gotten me into all kinds of trouble." Chris took a deep breath, and I plowed on, determined to finish before he stopped me. If he was going to turn me down, he would at least have heard me out, and that was the best I could hope for.

"The idea that I could get attached to someone. Like, actually attached. Not the this-is-convenient attached but the even-if-we-disagree-I-still-want-you attached. It made me so nervous, and I wasn't sure what to do with it or if you'd still be there feeling like I feel. So I put distance between us. I tried to box you out. But the truth is, I want you. All of you. And that's scary and I don't know how to do this. But I do know that I've never felt like this with anybody, and I'm sure that we can figure it out. If you'll have me."

For a second, he didn't move. I wasn't even sure he was breathing. Then he took a step and closed the front door behind him. Slowly, he came down the steps to stand in front of me, his dark eyes serious and unreadable.

"Here's the thing. I understand why you don't want to get attached. But I don't often go and get detention and then get grounded just because I have a minor crush on someone."

The memory of covering him in food came back to me. I groaned and hung my head. "I'm sorry about that."

"The truth is, I'm already attached to you." Chris tapped my chin, and I looked up to find him smiling down at me. "You were always holding my heart, whether or not you wanted it, and that scares me. So maybe there's a compromise here. You promise not to run off without talking to me. I agree to be patient. And we decide to figure it out together?"

"I think I could manage that."

Chris wrapped an arm around me, the corners of his mouth lifting slightly as he pulled me toward him. "Good. Because I really didn't want to stay home tonight."

"Watching *Murder, She Wrote* isn't your idea of a good time? That was originally my plan, you know." I wrapped my arms around his waist, feeling the planes of his back through his T-shirt.

"It was a decent plan, but I feel like you've got a better one. So tell me how homecoming ends for us."

I stepped a fraction of an inch closer to him, not even trying to hide my smile. "Russ made sure your grandpa has a suit, the hat, and the car ready."

"No wonder Grandpa insisted on staying at our house tonight." He laughed, the sound as delicious and rich as I remembered.

"We eat these chocolates for dinner. Then arrive at homecoming and not care how anyone feels, because we want to dance together."

"I think I can do all that." Chris pulled me closer to him.

Leaning into me, his voice was low and husky as he asked, "Anything else I should be aware of?"

"Just one thing."

"Which is?"

"I really want to kiss you right now. If you'll let me."

The smile that I loved, the one that could light up a whole city block, spread across his face. His embrace tightened around me, and he whispered, "Please, just kiss me."

Chapter Twenty-Four

"YOU READY FOR THIS?" CHRIS ASKED AS SOON AS HE opened my car door.

"As ready as I can be, I guess." I shrugged and took Chris's hand to get out of the car, the fabric of my dress rustling as I stood up and shook out its frills along with my jitters. I was determined not to let everyone's reactions to our being together ruin our night. But that didn't mean I wasn't nervous.

Chris adjusted the lapels on his grandfather's dark green suit and straightened his matching tie. Smiling at me, he said, "I mean, people may talk about us, but more realistically, they're gonna talk about what we're wearing."

"We do look a little ridiculous." When I was planning my "big romantic gesture," I may have let Mom nudge me a little too far with the vintage idea. That woman's commitment to a theme was the stuff of legends, and I should have known better.

"No. We look amazing, like a mobster movie and a teen-vampire movie had a baby." Chris adjusted his hat so it was at a jaunty angle. "Shall we?" he asked, holding his elbow out to me.

"Just a sec." I pulled the Tabbys out of my purse. My dad couldn't be with me physically. We wouldn't do father-daughter poses, and I wouldn't get to watch him threaten Chris when he picked me up for dates. But I could bring a little bit of him with me tonight.

"Oh yeah," Chris said, reaching into his pocket and taking out his Wayfarers, then popping them on. Reason number 152 that I adored Chris: He didn't think it was strange that I wanted us to wear sunglasses. In fact, he'd do it with me. No explanation required.

For a second, we stood in the parking lot and grinned at each other in near darkness. Then Chris held his arm out again. "Ready?"

I looped my arm through his and snuggled against his side. "Let's do this."

We sauntered toward the front of the gym, our pace slowing as we approached the flower arch and twinkle-light hedges that Nadiya had spent the last week painstakingly making. The bass from the song the DJ was playing vibrated through me, shaking out my nerves and making me giddy as we walked down a green carpet and into the gym's entryway. With the lights low, the place had been transformed from a bland, slightly stuffy gym into something magical.

Although I'd seen it on Friday, now that the gym was packed with people, it felt totally different. I was so proud of us. The Huntersville High junior class had done an amazing job. On one side of the gym foyer, we'd created a picture wall, complete with a butcher paper fence and a field of flowers, each with one student's name written on it. The flowers were taped to the wall so people could pull theirs off and take it home as a keepsake. Across from the picture wall was the formal photographer, who brought a bucolic backdrop and was taking formal posed photos or wacky ones with big sunglasses or funny hats. Directly in front of us was the gym, all done up with streamers, balloons, and a big sign that said HUNTERSVILLE COUNTRYSIDE HOMECOMING in a sparkly handwriting that looked suspiciously as though Mr. Bednarik had tried to clean it up after whoever made the sign went home.

The couple getting their photos taken spotted me and Chris and froze momentarily. So much for no one noticing us. At the same time, a group of sophomores over by the drinks started to gawk. I took a deep breath and looked over at Chris to make sure he was fine with being stared at. "You still okay with this?"

"Absolutely. Besides, we look good." He smirked and raised the volume of his voice so the couple taking pictures could hear. "They won't be the only ones staring at you in that dress."

We waited a beat as the couple frantically tried to look busy, then we busted up. Laughing shook the tension out of my shoulders. Tonight was going to be fun, if for no other reason than that I was with him. Looking him up and down, I asked, "So pictures first or—"

"There you two are!" Nadiya's voice ricocheted around the entrance, despite the loud music. Behind her, a somewhat stunned Kelly watched as Nadiya ran over and gave Chris a big hug. My heart swelled. She really did have my back, and she was determined to let everyone know it.

Chris froze in momentary surprise before returning the hug. "Hi, Nadiya. I told Meg you would like me someday."

"I'll like you as long as she does and not a second more. So don't mess up." Nadiya deadpanned the threat, then burst into giggles and took a step back so that Riley could give him a hug, too. To Tabitha's credit, she managed to maintain her chill. Riley must have given her a heads-up first.

"Hey, Prez!" Russ's voice boomed from the foyer. "You two look so nice together. Don't they?" He looked around at everyone who was staring. His voice was the usual warm teddy bear sound I'd gotten used to, but his scowl let everyone know that the only thing out of their mouths tonight better be "They look great" or he'd flatten them like a tackling dummy.

"They sure do." Tabitha smiled and came over to give me a side hug. "Should we take pictures before we get all sweaty from dancing?" she asked, fixing the bow on the front of her little black dress.

"Yes!" Nadiya and I said at the same time. Herding ourselves over to the photographer, we took turns posing for pictures our parents would want—the kind where everyone smiles and stands stick-straight with their date—and the ones we planned to keep, aka the ones with absolutely stupid poses and silly faces. Chris and I traded in our regular sunglasses for giant ones and had just finished taking pictures when the opening bars of a cover of "This Magic Moment" started playing.

"Dance with me?" Chris asked, casually setting down the glasses on the table as if our first dance was no big deal. I almost would have bought it except for the way he bit down on his lip just a second before smiling. The fact that he was still a little nervous around me, after everything we'd been through, made me melt.

"I was hoping you'd ask."

A big, goofy grin crossed his face. Taking my hand, he wove his fingers through mine, rubbing his thumb along the edge of my palm, sending tingles down my spine as he pulled me close to his side. Together, we made our way to the dimly lit gym.

As my eyes adjusted, I spotted Mr. Bednarik in his best shiny maroon suit and his fancy toe-running shoes, looking some combination of elated and surprised to see Chris and me together. I nudged Chris and nodded in Mr. B's direction. We waved and Warm Fuzzy's smile spread so big it looked like it was taking up his whole face. He was probably mentally congratulating himself on a bonding job well done. I laughed. Of all the people I expected to be right about the Huntersville High merger, Warm Fuzzy was not even on my list.

I could feel other eyes on us as we made our way toward an empty spot on the dance floor, but as Chris spun me slowly around and wrapped me in his arms, I realized just how much it didn't matter to me. People could think what they wanted. I knew exactly how I felt, and after all of the confusion of this year, knowing that I wanted to be here with him was more than enough for me. I leaned against him and closed my eyes, letting the music carry my thoughts away and out of the room.

For a brief moment, I was transported back to the first time I'd been in his arms, at my birthday party. Only tonight I didn't feel like I needed to find a place to hide during this slow song. Looking back on everything—the pranks, dodging Hungry Girls, sneaking out, getting detention, even Warm Fuzzy's lectures—it all seemed worth it. Sure, merging schools had been beyond difficult, and tomorrow would probably still be tricky. But all the hard stuff that came with leaving Hirono and my plan behind felt better than worth it; it felt right, as if I didn't need to run away from Huntersville to be happy. With my head against Chris's chest, our bodies swaying slowly to the music, I couldn't imagine a place I wanted to be more than here, with him. In short, tonight was nothing I'd planned for. And it was perfect.

I tilted my chin up so I could see Chris's face. "At the start of school, if you'd told me that I'd be here with you, I would have laughed. But now I can't imagine spending tonight with anyone else."

"This did work out pretty perfectly." Chris looked around at everything we'd worked to make happen, then pulled me in a little closer. "Except for one thing."

My heart skipped a beat, and I let the warmth of him wash over me. "Oh, really?" I asked, looking into his eyes. "What's that?"

A slow smile played with the corners of his mouth. He leaned in closer so that only I could hear him. "I haven't kissed you yet."

"You'd better fix that."

If a kiss could make promises, this kiss promised big dreams, a few questionable ideas, and vast adventures. It was scary and reassuring all at the same time. Most important, this kiss was a promise that no matter what, wherever he went, I'd be there, too.

ACKNOWLEDGMENTS

The feeling of writing *The End* never grows less meaningful or uncertain. It doesn't matter how many times I've done it before; with every story there is a moment where I wonder if this is the book that I finally truly can't finish. That is where community is most important—and trust that no book comes into this world without community—so bear with me while I thank mine.

First, a big thank-you to my agent, Nalini Akolekar, who paid attention to the internet when I was busy wearing a pink wig and celebrating. Second, I'd like to thank Wendy Loggia, my wonderful editor, for tracking me down, and then tracking down Nalini when I was in the aforementioned wig state. Also, a special thank-you to Alison Romig for your enthusiasm and appreciation of the *Bring It On* universe. Similarly, thank you to Casey Moses and Ana Latese for my wonderful cover and to the entire team at Delacorte Press/Underlined for their keen eyes and their work bringing this book into the world. I'd also like to thank Kelsea Reeves for her thoughtful cultural read.

And a big thank-you to Candice Gianetti, Colleen Fellingham, and Annette Szlachta-McGinn for their thoughtful copy edits.

As always, a thank-you to the Struggle Bus writers. A piece of every book belongs to you all, and I'm deeply grateful to have you in my corner. Another debt of gratitude is owed to my Day Ones, Angie and Ashley. I wish for this level of friendship for everyone. Love you, boos. Similarly, to The Coven and the Bay Area homies, you all remain my saving grace. And a shout-out to Mary and Cosimo for letting me crash with them in Paris and exposing me to the world of vintage sunglasses. Meg wouldn't have been half as cool without you two.

I also have some elders to thank. First, as with every book I have written, I'm grateful to GAP (Great-Aunt Patty), to whom this book is dedicated. She gave me some of my first books, showers me with love, and is still crushing the book recommendation game at ninety-eight. Libraries dream of patrons like her. Also, a thank-you to my granddaddy, who taught me the true value of self-sufficiency while he was alive and the lasting impact of style in his passing. Chris's vintage car is accurate thanks to granddaddy's hustle and swagger.

Finally, to my family. The first draft of this book was written during a hard time for us, and I remain overwhelmed by how you all showed up for me. Your thank-yous are as follows: Dad, thank you for regaining consciousness; Mom, for literally reading this thing chapter by chapter as I wrote them; CoCo, for gifting me Juni snuggles; and Marshall, for laughing at the most unlaughable things with me (also, I'm sorry I finished *Sandman* without you . . . or I would be if you stopped stealing my chargers). I love you all.